"MIGHT I INQUIRE AS TO YOUR NAME, MISS?"

"OH, UM, MY APOLOGIES."
—NORAH ARENDT, THE SHEPHERDESS

"IF ONLY YOU HADN'T—" HE SHOUTED. BUT BY THE TIME HE REALIZED HIS ERROR, HE WAS TOO LATE.

UNLESS THEY NAVIGATED THE PASS AND ARRIVED SAFELY IN LAMTRA, AND UNLESS THEY RETURNED WITH GOLD, NONE OF THEM HAD A FUTURE. THEIR FACES MET, AND THEY ALL NODDED WITH UNSPOKEN UNDERSTANDING.

"GOD'S PROTECTION
BE WITH US."
—MARTEN LIEBERT OF THE
REMELIO COMPANY

Contents

SPICE & WOLF

VOLUME II

ISUNA HASEKURA

Yen
Press

NEW YORK

SPICE AND WOLF, Volume 2

ISUNA HASEKURA

Translation: Paul Starr

OOKAMI TO KOUSHINRYO © Isuna Hasekura /
ASCII MEDIA WORKS Inc. 2006. All rights reserved.
First published in Japan in 2006 by MEDIA WORKS
INC., Tokyo. English translation rights in USA, Canada,
and UK arranged with ASCII MEDIA WORKS INC.
through Tuttle-Mori Agency, Inc., Tokyo.

English translation © 2009 by Hachette Book Group, Inc.

Yen Press
Hachette Book Group
237 Park Avenue, New York, NY 10017

Visit our websites at www.HachetteBookGroup.com and
www.YenPress.com.

Yen Press is an imprint of Hachette Book Group, Inc.
The Yen Press name and logo are trademarks of Hachette
Book Group, Inc.

First Yen Press Edition: June 2010

Library of Congress Cataloging-in-Publication Data

Hasekura, Isuna, 1982–
    [Ookami to Koushinryo. English]
    Spice and Wolf, II / by Isuna Hasekura ; illustrated by
Jyuu Ayakura. — 1st Yen Press ed.
        p. cm.
    Summary: Twenty-five-year-old merchant Kraft Law-
rence and his traveling companion Holo, the ancient pagan
wolf-goddess of the harvest, embark on a risky scheme even
as their relationship grows closer.
    ISBN 978-0-7595-3106-2
    [1. Fantasy — Fiction. 2. Merchants — Fiction.
3. Goddesses — Fiction. 4. Wolves — Fiction.]
I. Ayakura, Jyuu, 1981– ill. II. Title. III. Title:
Spice and wolf two.
    PZ7.H2687Spi 2010
    [Fic] — dc22
                                2009054431

10 9 8 7 6 5 4

BRR

Printed in the United States of America

SPICE & WOLF

CHAPTER ONE

The rolling hills continued endlessly.

Boulders were prominent; grass and trees were few.

The road wound thinly between the hills, frequently becoming so narrow that even the single cart was enough to block it entirely.

Just when it seemed the climbing would continue forever, the road turned down, and the seemingly endless naked rocks and dried shrubs suddenly changed to a wide awaiting vista.

While the journey had been more interesting than endless grass plains, most anyone would find the travel tiresome by the fifth day.

From the road, tinged with a loneliness that suggested the coming winter, the voice that once sounded its delight at the undulations of the stony, ocher path was now gone. Its owner was now apparently too bored to even sit on the bench of the cart; she lay instead in the bed, grooming the fur of her tail.

A young man drove the cart, apparently used to such selfish behavior on the part of his companion. The man, Kraft Lawrence, was instantly recognizable as a traveling merchant. This year made the seventh since he'd struck out on his own, and he appeared to be around twenty-five. As if in acknowledgment of the chill that came with the deepening autumn, he tightened the fur coat that was wrapped around his body.

Occasionally, the chill also caused him to stroke his chin, covered in the sort of beard one often saw on traveling merchants, since when he sat still, he became slightly cooler. Letting a breath escape that would have turned foggy once the sun set, Lawrence glanced over his shoulder at the bed of the cart.

Normally filled to the brim with various goods, the bed was enjoying a brief respite. All that stood out was the firewood and straw that provided warmth at night, along with a single bag, small enough for a child to carry.

However, the contents of the bag were more valuable than an entire cart full of wheat would have been. The bag was full of high-grade pepper worth roughly one thousand silver *trenni*. If it could be sold in a mountain town, it might fetch as much as seventeen hundred pieces, but the bag was currently being used as a pillow by Lawrence's companion, who continued lazily grooming her tail.

She was small with a face that was somehow imperious despite its apparent youth, reminiscent of a queen relaxing in her palace. The hood of her robe was thrown back, exposing her pointed ears as she attended to her tail, her expression listless.

Given the tail, the pointed ears, and the fact of her status as a merchant's traveling companion, one might reasonably think of a dog, but unfortunately she was no dog.

She was apparently a "wisewolf," a wolf-god from the taiga in the distant north — but Lawrence felt there was some question as to whether she could be properly called a wolf.

After all, this "wolf" appeared to be a young girl. Calling her a wolf seemed slightly inaccurate.

"We'll be reaching the town soon. Be careful," he said.

It would be disastrous for the girl's ears and tail to be seen by others. The truth was, her canniness would put the instincts of even the sharpest merchant to shame, thus Lawrence didn't need to warn her of the danger. However, she was so thoroughly relaxed that he simply had to speak up.

Not so much as glancing at him, she only yawned hugely.

Her yawn concluding with a vacant exhalation, she now nibbled puppylike on the snow white tip of her dark brown tail, as though it itched. She did not appear to have the slightest inclination to "be careful."

Having introduced herself as a wolf and possessing these ears and this tail, Holo certainly relaxed with the carelessness of an animal, if nothing else.

"...Hrm."

A slight vocalization that could have been a reply (or it could simply have been a small utterance of satisfaction at having conquered the itch) reached Lawrence's ears. Tired of waiting for her reply, he looked forward again.

Holo and Lawrence had met two weeks earlier. Owing to a strange event in one of the villages Lawrence stopped at, Holo had joined him, and the two had been traveling together since. With her ears and tail, she was currently regarded as an evil spirit, and the Church sought to end her life to preserve order.

Lawrence had not a shred of doubt that she was in fact a wolf rather than a simple girl, who happened to have a wolf's ears and a tail.

Just nine days earlier, in the river town of Pazzio, as a riot of silver chasing had come to a close, he had seen her true form.

The huge brown wolf named Holo had understood human speech and possessed an overwhelming presence that was undeniably that of a god.

Yet Lawrence believed his relationship with Holo the Wisewolf to be one of money, of partners in lending and borrowing, of companions in travel, and of friends.

He looked behind him again, and Holo appeared to be curled up in sleep. Although her legs were covered by the pants she wore under her robe, the robe was still hitched up around her waist from her earlier tail grooming, and there was no denying the fact that the sight was slightly lascivious.

Her sleeping expression was the very picture of defenselessness, and coupled with her slight form, Holo looked less like a wolf and more like the sort of girl a wolf was likely to eat.

Nevertheless, Lawrence did not take her lightly.

Her wolf ears pricked suddenly, and she stirred, pulling her hood over her head and drawing the edge of her robe down to cover her tail.

Lawrence looked ahead just as the road drew near the face of a hill and curved. Before them, the figure of a single merchant on foot could be seen.

Cautioning Holo had indeed been unnecessary.

Holo the Wisewolf was hundreds of years old, and the young man's twenty-five years of experience were far from sufficient to make him her equal.

However, Holo looked to be the younger of the two, with her true age being many times greater than what she appeared to be, a fact that occasionally irritated Lawrence.

It was Lawrence's hope that Holo would act more in keeping with the apparent difference between their ages, obediently minding him when she was told. A variety of problems could have been avoided this way, and the wolf would have him to thank for this — but unfortunately, the opposite was much more common.

Lawrence glanced back at the cart bed once more.

Despite the surreptitious nature of Lawrence's backward peek,

Holo returned his look from where she lay, curled up around the bag of pepper.

She threw him a mean-spirited grin as if to say that yes, she could see everything ahead just fine, before closing her eyes once more.

Lawrence looked back to the road.

Perhaps enjoying the cart ride, Holo's tail flicked back and forth.

The town ahead bore the strange name of Poroson.

Beyond the town to the north and east (they would travel toward towns and villages that lay many days beyond the highlands in the foreground), the dress and food of the people would change — even the gods worshipped would be different. The pair would find themselves in a truly foreign land.

Lawrence had heard that Poroson was until recently known as a gateway to another world.

Descending to the west of these rock-strewn highlands, one would find abundantly fertile, forested land in all directions. Yet the land, hemmed in as it was by the surrounding rocks, which yielded little springwater, was difficult to farm. The only reason to take the trouble of founding a town here was its position as this gateway to another world.

They continued through the fields. Lawrence could hear the faint cries of goats through the morning haze as he counted the many gravestone-like posts he saw. The posts were carved with the names of many generations of sages in the Church's long history and continued to purify the land even now.

Long before it was known as a gateway to another world, Poroson was a holy land to a certain pagan faith.

Many years had passed since the Church, following the will of its god, sent missionaries to convert the heathens, starting a war to purify this land tainted by impure beliefs. Poroson was a psychological turning point in the process of the destruction of the old faith. Once the Church was on the verge of wiping out the pagan faith in the area, the priests commanded that a town be founded there.

Poroson soon became the staging area for the missionaries and knights heading north and east after the remaining pagans, and it came to have a reputation as a crossroads for both goods and people.

The missionaries with their tattered, hermit-like robes and the knights with righteous swords in hand, ready to reclaim land in the name of their god, were now gone.

All that passed through the town these days were woven goods, salt, and iron from the north and east and grain and leather from the south and west. The holy wars of the past were long gone, replaced by the continuous comings and goings of shrewd merchants.

Holo's presence made it necessary for Lawrence to take roads with little traffic, but along certain ancient trade routes, they continually passed carts laden with rare goods. Many of the textiles they saw were of particularly fine quality.

Despite the brisk trade, Poroson was rather modest, thanks to the habits of its residents. The wealth of commerce provided for a magnificent wall around the town, but the buildings within it were of humble stone construction, their roofs thatched with straw. It's true that wherever goods and people intersect, money will be left behind and the area will prosper, but Poroson's circumstances were slightly different.

The residents were all highly devout and gave most of their money to the Church. Furthermore, Poroson was not the holding of a particular nation, but rather of the religious capital of Ruvinheigen to the northwest, so tithes did not stay in the town's own church, but instead flowed to the larger city. In fact, the Church offices managed land taxes as well, so Poroson did not even control its own tax revenue.

The residents of the town had no interest in anything beyond their own humble lives.

When a bell sounded through the morning haze, the workers in the fields paused in their labors and turned to face the sound, putting their hands together and closing their eyes.

In a typical town at this hour, red-faced merchants would be busy jockeying for position in the town square, but here there was no such rude commotion.

Not wanting to intrude upon the residents' prayers, Lawrence stopped his cart horse. Then, putting his hands together, he offered a prayer to his own god.

The bell rang a second time, and when the people returned to their work, Lawrence made his cart horse walk again. Suddenly, Holo spoke.

"Oh, so you are a religious man now, are you?"

"I'll pray to anyone who can promise me safe travels and tidy profits."

"I can promise you a fine harvest."

Holo faced Lawrence as he glanced at her out of the corner of his eye.

"You want me to pray to you, then?"

Holo knew and hated the loneliness felt by gods. Lawrence believed she couldn't possibly be serious, but he ventured to ask.

He suspected she was joking with him out of boredom.

As expected, her reply came in a purposefully sweet voice.

"Yes, I certainly do."

"What shall I pray for, then?" asked Lawrence, by now used to this sort of treatment from Holo.

"Whatever you like. I can provide a bountiful harvest, naturally, but safe travels are also no problem for me. I can predict the

9

winds and rain and tell whether springwater is good or bad. And I'm just the thing for getting rid of wolves and wild dogs."

She sounded just like a village youth extolling his virtues to a merchant guild, but Lawrence thought for a moment before answering.

"I suppose safe travels would be worth praying for."

"They would, would they not?" answered Holo with a self-satisfied smile, inclining her head slightly.

Seeing her carefree, innocent smile, Lawrence wondered whether she wasn't simply trying to praise her own abilities over the god of the Church. Every once in a while, Holo exhibited a certain childishness.

"Well, I suppose I'll ask for safe travels, then. It would be heartening to be able to avoid wolves."

"Mm. Safe travels, is it?"

"Indeed."

Lawrence tugged on the reins to avoid a donkey grazing on the grass.

The gateway to the town walls would be upon them soon. The end of a line of people waiting for inspection was visible even in the morning mist.

Though the entire town was part of the Church, many merchants came to it from pagan lands, so Poroson was remarkably accommodating — its inspection of goods was much stricter than its inspection of people. Lawrence was considering the tax likely to be levied on the pepper he carried when he became aware of someone looking at him from the side. There was only Holo.

"What, is that all?" Her voice sounded slightly irritated.

"Hm?"

"I am asking you if all you require is safe travel."

Staring blankly at Holo for a few moments, Lawrence realized what she was talking about.

"What? You wanted me to put my hands together and pray?"

"Don't be ridiculous," she said with a vexed glare. "I'm guaranteeing you safe travel — surely you don't think that a single, useless prayer is compensation enough."

Lawrence's mind turned like a waterwheel as he arrived at the obvious conclusion.

"Ah, you want an offering."

"Hee-hee-hee." Holo gave a self-satisfied chuckle.

"What do you want?"

"Dried mutton!"

"You gorged yourself on the stuff yesterday! It must've been a week's worth that you ate."

"I've always room for mutton."

Never shy, Holo licked her chops at the memory of the meat. It seemed even the noble wolf was a mere dog when presented with dried victuals.

"Cooked meat is good, too, but I simply cannot resist the texture of dried meat. If you would pray for safe travels, dried mutton is the price."

Holo's eyes blazed, and her tail switched restlessly underneath her robe.

Lawrence ignored this completely, instead looking at the goods loaded on the horse that was being led by the merchant in front of them. The horse's back was piled high with a mountain of wool.

"What about that wool — is it good or bad?"

Wool evidently suggested sheep. Holo looked at the mountain of wool, her eyes brimming with anticipation, before answering quickly.

"It is quite good — so good I can almost smell the grass they ate."

"I thought as much. My pepper should fetch a good price here."

If the wool was of high quality, the meat would be excellent,

11

too. And as the quality of meat rose, so did its price. Expensive meat made his pepper, which could be used to flavor and preserve it, all the more valuable, and Lawrence began to look forward to selling his wares.

"Also, dried meat with lots of salt is good. Just a little bit of salt will not do. Also, meat from the flanks is the best, better than meat from the legs. Here now, are you listening?"

"Hm?"

"Salted meat! From the flanks!"

"You have excellent taste. That'll cost us."

"Hah, 'tis a bargain at twice the price."

It was true that some good mutton was a bargain if it meant Holo would guarantee safe travels. After all, her true form was a giant talking wolf. She could probably even protect him from the kind of ill-mannered soldiers that were hard to distinguish from out-and-out thieves.

Nonetheless, Lawrence assumed a purposefully blank expression as he regarded Holo.

Her eyes were fixed greedily upon the imagined food. He couldn't help but tease her.

"Well, now, you must have quite a bit of money indeed. If you've got so much, perhaps you should repay me."

Yet his opponent was a canny wisewolf. She soon discerned his motive.

Her demeanor tightened suddenly as she glared at him.

"That approach will no longer work."

Apparently she had learned from the apple incident. Lawrence clicked his tongue in irritation, his face grim.

"You should've just asked nicely in the first place, then. It would've been so much more charming."

"So if I ask charmingly enough, you will buy some for me, then?" asked Holo without a trace of charm.

Lawrence eased the horse forward as the line moved, answering flatly, "Of course not. You could stand to learn something from those cows and sheep — try chewing your cud, hm?"

He grinned to himself, proud of his wit — but Holo's face went blank with anger, and without a word, there on the driver's seat of the wagon, she stomped on his foot.

The road was nothing more than hard-packed dirt, the simple houses made of rough-hewn stone and thatched with grass.

The people of Poroson bought nothing but the barest necessities from the merchant stalls, so there were surprisingly few such stalls.

A goodly number of people moved about the town, among them merchants with carts or backs fully loaded, but the atmosphere seemed to suck up the normal town chatter like cotton, so it was oddly quiet.

It was hard to believe this quiet, simple, proud town was a nexus of foreign trade that earned dizzying amounts of money every day.

After all, missionaries whose street-corner sermons went largely ignored in other cities could count on gratefully attentive crowds here — so how was profit so effectively made?

To Lawrence, the town was nothing less than a mystery.

"'Tis a tedious place," came Holo's assessment of the uniquely religious town.

"You're only saying that because there's nothing to eat."

"You speak as though I think of nothing else."

"Shall we take in a sermon, then?"

Just ahead of them, a missionary preached to a crowd, one hand on a book of scripture.

The listeners were not only townspeople — there were several merchants whose prayers were normally for naught but their own profit.

Holo regarded them distastefully and sniffed.

"He's about five hundred years too young to be preaching to me."

"I daresay you could stand to hear a sermon on frugality."

Toying idly with the silken sash at her waist, Holo put her hand to her mouth and yawned at Lawrence's suggestion. "I'm a wolf yet. Sermons are complicated and difficult for us to understand," she said shamelessly, rubbing her eyes.

"Well, as far as the teachings of the god of frugality go, they're more persuasive here than anywhere else, I'd reckon."

"Hm?"

"Nearly all the money made here flows to the seat of the Church northwest of here, Ruvinheigen — now *there's* a place I've no desire to hear a sermon."

The Church capital of Ruvinheigen was so prosperous some said its walls had turned to gold. The upper echelons of the Church Council that controlled the region had turned to commerce to support their subjugation of the heathens, and the priests and bishops of Ruvinheigen put the merchants to shame.

Lawrence wondered if that was precisely why opportunities for profit there were so absurdly plentiful.

Just then, Holo tilted her head quizzically. "Did you say Ruvinheigen?"

"What, do you know it?" Lawrence gave Holo a sidelong glance as he steered the wagon to the right once the street forked.

"Mm, I remember the name, but not as a city — it was a person's name."

"Ah, you're not wrong. It's a city now, but it was the name of a saint who led a group of crusaders against the pagans. It's an old name — you don't hear it much anymore."

"Hmph. Maybe 'tis him I'm remembering."

"Surely not."

Lawrence laughed it off but soon realized—Holo had set out on her travels hundreds of years ago.

"He was a man with flaming red hair and a great bushy beard. He'd hardly gotten a glance at my lovely ears and tail before he set his knights after me with spear and sword. I'd had enough, so I took my other form and kicked his knights around before sinking my teeth into that Ruvinheigen's backside. He was rather lean and far from tasty."

Holo sniffed proudly as she related the gallant tale. The surprised Lawrence had no response.

In the holy city of Ruvinheigen, there were records of Saint Ruvinheigen having red hair and the city itself having originally been a fortress that fought against pagan gods.

However, in his battles against the heathen deities, Saint Ruvinheigen was said to have lost his left arm. That is why on the great mural in the city cathedral he was pictured with no left arm, his ragged clothing smeared with blood, resolutely ordering his crusaders forward against the pagans, the protection of God at their backs.

Perhaps the reason Saint Ruvinheigen was always pictured in clothes so ragged he might as well be nude was because Holo had shredded them. Her true form was that of a massive wolf, after all. It was easy to imagine her bloodying someone after a bit of sport.

If what Holo said was true, Saint Ruvinheigen had probably been ashamed of being bitten on his rear and had omitted that bit from the story. In that case, the tale of the saint losing his left arm was pure fabrication.

Had Holo bitten the real Saint Ruvinheigen?

Hearing the story behind the history, Lawrence chuckled.

"Oh, but wait a moment —," said Holo.

"Hm?"

"I only bit him, I'll have you know. I did not kill him," said Holo quickly, anticipating Lawrence's reaction.

For a moment, Lawrence didn't understand what she was getting at, but soon he realized.

She must have assumed he would be angry if she killed one of his fellow humans.

"You're considerate at the strangest of times," said Lawrence.

"'Tis important," said Holo, her face serious enough that Lawrence capitulated without any further teasing.

"Anyway, this surely *is* a tedious city. The middle of the forest is livelier than this."

"I'll unload my pepper, pick up a new commodity, and we'll be on our way to Ruvinheigen, so just bear it until then."

"Is it a big town?"

"Bigger even than Pazzio — more properly a city than a town really. It's crowded, and there are lots of shops."

Holo's face lit up. "With apples even?"

"Hard to say if they'll be fresh. With winter coming, I'd think they'd be preserved."

"...Preserved?" said Holo, dubious. In the northlands, salt was the only method of preservation, so she assumed preserved apples would also use salt.

"They use honey," said Lawrence.

Pop! went Holo's ears, flicking rapidly under the hood she wore.

"Pear preserves are good, too. Also, hmm, they're a bit rare, but I've seen preserved peaches. Now *those* are fine goods. They slice the peaches thin, pack them in a cask with the odd layer of almonds or figs, then fill up the spaces with honey, and seal it shut. Takes about two months for it to be ready to eat. I've only had it once, but it was so sweet the Church was considering banning the stuff...Hey, you're drooling."

Holo snapped her mouth shut as Lawrence pointed it out.

She took a nervous glance around, then looked back at Lawrence dubiously. "You...you're toying with me, though."

"Can't you tell if I'm lying or not?"

Holo set her jaw, perhaps at a loss for words.

"I'm not lying, but there's no telling whether they'll actually have the preserves. They're mostly for rich nobles, anyway. The stuff isn't just lined up in a shop."

"But if it is?"

Swish, swish — Holo's tail was switching back and forth beneath her robe so rapidly it almost seemed like a separate animal altogether. Her eyes were moist and blurred with overflowing anticipation.

Holo's face was so close to Lawrence that she rested her head on his shoulder.

Her eyes were desperately serious.

"...Fine, fine! I'll buy you some!"

Holo gripped Lawrence's arm tightly. "You have to!"

He felt that if he looked sideways at her, he'd be bitten on the spot.

"A little, though. Just a little!" Lawrence said. It was not clear if Holo was listening or not.

"That's a promise, then! You've promised!"

"Okay, okay!"

"So let us hurry on, then! Hurry, now!"

"Stop grabbing me!"

Lawrence shrugged her off, but Holo's mind had wandered elsewhere. She seemed to look off into the distance and muttered as she nibbled on the nail of her middle finger.

"They may sell out. Should it come to that..."

Lawrence was beginning to regret having said anything about honeyed peach preserves, but it was too late for such regrets. If he

dared to suggest he had decided not to buy any after all, it seemed likely she'd tear out his throat.

It didn't matter that honeyed peach preserves weren't something that traveling merchants could afford.

"It's not a question of selling out — they may not have any at all," Lawrence said. "Just understand that."

"We are talking about peaches and honey, sir! It beggars belief. Peaches *and honey.*"

"Are you even listening to me?"

"Still, it's hard to give up pears," said Holo, turning to Lawrence and looking up at him.

Lawrence's only reply was to heave a long-suffering sigh.

Lawrence planned to sell his pepper to the Latparron Trading Company, whose name was every bit as odd as the town in which it was located — Poroson.

If one were to trace the name, it would surely hearken all the way back to the time before Poroson was a town and only pagans inhabited the area. The strange names were all that remained of the past, though. After all, everyone here was a true believer in the Church, from the tops of their heads to the tips of their toes. The Latparron Company would soon have its fiftieth master, and each seemed to be more devout than the last.

Thus it was that no sooner had Lawrence called upon the company — which he'd not visited in half a year — than he was regaled with praise for the newly arrived priest, whose sermons he simply had to hear, as would they not save our very souls?

Still worse, the master of the Latparron Company seemed to take Holo in her robes for a nun on pilgrimage and exhorted her to minister to Lawrence as well.

Holo took the opportunity to rail at Lawrence at length, occasionally grinning in a way that only he could see.

After some time, their preaching ended, and Lawrence swore to himself that he wouldn't spare so much as a single coin for any honeyed peach preserves.

"Well, then, that went a bit long, but shall we talk business now?"

"I await your pleasure," said Lawrence, clearly tired — but the Latparron master had put on his business face now, so Lawrence couldn't let his guard down.

It was possible that the master's lengthy sermon was a tactic to wear his opponents down, making them easy prey.

"So, what goods have you brought me this day?"

"Right here," said Lawrence, regaining his composure and bringing out the pepper-stuffed sack.

"Oh, pepper!"

Lawrence kept hidden his surprise at the master's correct guess of the bag's contents. "You know your goods," he said.

"It's the smell!" said the master with a mischievous smile — but Lawrence knew pepper yet to be ground has little scent.

Lawrence stole a sidelong glance at Holo, who looked on amused.

"It seems I'm still a novice," said Lawrence.

"Just a matter of experience," said the master. As far as Lawrence could tell from the man's broad, easy manner, his mistaking Holo for a nun might also have been an act.

"Still, Mr. Lawrence, you always bring the best goods at the most opportune time. By God's grace, the hay grew well this year, and the pork has gotten fat merely walking the streets. Demand for pepper will be high for a while. Had you gotten here even a week sooner, I'd have been able to take it off your hands for a pittance!"

Lawrence could only offer a pained smile in response to the cheerful man. The Latparron master had taken complete control of the conversation. He could now use strong-arm negotiating tactics. It would be hard for Lawrence to regain the upper hand.

Traders like these in small companies were why the life of the merchant was a hard one.

"Right, then, let's take its measure. Have you a scale?"

Unlike the money changers whose reputations depended on the accuracy of their scales, the scales that merchants carried were doctored as a matter of course. With commodities like pepper or gold dust, a small "adjustment" to a scale's gradations could make a large difference, so both buyer and seller weighed items on their own scales.

However, it wasn't every day that Lawrence dealt with high-priced goods like pepper, so he had no scales.

"No, I don't have a scale — I trust in God."

The master smiled and nodded at Lawrence's reply. There were two sets of scales on a shelf, and he deliberately brought out the set farther away.

Though he was careful not to show it, Lawrence internally sighed in relief.

Be he the most devout, faithful follower of the teachings of the Church, a merchant was still a merchant. Undoubtedly the first set of scales had been doctored. If Lawrence's pepper was weighed on such scales, there was no telling how much of a loss he might sustain. It could be as bad as a silver piece for every peppercorn.

Lawrence gave God his thanks.

"Even if you believe in a just God, man should be able to discern whether the scripture before him is true or false. A righteous man still trespasses against God if he commits to memory false scripture, after all," said the master, setting the scales down on a nearby table.

He was probably trying to reassure Lawrence that his scales were accurate.

Although merchants were always trying to outsmart one another, that didn't mean trust was never necessary.

"If you'll excuse me for a moment," said Lawrence, at which point the master nodded and took a step back.

On the table was a beautiful set of brass scales, which gleamed a dull gold. It was the sort of set one would expect to see in the offices of a wealthy cambist in a large city and seemed a bit out of place in this shop.

The Latparron Trading Company's storefront was so plain it was easily mistakable for a simple home, and the only employees were the master and a few men. The interior of the shop was also plainly furnished with two shelves situated against the wall, one holding jars that seemed to contain spices or dried foodstuffs and another holding bundles of documents, paper, and parchment.

While the scales seemed not in keeping with the rest of the shop, the balance of those scales was clear.

The scales balanced in the center with plates of counterweights to the left and right.

They did not seem to have been tampered with.

Relieved, Lawrence looked up and smiled. "Shall we proceed to weigh the pepper, then?"

There was no reason not to.

"Let's see, we'll need paper and ink. Wait just a moment, please," said the master, walking to the corner of the room and retrieving an ink pot and paper from the shelf. Lawrence was idly looking on when a tug at his sleeve pulled him out of his reverie. There was no one else there—it was Holo.

"What is it?"

"I'm thirsty."

"You'll have to wait," said Lawrence shortly—but he immediately reconsidered.

She was Holo the Wisewolf after all. She wouldn't make a complaint like that out of the blue. There had to be some kind of reason behind it.

Having changed his mind, Lawrence was about to ask her to explain herself when the master spoke again.

"Even the saints themselves needed water to live. Would you like water or perhaps wine?"

"Water, if you please," said Holo with a smile. Evidently she had only been thirsty after all.

"Just a moment, then." The master left the contract paper, ink, and quill on the table and walked out of the room, going to fetch the water himself.

In this regard he seemed to be no merchant, but the model of a devout adherent of the Church.

Yet even as Lawrence was impressed at the master's faith, he gave Holo a sidelong glare.

"I know this may seem like nothing to you, but to us merchants this is a battleground. You could have had as much water as you wanted later."

"But I am *thirsty*," said Holo, looking away stubbornly — she hated being scolded. Despite her frightening intelligence, she could be strangely childish at times. There was no point in saying anything more.

Lawrence sighed, and to chase away his frustration with Holo, he set his mind on estimating how much pepper he had.

At length the master returned, carrying a wooden tray with an iron pitcher and cup. Lawrence's shame at having made a business associate and an elder perform such a menial task was very real, but the master's smiling face seemed to have dispensed with business for the moment.

"Well, then, shall we proceed with the weigh?"

"Indeed."

They began to weigh the pepper as Holo looked on, leaning against a wall a short distance away, iron cup clasped between her hands.

The weigh was a simple enough task, with a set weight being prepared on one side of the scales and the other being loaded with pepper until it balanced.

It was simple, but if one grew tired of seeing the counterweight sink and was tempted to call it good enough and proceed to the next load, a merchant could unwittingly sustain a significant loss.

So both the master and Lawrence carefully balanced each load until each was satisfied before proceeding to the next.

For all its simplicity, the weighing was sensitive work, and it took forty-five loads to finish. Pepper varied depending on its origin, but a load of Lawrence's product balanced roughly with a single counterweight should have been worth about one gold *lumione* piece. Based on his most current knowledge of exchange rates, one *lumione* equaled thirty-four and two-thirds *trenni*, the silver coin commonly used in the port town of Pazzio. Forty-five loads at that rate would come to 1,560 *trenni*.

Lawrence had bought the pepper for a thousand *trenni*, so that meant a profit of 560 pieces. The spice trade was indeed delicious. Of course, gold and jewels — the raw materials for luxury goods — could fetch two or three times their initial purchase price, so this was a meager gain in comparison, but for a traveling merchant who spent his days crossing the plains, it was profit enough. Some merchants would haul the lowest-quality oats on their very backs, destroying themselves as they crossed mountains, only to turn a 10 percent profit when they sold in the town.

Indeed, compared with that, clearing more than five hundred silver pieces by moving a single light bag of pepper was almost too savory to believe.

Lawrence grinned as he packed the pepper back into its leather sack.

"Right, that's forty-five measures' worth, then. Where does this pepper come from?"

"It was imported from Ramapata, in the kingdom of Leedon. Here's the certificate of import from the Milone Company."

"From Ramapata, then? It's come quite a ways, then — I can scarcely imagine the place," mused the master, narrowing his eyes and smiling as he took the certificate parchment Lawrence offered him.

Town merchants often spent their entire lives in the villages of their birth. There were some who would go on pilgrimages after their retirement, but there was no time for such things when they were actively working.

However, even Lawrence the traveling merchant knew little of the kingdom of Leedon, save that it was famous for its spices. To get there from Pazzio, one had to take the river all the way to the coast and then board a long-distance sailing ship south across two separate seas, a journey of roughly two months.

The language was different, of course, and apparently it was hot like summertime year-round in Leedon, and the population was permanently tanned near black from the time they were born.

It seemed unbelievable, but there was spice, gold, silver, and iron that supposedly came from the place, and the Milone Company vouched for the origin of the pepper, which the certificate claimed was Ramapata.

Was it a real country?

"The certificate seems authentic," said the master.

The kinds of bills of exchange, trusted promissory notes and contracts that passed through town merchants were huge. Supposedly they could even recognize bills signed by small companies in faraway lands to say nothing of huge organizations that had their main branches in a foreign country.

Recognizing the seal of a company as large as Milone would be but the work of a moment. Signatures were important, but the soul of a contract was the seal.

"Right, then, it'll be one *lumione* per measure. Will this do?"

"Can you tell me what the *lumione* is trading at currently?" Lawrence asked suddenly, even though he had some grasp of the coin's market value.

Gold coin was generally used as an accounting currency — that is to say it was the basis for calculating the values of the many other currencies in the world. Calculations were performed in gold currency and then remitted in other, more convenient forms. Of course, in that situation the market value of the currency in question became an issue.

Lawrence was suddenly very nervous.

"Mr. Lawrence, as I recall, you follow the path of Saint Metrogius in business, like your teacher did, correct?"

"Yes. Perhaps it's the protection of Saint Metrogius that's kept my travels safe and my business sound."

"So I presume that you'll take payment in *trenni* silver?"

Many traveling merchants wanted to repeat the successes of the past, and so rather than move randomly from one town to another, they trod the paths of the saints of old.

Thus it was that the currency they used at a given time was quite predictable.

For the master of the Latparron Trading Company to come to that conclusion so quickly meant he was very shrewd merchant indeed.

"In *trenni* silver," he continued, "the current rate is thirty-two and five-sixths."

The rate was lower than Lawrence remembered. But given this

town's importance as a trade center, it was within the realm he could allow.

In places where currencies from many different places all converged, the exchange rate with respect to accounting currencies tended to be lower.

Lawrence did the calculations in his head at lightning speed. At this rate he'd get 1,477 *trenni* for his pepper.

The amount was less than he'd anticipated but a tolerable price nonetheless. It would be a huge step toward realizing the dream of opening his own shop.

He took a deep breath and extended his right hand toward the master. "That price will be fine, sir."

The master's face broke into a smile, and he accepted Lawrence's hand. A merchant's spirits were never better than at the moment of a successful contract.

This was one such moment.

"Ughh…," Holo cut in with a listless voice.

"Whatever is the matter?" asked the master worriedly as he and Lawrence looked to Holo, who leaned unsteadily against the wall.

In that instant, Lawrence remembered the sale of his furs to the Milone Company and grew suddenly nervous.

The master of the Latparron Company was a canny merchant who managed his shop alone. Trying to outwit him was likely to end badly. Having Holo around didn't mean they had to try to trick their trading partners every single time.

Even as Lawrence thought this, he stopped short. Holo was acting strangely.

"U-ugh…I'm, I'm dizzy…"

Holo held on to the cup as her unsteadiness grew worse, and the water seemed like it would spill out at any moment.

The master walked up to her, looking worried as he stilled the cup and supported her slim shoulders.

"Are you recovered?"

"…A bit. Thank you," said Holo weakly, finally standing straight again with the master's help.

She looked every bit the fasting nun suffering from a bout of anemia. Even someone who wasn't as devout as the master would have wanted to help her, but Lawrence noticed something strange.

Underneath Holo's hood, her wolf ears had not drooped very much.

"A long journey will tire even the strongest man," declared the master.

Holo nodded slightly, then spoke. "I may well be tired from the travel. My vision seemed to tilt suddenly…"

"That won't do. Ah, I have it — shall I bring some goat milk? It's fresh from yesterday's milking," he said, offering her a chair and briskly going to fetch the milk without waiting for her response.

Lawrence was surely the only one who had any premonition that Holo was going to do something else when she did not sit in the offered chair and instead went to set the iron cup on the table.

"Sir," she said to the master, whose back was turned. "I believe I am yet a bit dizzy."

"Heavens. Shall I call a physician?" asked the master, looking over his shoulder with heartfelt concern.

Underneath the hood, Holo's expression was anything but the weak dizziness she feigned.

"Look here. It's tilting before my very eyes," said Holo, taking the cup and spilling a few drops on the surface of the table — whereupon it flowed smoothly to Holo's right and off the edge of the table, dripping to the floor with a small *plip* sound.

28

"Wha —!" Lawrence walked swiftly to the table and put his hand on the scales.

It was the same set of scales he'd so carefully gauged the accuracy of earlier. If they were even slightly off, it would mean a large loss for him, and so he'd checked the scales' accuracy carefully — but they aligned perfectly with the direction in which the water had flowed off the table.

This led to a single conclusion.

The weighing was over, and the plates of the scale were empty save for the counterweights on them. Lawrence took the set of scales and rotated it to face precisely the opposite direction.

The scales tipped this way and that owing to the sudden movement, but when set back on the table, their movement slowed and eventually stopped.

According to the gradations, the scales balanced perfectly — despite the incline of the table. If they had been accurate, the reading would have been skewed by the slant of the table.

The scales had clearly been tampered with.

"So, then, did I drink water, or was it wine?" inquired Holo. She looked back to the master — as did Lawrence.

The master's expression froze, and sweat appeared on his forehead.

"What I drank was wine. Was it not?" Holo's voice sounded so amused that even her smile was practically audible.

The master's face paled to a nearly deathly pallor. If the fact that he used fraudulent scales to swindle merchants was made public in a god-fearing town like this, all his assets would be forfeit, and he would face instant bankruptcy.

"There's a saying that 'no one drinks less than the master of a full tavern' — this must be what that means," said Lawrence.

The stricken master was like a cornered hare, unable to cry out even as a predator's fangs pierced its skin.

Lawrence walked back toward the master with an easy smile.

"The secret to prosperity is being the only sober one, eh?"

So much sweat beaded up on the master's forehead that you could trace a picture in it.

"It seems I'm drunk on the same wine as my companion. I doubt we'll be able to remember anything we've seen or heard in here...though in exchange I may be a bit unreasonable."

"Wh-what do you...?" The master's face shivered in fear.

Taking easy revenge here would be failing as a merchant, though.

There wasn't even a mote of anger at being deceived in Lawrence's mind.

All he thought of were cold calculations of how much more profit he could extract from his opponent's fear.

This was an unexpected opportunity.

Lawrence drew near the man, his expression still smiling, his tone still every bit the negotiating merchant.

"Let's see...I think the amount we agreed to, plus the amount you were going to gain, plus, oh...you'll let us buy double on margin."

Lawrence was demanding to be allowed to buy more than he had the cash to secure. It's self-evident that the more money a merchant can invest, the greater profit he can realize. If he can buy two silver pieces' worth of goods with a single piece, he will double his profit, pure and simple.

But to buy two pieces' worth with one piece, he would obviously need collateral. Since the merchant is essentially borrowing money, the lender has the right to demand collateral from the borrower.

However, the master was in no position to make such a demand, which is why Lawrence pushed such an unreasonable position. It's a third-rate merchant that doesn't take advantage of weakness.

"I, uh, er, I can't possibly…"

"You can't do it? Oh, that's a shame…I'm feeling significantly less drunk."

The master's face was so wet it seemed to nearly melt as the sweat mixed with tears.

His face a mask of despair, he slumped, defeated.

"As for the goods, let's see. Given the amount, perhaps some high-quality arms? Surely you have lots of goods bound for Ruvinheigen."

"…Arms, you say?"

The master looked up, seeming to see a glimmer of hope. He had probably been assuming that Lawrence never planned to pay him back.

"They're always a good bet for turning a tidy profit, and I can get the loan back to you quickly that way. What say you?"

Ruvinheigen served as a resupply base for the efforts to subjugate the pagans. Any items that served in the fighting flew off the shelves year-round. It was difficult to sustain depreciation losses when selling such goods.

Since Lawrence would be able to purchase double the normal amount on margin, he'd have double the insurance against depreciation, which made weapons a good choice for a margin buy.

The master's face shifted to that of a shrewdly calculating merchant. "Weapons…you say?"

"Since I'm sure there's a trading company in Ruvinheigen with connections to yours, selling them there will balance out the books."

In short, after Lawrence sold the weapons he bought with money borrowed from the Latparron Company to another company in Ruvinheigen, he wouldn't have to come all the way back to Poroson to return the money.

In certain situations, the give-and-take of money could be accomplished with nothing more than entries in a ledger.

It was the great triumph of the merchant class.

"What say you?"

At times, the business smile of a merchant could be an intimidating thing. Even among such smiles, Lawrence's was exceptionally intimidating as he cornered the manager of the Latparron Trading Company, who — unable to refuse — finally nodded.

"My thanks! I'd like to arrange for the goods immediately, as I hope to depart for Ruvinheigen very soon."

"U-understood. Er, as for the valuation..."

"I shall leave that to you. After all, I trust in God."

The master's lip twisted bitterly in what must have been a pained smile. It was unavoidable that he'd appraise the weapons rather cheaply.

"Are you two quite finished?" said Holo, guessing that the strong-armed "negotiation" was over. The master gave a sigh of dismay. It seemed there was still one person who wanted a say.

"I daresay my drunkenness is lifting as well," said Holo, her head tilted charmingly to one side — but she must've seemed like a devil to the master.

"Some fine wine and mutton would do much for my spirits. Make sure the mutton's from the flanks now!"

The master could only nod his head at her casual imperiousness.

"Make it quick now," said Holo, partially in jest, but hearing these words from the girl who adroitly saw through his doctored scales, the master turned around and scampered from the room like a pig smacked on the rear.

One couldn't help but feel the master was overdoing it a bit, but if his fraud was made public, he would be ruined. To that extent, a little bowing and scraping was a small price to pay.

Lawrence would have taken a huge hit to his own assets if the trick hadn't been noticed.

"Hee-hee. Poor little man," said Holo with a delighted chuckle that made her seem even nastier.

"You've certainly a keen eye, as usual. I didn't notice a thing."

"I'm beautiful and my tail fur is sleek, but my eyes and ears are also keen. I noticed the moment we entered the room. I suppose he would've been sly enough to fool the likes of you, though," said Holo, sighing and waving her hand dismissively.

Lawrence would have been happier if she'd said something sooner, but the reality was he had not noticed the fraud, and the fact that Holo did had turned a great loss into a great gain.

It wouldn't kill him to be polite.

"I've nothing to say for myself," Lawrence admitted. Holo's eyes twinkled at his unexpected meekness.

"Oh ho! I see you've matured a bit."

Lawrence — indeed having nothing to say for himself — could only smile, chagrined.

There is something known as "spring fever."

It is most common during the winter in places far from rivers or seas. The streams freeze, and people survive on salted meat and stale bread day in and day out. It's not that no vegetables can survive the frost, but rather that such produce is better sold than eaten. Eating the produce does nothing for the chill, but with the money gained from its sale, firewood can be bought and furnaces stoked.

Eating naught but meat and drinking nothing but wine takes its toll, and by spring, many have broken out in rashes.

This is spring fever, and it is proof of neglect for one's health.

Naturally it is well-known that resisting the temptation of meat and the comfort of wine will spare one this fate. Eat vegetables and meat only in moderation — such will the Church's sermon be every Sunday.

Thus come spring, the sufferers of spring fever will often find themselves being terribly scolded by the priest. Gluttony is, after all, one of the seven deadly sins — whether or not the glutton knows it.

Lawrence heaved a long-suffering sigh at Holo's overindulgence.

She burped. "Whew...that was tasty." She was in high spirits after washing down the fine mutton with some fine wine.

Not only was it all free of charge, but after eating and drinking her fill, she could curl up in the wagon bed for a nap.

Even the most extravagant merchant will, as a matter of course, think ahead and limit his excesses, but not Holo.

Tapping her feet in delight, she had eaten and drunk with glee and only stopped to take a break.

Lawrence reckoned that if it had been their travel provisions, she would've eaten three weeks' worth — and she drank so much wine he began to wonder where it was going.

If she had turned around and sold the food she extorted from the Latparron master, she would have put a big dent in her own debt to Lawrence.

This was yet another reason Lawrence was stunned.

"Now, then, I daresay I'll take a nap," said Holo.

Lawrence didn't even bother to look at the source of this exemplar of depravity.

In addition to squeezing some fine wine and mutton from the Latparron Company master, Lawrence had obtained a large load of arms at a very reasonable price. He and his companion left the town of Poroson without so much as waiting for the noontime bells. Little time had passed since then, and the sun was just now overhead.

With the clear skies and warm sunshine, it was perfect weather for a midday drink, followed by a nap.

Owing to the load, the wagon bed was in a state of disarray, but with wine enough in her, Holo probably wouldn't mind.

The trade road that they took to Ruvinheigen was full of steep inclines and sudden turns just outside of Poroson but smoothed out and gave a grand view as it slowly descended.

The road meandered on.

It was well traveled, which made for a firmly packed surface with holes being quickly filled.

Even though her "bed" was packed full of sword hilts, Holo was easily able to nap on top of them and pass the afternoon away since the road was so smooth.

Then there was Lawrence, who had drunk no wine and spent the day looking at a horse's backside, reins in hand. His jealousy made it easy for him not to look at Holo.

"Mm, I ought to tend to my tail," said Holo — her tail the only thing she was diligent about. She pulled it out of her robes without a hint of concern.

Not that any was warranted; the expansive view meant there was no danger of being surprised by an approaching traveler.

Holo began to comb her tail, occasionally picking a flea out or pausing to lick the fur clean.

The care she took with her tail was visible in her silent, single-minded attention to the job.

She worked from the very base of the tail, which was covered in dark brown fur, finally reaching its fluffy white tip, and then suddenly looked up. "Oh, that's right."

"…What?"

"When we get to the next town, I want oil."

"...Oil?"

"Mm. I've heard it would be good to use on my tail."

Lawrence turned away from Holo wordlessly.

"So will you buy some for me?" asked Holo with a charming smile, her head tilted.

Even a poor man would be hard-pressed to resist that smile, but Lawrence only glanced at her out of the corner of his eye.

Figures larger than her smile danced before his eyes — specifically, the debt she owed him.

"The clothes you're wearing now, plus the extras, the comb, the travel fee, the wine and food — have you added them all up? There's the head tax when we enter a town, as well. Surely you're not telling me you can't do sums," said Lawrence, mimicking Holo's tone, but Holo still smiled.

"I can surely do sums, but I'm still better at subtraction," she proclaimed, then laughed at some private amusement.

Lawrence knew she was hiding some kind of comeback, but her manner was strange. Perhaps she was still drunk.

He glanced at the wineskins that lay in the wagon bed. They'd taken the Latparron master for five skins of wine, two of which were now empty.

It wasn't impossible that she was drunk.

"Well, perhaps you should try adding up all you've used. If you're such a wise wolf, you should be able to work out my answer from that."

"All right, I shall!" said Holo with a smile and a cheerful nod.

Just as Lawrence looked forward again, thinking how nice it would be if she were always so agreeable, Holo continued.

"You will definitely buy me some," she said.

Lawrence cast his eyes askance to spy her grinning at him. Maybe she really *was* drunk. It was a very charming smile.

"Just look what happens to the wits of the proud wisewolf when she has too much wine," muttered Lawrence to himself. Holo's head flopped from one shoulder to the other.

If she fell drunkenly out of the wagon, she could be injured. Lawrence reached out to steady her slim shoulder, and Holo grabbed his hand with a quickness that was nothing short of wolflike.

Surprised, Lawrence looked into her eyes. She was neither drunk nor laughing.

"After all, it's thanks to me that your wagon bed was so cheaply filled. You'll pull in a tidy profit."

Her charm had vanished.

"O-on what basis — "

"I won't have you belittle me. Surely you don't think I missed you strong-arming that master? I've a sharp mind, keen eyes, aye; but don't forget, my ears are good, too. I couldn't have missed your negotiations." Holo grinned unpleasantly, showing her fangs. "So you'll buy some oil for me, yes?"

In fact, Lawrence had taken advantage of the master's weakness during his negotiations, and it was also true that things had gone just as Lawrence had hoped.

He cursed himself for being so obviously pleased upon signing the contract. Once it was known that someone was going to make a lot of money, they were obvious targets for sponging and wheedling — it was human nature.

"Uh, er, well, how much do you think you're in debt to me for? It's one hundred forty silver! Have you any idea how much money that is? And now you think I'm going to spend more on you?"

"Oh? What, you want me to pay you back?" Holo looked at Lawrence with an expression of mild surprise, as if to say she could pay him back at any time she chose.

There are none in this world who don't wish to be paid back money they have lent. Lawrence gritted his teeth and glared at Holo, enunciating his response very carefully. "Of. Course. I. Do."

If Holo paid back what she owed in a lump sum, he'd be able to fill his wagon bed with more and better goods, which would mean improved profits. More investment equaled greater return — it was at the very center of a merchant's world.

Yet Holo's expression changed completely at Lawrence's words. She regarded him coldly, as if to say, "Oh, that's how it is."

Lawrence faltered at the completely unexpected change.

"So that's how you've been thinking," said Holo.

"Wh-what do you — "

Lawrence would have finished with *mean,* but Holo's rapid-fire response cut him off.

"Well, I suppose if I pay my debts, that makes me a free wolf. I see. I'll just pay you back, then."

Hearing these words, Lawrence understood what Holo wanted to say.

Some days earlier, during a disturbance in Pazzio, Lawrence had seen Holo's wolf form and retreated in fear. Deeply hurt, Holo tried to leave Lawrence, but Lawrence stopped her by saying he would follow her all the way to the north country to collect the money she owed him for destroying his clothes.

"Come what may, you'll pay me back," he had said. "So leaving me now won't get you anything."

Holo stayed with Lawrence based on the reasoning that making him come all the way out to the north country would be a bother, and Lawrence had thought that the business about debt repayment was just a pretense for both of them.

No, he'd believed it.

He believed that even if she were to repay the debt, she would still wish for him to travel with her to the forests of the north

38

country — though her bashfulness would prevent her from admitting it.

And Holo had now turned the tables on him. She used the fact that the debt *was* his own pretense against him.

A single word jumped into his mind.

Unfair. Holo was truly unfair.

"In that case, I'll just give your money back and hie myself north, shall I? I wonder how Paro and Myuri are faring."

Holo looked away, purposefully letting a small sigh escape.

Lawrence, at a loss for words, glared sourly at the wolf girl that sat beside him and wondered how to retort.

He imagined that if he was stubborn and demanded that she pay him now and go on her merry way, Holo would really do it — and that wasn't what Lawrence wanted. This was where he'd have to cry uncle.

There really wasn't anything charming about Holo.

Lawrence stared at her, furiously trying to think of a comeback, but Holo looked away from him obstinately.

Some time passed.

"...We didn't decide the due date for repayment. Just as long as I get it by the time we arrive in the north country. Will that do?"

Some part of Lawrence was still stubborn. He simply couldn't let the cheeky wolf girl have everything she wanted. This was as far as he could give in.

Holo seemed to understand that. She slowly turned toward him and smiled, satisfied.

"I should think I'll be able to repay you by the time we've arrived in the north country," she said purposefully, drawing near him. "And it's my intention to pay you back with interest, which means the more I borrow, the greater profit for you. So you'll do it for me, yes?"

Holo's eyes met Lawrence's as she looked up at him.

They were beautiful eyes with red-brown irises.

"The oil, you mean?"

"Yes. Make it part of my debt, but please — buy it for me, won't you?"

The plea was strangely rational, and Lawrence couldn't think of a good rejoinder.

All he could do was slump his head sideways as if exhausted.

"My thanks," said Holo, brushing against Lawrence's arm like a cat asking for affection — which wasn't a bad feeling at all.

He knew that was what Holo wanted, and it was an unavoidable part of his long, lonely time as a traveling merchant.

"Still, you really did haggle him down, didn't you?" asked Holo, attending once more to her tail as she reclined against Lawrence.

This particular wolf could sense lies, so Lawrence didn't bother lying and answered truthfully. "Rather he put himself in the position of having no choice but to *be* haggled down."

Yet the interest rate on the arms was not good. The most profitable method would be to import the materials and then assemble and sell the weapons. As far as the business of selling completed weapons went, simply by going somewhere with a constant demand for large amounts of weaponry and turning a fair profit, the amount by which the goods could be bargained down was limited.

Lawrence headed to Ruvinheigen for that very same fair profit.

"How much?"

"What's the point of asking that?"

Holo glanced up at Lawrence from her position leaning against him and then looked quickly away.

At which point Lawrence more or less understood.

Despite her forcing of the oil issue, she was actually quite concerned about his profits.

"What? I was just worried about sponging off a traveling merchant, who is barely scraping by. That is all."

Lawrence tapped Holo's head lightly at the nasty comment.

"Weapons are the best-selling product in Ruvinheigen, but many merchants bring them into the city. Thus, the interest rate on them drops, and the amount I could bargain him down is limited."

"But you bought so much, you'll yet come out ahead, yes?"

The wagon bed was not full, strictly speaking, but it was well laden. The goods were solid, and though the interest was low, in comparison to Lawrence's initial investment, the actual amount of material was nice indeed. The fact that he was getting double the material for his investment was icing on the cake. Like the saying goes, "One raindrop raises the sea," and so Lawrence's gain might be second only to his profit from the pepper.

In truth, the proceeds would be enough to buy more apples than would fit in the wagon bed, to say nothing of oil, but if Lawrence told Holo that there was no telling what demands she might make — so he held his tongue.

Holo, blissfully ignorant, simply groomed her tail.

Looking at her, Lawrence couldn't help but feel a bit guilty.

"Well, I should think we'll make enough to pay for some oil, anyway," he said.

Holo nodded, apparently satisfied.

"Still, now that I think about it, some spice would be quite tasty," Lawrence murmured, as he estimated the likely gain against the cost of the weapons.

"You've eaten it?"

"I'm not like you, you glutton. I'm talking about the profit."

"Hmph. Well, why don't you load up on spice again, then?"

"The prices in Ruvinheigen and Poroson aren't so very different. I'd take a loss after paying the tariff."

"Then give it up, I say," said Holo shortly, nibbling the tip of her tail.

"If I could get a rate about like what I'd normally get for spices or maybe a little more, I'd make enough to open a shop."

Saving enough money to open his own shop was Lawrence's dream. Though he'd made a sizable amount in the kerfuffle in Pazzio, the goal remained distant.

"Surely there's something," said Holo. "Say…jewels or gold. Those are sure things, no?"

"Ruvinheigen is not a profitable place for such things really."

Perhaps catching a bit of fluff in her nose, Holo gave a small sneeze as she licked her fur. "…Why's that?" she asked.

"The tariff is too high. It's protectionism. They levy serious taxes on all but a certain group of merchants. There's no business to be had there."

Towns that weakened the foundation of commerce with this kind of protectionism were not uncommon.

But Ruvinheigen's policy was aimed at turning monopolistic profits. Gold brought to the Church in Ruvinheigen could be stamped with the Church's holy seal, and such gold would bring safe travels, happiness in the future, or triumph in battle, all by the grace of God. There was even gold for guaranteeing happiness in the afterlife, and it all sold for exorbitant prices.

The Church Council that controlled Ruvinheigen colluded with the merchants under their power to preserve the monopoly, so taxes on gold entering the city were terrifying and punishments for smuggling harsh.

"Huh."

"If we somehow smuggled gold in, we'd be able to sell it for, oh, ten times what we paid. But the danger rises with the profit, so I've no choice but to make money bit by bit."

Lawrence shrugged, thinking wistfully of the end of his road.

In a city like Ruvinheigen, there were plenty of merchants who made in a single day what Lawrence had spent his entire life striving for.

It seemed unfair — no, worse than unfair, it was downright strange.

"Oh truly?" came Holo's unexpected reply.

"Do you have some idea otherwise?"

This was Holo the Wisewolf, after all. She might have come up with some unheard-of scheme.

Lawrence turned to her expectantly. Pausing in her grooming for a moment, Holo looked up at him.

"Why don't you just sneak it in?"

If she was always this foolish it would be charming, thought Lawrence to himself upon hearing her suggestion.

"If that were possible, everyone would do it."

"Oh, so you can't do that."

"When tariffs go up, smuggling does, too — it's a basic principle. Their inspections are very thorough."

"Surely a small amount wouldn't be found."

"If they *do* find anything, they'll cut off your hand at the very least. It's not worth the risk. It would be worth it if you were bringing a larger amount in…but that's impossible."

Holo smoothed her tail fur and nodded, satisfied with her grooming. Lawrence couldn't see much difference, but apparently Holo had her standards.

"Mm, 'tis true," she said. "Well, your business is steady enough. It is well as long as you make steady coin."

"Right you are, but I seem to have a certain companion bent on wasting that same steady coin."

Holo yawned, pretending not to hear the gibe as she squirmed to hide her tail. She rubbed her eyes and crept back to her place in the wagon bed.

Lawrence had not been terribly serious. He stopped following Holo's movements and looked to the road ahead. Trying to talk to her once she decided to sleep was an exercise in futility, so he abandoned the prospect.

For a while he could hear the clattering of weapons as she pushed them aside to make a place to nap, but soon silence returned, and he heard her sigh contentedly.

Lawrence glanced back and saw her curled into a ball, just like a dog or cat. He couldn't help smiling.

He couldn't very well say what he thought for many reasons, but he did want her to stay with him.

As Lawrence pondered this, Holo suddenly spoke.

"I forgot to say it earlier, but the wine we got from the master — I've no intention of drinking it all myself. This evening we must drink together — and enjoy that mutton, too."

Mildly surprised, Lawrence turned to look at her, but she was already curled back up.

But this time, she was smiling.

Lawrence looked ahead, holding the reins, and drove the horse carefully, so as not to shake the wagon any more than he had to.

CHAPTER TWO

The rolling hills ended, replaced by undulations in the landscape that barely rated the term, which made for easy traveling.

Lawrence hadn't yet shaken the effects of the previous night's wine, so the easy road suited him just fine.

With a companion to partake of the fine wine and food, he had overindulged. If he'd had to navigate a mountain trail in his current state, he would likely have tumbled straight to the bottom of the valley.

But here, there wasn't so much as a river, let alone a valley, so Lawrence could safely leave the horse to simply follow the road.

Occasionally he would nod off for a brief moment, and in the wagon bed Holo was sound asleep, snoring away without a care in the world. Every time Lawrence started awake, he thanked God for such peaceful times.

After passing many quiet hours this way, Holo finally stirred herself awake just past noon. She rubbed her eyes, her face still clearly bearing the marks of whatever she had slept against.

She hauled herself up to the driver's seat and gulped some water from a water-skin, a blank expression on her face. Happily, she did not seem hungover. Had she been, Lawrence might have had to stop the wagon — otherwise, she might wind up vomiting in the wagon bed, an outcome that didn't bear thinking about.

"'Tis good weather today," said Holo.

"It is."

The two exchanged lazy pleasantries, then both yawned hugely.

The road that they were on was one of the major northbound trade routes, so they encountered many other travelers while following it. Among them were merchants flying flags of countries so far away that Lawrence only knew of them from import receipts. Holo saw the flags and seemed to think they were simply advertising the merchant's home country, but generally the small flags were displayed so that merchants from the same nation could identify a fellow countryman should he pass. Generally such encounters would give way to exchanges of news from the old country. Arriving in a foreign land, where the language, food, and dress were all different, could lead even a constantly traveling merchant to homesickness.

Lawrence explained this to Holo, who then gazed at the small flags of passing merchants, deep in thought.

Holo had left her homeland hundreds of years ago, and her desire to speak to someone from her birthplace was stronger than any traveling merchant's homesickness.

"Ah, well, I'll be back soon enough, eh?" she declared with a smile, but there was a touch of loneliness in it.

It seemed to Lawrence that he should have some response to this, but none came to mind, and as he drove the horse along the road, the afternoon sun made the thought hazy in his mind.

There was nothing finer than warm sunlight in the cool season.

But the stillness was soon shattered.

Just as Lawrence and Holo started to doze off in the driver's seat, Holo spoke abruptly.

"Hey."

"…Mm?"

"There is a group of people."

"What'd you say?" Lawrence asked as he scrambled to grab the reins, his sleepiness gone in an instant. He narrowed his eyes and looked ahead into the distance.

Despite the slight undulations in the road, the generally flat terrain offered a good view ahead.

But Lawrence saw nothing. He looked to Holo, who now stood, staring forward intently.

"They are certainly there. I wonder what happened."

"Are they carrying weapons?"

There were only a few ways to explain a group of people on a trade road. Lawrence hoped for a large caravan of merchants, a column of pilgrims all visiting the same destination, or a member of the nobility visiting a foreign country.

But there were other, less-pleasant possibilities.

They could be bandits, rogues, hungry soldiers returning home, or mercenaries. Encountering returning soldiers or mercenaries might mean giving up everything he owned — if he was lucky. His life could well be forfeit.

What would happen to his female companion went without saying.

"I…do not see any weapons. They don't seem to be annoying soldiers, at any rate."

"You've encountered soldiers?" asked Lawrence, slightly surprised.

"They had long, sharp spears, which made them quite a bother. Though they couldn't keep up with my wits," Holo said so proudly that Lawrence didn't venture to ask what had happened to the unlucky mercenaries.

"There's…no one about, yes?" Holo looked around quickly, then pulled her hood back, and exposed her wolf ears.

Her pointed ears were the same brown as her tail, and like her tail, they expressed her mood so effectively that they were a good way to tell when she was (for example) lying.

Those same ears pricked forward intently.

Holo's attitude was every inch the wolf searching out its prey.

Lawrence had encountered such a wolf once before.

It had been a dark, windy night. Lawrence had been following a road across a plain, and by the time he heard the first howl, he was already within the wolves' territory. Baying sounded from every direction, when he realized he was surrounded, and the horse that pulled his wagon was half-mad with fear.

Just then, Lawrence caught sight of a single wolf.

Its posture was fearless as it had looked straight at Lawrence, its ears so keenly fixed upon him that he was sure it could hear him breathe. He had known that forcing his way free from the wolves' snare would be impossible, so he immediately took out a leather bag and, making sure the wolf could see, dumped all the meat, bread, and other provisions he had onto the ground. Then he urged his horse onward, the wolf watching him all the while.

He could feel the beast's gaze on his back for some time, but eventually the howls seemed to cluster around the food he had dropped, and he escaped unscathed.

Lawrence would never forget that wolf. And at this moment, Holo looked just like it.

"Hmm...seems there's some kind of to-do," said Holo, bringing Lawrence out of his reverie; he shook his head to clear it.

"Is there a market I've forgotten about?" said Lawrence. Roadside meetings to exchange information and advance trade were not unheard of.

"I wonder. It doesn't smell of a fight. That's for sure."

Holo pulled her hood back over her head and sat down.

Lawrence was preoccupied with driving the cart as she regarded him with an expression that said, "So what shall we do?"

The merchant was deep in thought as he visualized a map of the area.

Lawrence knew he had to get the arms in his wagon bed to the Church city of Ruvinheigen. He had signed a contract to that effect with a company in Ruvinheigen. If he detoured now, he would have to backtrack along a very roundabout route — the only other roads were so poor as to be passable only on foot.

"You don't smell any blood, do you?" asked Lawrence.

Holo shook her head decisively.

"Let's go, then. The detour is a bit too far."

"And even if they should be mercenaries, you have me," said Holo, pulling out the leather pouch filled with wheat that hung from her neck. A better bodyguard didn't exist.

Lawrence smiled trustingly as he drove the horse down the road.

"So, to detour around here, take the path of Saint Lyne?"

"No, it's surely shorter to take the road that crosses the plains to Mitzheim."

"Anyway, is that talk about the mercenary band true?"

"Buy this cloth, won't you? I'll take salt in exchange."

"Anyone here speak Parcian? I think this guy's got a problem!"

Lawrence and Holo caught snatches of conversation as they reached the throng of people.

Some of the people stopped in the road were recognizable at a glance as merchants. Others were artisans from different lands on pilgrimages to improve their skills.

Some walked; others traveled by wagon or carriage. Some led donkeys loaded with bundles of straw. Conversation was everywhere, and those who didn't share a common language gesticulated wildly in efforts to make themselves understood.

51

Getting into a confrontation because of a language barrier is a terrifyingly unforgettable experience — all the more so when you happen to be carrying your entire fortune with you.

Sadly, Lawrence didn't understand the man, either. He empathized, but there was nothing he could do, and he didn't know what the precise problem was anyway.

Lawrence glanced at Holo — a sign that she should stay quietly sitting in the driver's seat — and hopped out of the wagon, hailing a nearby merchant.

"Excuse me," he said.

"Hm? Oh, a fellow traveler. Have you just arrived?"

"Yes, from Poroson. But what's going on here? Surely the local earl hasn't decided to open a market here."

"Hah! Nay, were that so, we'd all have mats spread on the ground and be trading the day away. In truth, there's tell of a mercenary band crossing the road to Ruvinheigen. So we're all stopped here."

The merchant wore a turban and loose, baggy pants. The man had a heavy mantle wrapped about his neck and large knapsack slung over his back. Judging by his heavy clothes, the merchant frequented the heart of the northlands.

The dust of the road lingered on his snow-burned face. The many wrinkles and the tanned leather pallor of his skin were proof of a long life as a traveling merchant.

"A mercenary band? I know General Rastuille's group patrols these parts."

"No, they were flying crimson flags with a hawk device upon them."

Lawrence knitted his brow. "The Heinzberg Mercenary Band?"

"Oh ho. I see you've traveled the northlands. Indeed, they say it's the Hawks of Heinzberg — I'd sooner run into bandits than them when carrying a full load of goods."

It was said that the Hawks of Heinzberg were so hungry for wealth that wherever they passed, not so much as a single turnip leaf would be left behind if they thought it could be sold. They had made their name in the northlands, and if they were on the road ahead, trying to pass it would be suicidal.

The Heinzberg mercenaries were reputed to spot their prey faster than a hawk on the wing. They would be upon a lazily traveling merchant in an instant, surely.

However — mercenaries acted purely out of self-interest, and in that sense, they were not far from merchants. Essentially, when they behaved strangely, there was often something similarly unexpected happening in the marketplace.

For example, a sharp jump or drop in the price of goods.

Being a merchant, Lawrence was naturally pessimistic, but pessimism would get him nowhere, he knew — he was already on the road, loaded with goods. All that mattered now was how he would get to Ruvinheigen.

"So it seems taking a long detour is the only course," said Lawrence.

"Most probably. Apparently there's a new road to Ruvinheigen that heads off from the road to Kaslata, but it's been on the unsafe side lately, I hear."

Lawrence had not been in this region for half a year, so this was the first he had heard of a new road. He seemed to recall that on the northern side of the plains that stretched out, there was an eerie forest that was the source of constant unpleasant rumors.

"Unsafe?" he asked. "Unsafe how?"

"Well, there have always been wolves in the plains, but it's been especially bad lately, they say. There's a story going around that an entire caravan was taken two weeks ago—and the wolves were summoned by a pagan sorcerer."

Lawrence then remembered that the unpleasant rumors were mainly of wolves. He realized Holo was probably listening in on this conversation and stole a glance at her. A smile danced around the corners of her mouth.

"How do you get to this new road?"

"Hah, you're going to go? You're quite the rash one. Take this road straight, then turn right when it forks. Keep going for quite a while, then it will split again, and you bear left. Though peacefully whiling away two or three days here should be all right. It'd take but five minutes to tell if the mercenaries really are there, but by the time you saw them, it'd be too late. The merchants with fish or meat will have to head to a different city, but I'll play it safe."

Lawrence nodded and looked back to the contents of his own wagon. Fortunately his cargo was in no danger of spoiling, but he still wanted to sell it in Ruvinheigen.

He pondered silently for a moment, then gave his thanks to the other merchant, and returned to the wagon.

Holo had behaved herself, but once Lawrence sat down in the driver's seat, she started giggling. "Summoned, eh?"

"So, what is Holo the Wisewolf's take on this?"

"Hm?"

"The wolves in the plains," Lawrence clarified as he took up the reins and mulled over the question at hand—to go or not to go.

"Mm," sniffed Holo, idly biting her little fingernail with a sharp fang. "I think they'd be more interesting than humans. At the very least, we'll be able to talk."

It was a good joke.

"That decides it, then." Lawrence flicked the reins and turned the wagon around, heading down the road and away from the chattering merchants.

A few of them saw and raised their voice in surprise, but most simply took off their hats or capes and waved.

"Good luck," their gestures said.

There was no merchant that would shy away from a dangerous bridge — if across that dangerous bridge waited a larger profit.

The news of a mercenary band traveling the roads would spread faster than a plague. Such was the threat that they posed.

But for a merchant, time was an indispensable tool. Wasting it always led to loss.

This is why Lawrence decided that with Holo along, he would risk traveling the plains, despite the rumors of wolves.

The stories of a nearby mercenary band would surely have an impact on the Ruvinheigen market, and Lawrence meant to take advantage of that to make a nice bit of pocket money. At first he'd jumped to the assumption that things had taken a turn for the worse, but in reality, it was just the opposite.

And in any case, unexpected developments were part and parcel of the life of a traveling merchant — that's what made it fun.

"You certainly seem happy," remarked a bemused Holo.

"I suppose" was Lawrence's short reply.

The road ahead led to profit, the watchword of the traveling merchant.

They arrived at the plains in question before noon the next day.

There were times when new trade routes naturally occurred, and other times when the powers that be in the region created them. Sometimes grass was cleared to make the road, but in extreme cases, gravel would be laid, then topped with wooden planks, allowing carts to cross the terrain at relatively high speeds.

Such roads did not come cheaply, of course, and tolls to use them were high, but since robbers along these roads were dealt with harshly, the price was a good value in terms of time and safety.

The road ahead, with its rumors of wolf appearances, was somewhere between the two types.

A sign had been erected, indicating the destination of the road that now branched off. There at the fork was a pile of weather-beaten planks, as if there had once been a plan to build something at this junction. Perhaps the builders had intended to collect a toll to maintain the road well, but now all that remained was that one lonely sign.

The junction sat atop a small hill, and from its crest, one could see down the road as far as one cared to. This seemed like a good spot for lunch. Despite the approaching winter, the grass was still quite green, and Lawrence could look out across plains that he would have rushed to pasture his sheep upon were he a shepherd.

All that was left of the road that cut through the plains was a pair of wagon tracks, mostly overgrown with grass. Naturally, there were no other travelers.

According to Lawrence's mental map, the forest to the north of this road was the most suitable spot for the wolves to make their home, but it was hardly true that all wolves lived in forests. In the distance stood patches of tall grass, and this looked more and more like an ideal plain for wolves.

Lawrence could guess that much without asking Holo, but he went ahead and consulted her anyway.

"What do you think? Any wolves about?"

Holo, who was in the process of devouring a piece of dried mutton, gave Lawrence an exasperated look. "We wolves are hardly so foolish as to be spotted from a place with such an obviously good vantage," she said, sniffing with disdain. Her fangs occasionally showed as she chewed the meat, revealing her non-human nature.

Holo's statement and her fangs brought her essential wolf nature to the forefront of Lawrence's mind, and he considered complications.

If they did encounter wolves, the situation would become problematic.

"It should be well, though. Should we happen into a pack, we'll just throw them some jerky. We wolves don't get into pointless fights, after all."

Lawrence nodded and snapped the reins to start across the plains; the gentle breeze smelled faintly of wild beasts. Lawrence murmured a quiet prayer for safe travels.

"A *faram* silver piece."

"Nope. It's a counterfeit *marinne*."

"Wait, was not the counterfeit *marinne* this one?"

"No, that's a piece of late Radeon bishopry silver."

"..."

Holo fell silent, holding several pieces of silver in her hand.

Lawrence was teaching her the names of various currencies as a way to combat boredom, but even Holo the Wisewolf struggled with coins whose size and design were so similar.

"Well, you'll pick it up as you use them, no doubt," said Lawrence.

Holo was so serious that Lawrence was afraid to tease her, but his effort to be considerate only seemed to hurt her pride even more. She glared up at him, her ears flicking angrily under her hood.

"Once more, then!" she said.

"All right, from the top."

"Mm."

"*Trenni* silver, *phiring* silver, *ryut* silver, fake *marinne* silver, *faram* silver, bald king Landbard silver, Mitzfing temple silver, fake Mitzfing temple silver, Saint Mitzfing silver, Miztfingmas silver, and this one is…"

"…W-wait, now."

"Hm?"

Lawrence looked up from Holo's palm, where he'd been pointing at the various coins. Her expression was complicated — angry and on the verge of tears.

"Y-you're making sport of me," she said.

Lawrence remembered accusing his own teacher of the same thing, when he'd had to learn the names of all the different currencies — so without thinking, he laughed.

"Rrrrrr."

Holo growled and flashed her fangs, and Lawrence quickly composed himself. "The Mitzfing diocese in particular issues a lot of coin. I'm not teasing you, truly."

"Then don't laugh," Holo grumbled, looking back down at the coins. Lawrence couldn't help but smile.

"Anyway," Holo continued, "why are there so many coins? It seems such a bother."

"They're made when a new nation is established — or collapses. A powerful regional lord or church can issue coin, and of course, there's no end to counterfeiting. Even the *ryut* silver started out as a fake *trenni* piece, but it was so widely used it became an independent currency."

"But when pelts were used, you always knew what you were dealing with," said Holo, sniffing and then finally heaving a sigh of irritation. She might be able to tell the coins apart by scent, but Lawrence didn't know how serious she was about it.

"Still, it's a good way to kill time, eh?" he offered.

Without so much as a smile, Holo thrust the collection of coins back into Lawrence's hands. "Hmph. Enough. 'Tis time for a nap."

Holo stood, ignoring Lawrence's pained smile. He spoke to her as she made her way to the wagon bed.

"Even napping, you'll know if wolves come near?"

"Of course I shall."

"It'll be a hassle if we're surrounded."

To be cornered by mercenaries or bandits was, of course, troubling, but at least they could be reasoned with. Wolves, on the other hand, cared little for human words. One never knew what might cause them to attack.

Even with Holo at his side, Lawrence was uneasy.

"You worry excessively," said Holo, turning around with a grin, perhaps sensing his concern. "Most animals are quite aware, be they sleeping or awake. 'Tis only you humans who are defenseless in slumber."

"You'd be more convincing if you snored less."

Holo's face hardened at Lawrence's words. "I do not snore!"

"...Well, it's not too loud, I suppose," admitted Lawrence. He found her snoring rather charming, but the furrows in Holo's brow only deepened.

"I do *not* snore, I say."

"Fine, fine," said Lawrence, chuckling, but Holo came back up to the driver's seat and leaned close to him.

"I *do not*."

"All right! Fine!"

Holo seemed to consider this a question of honor, and Lawrence found her sharp expression irritating. She had constantly gotten the best of him since they'd met, and he realized he was generally used to her treatment.

She seemed to have nothing more to say; her expression sour, she turned her back on Lawrence unceremoniously.

"Still, there really doesn't seem to be anyone around," murmured Lawrence casually, smiling to himself at Holo's antics.

In truth there wasn't a single soul on the expansive plain, as far as the eye could see.

Even given the rumors of wolves, Lawrence would have expected a few people to be taking the shortcut to Ruvinheigen, but when he looked back, there was no one to be seen.

"Rumors are a powerful force," said Holo.

Even when her back was sullenly turned, her way of carrying on the conversation was amusing, and Lawrence chuckled in spite of himself. "True enough," he said with a nod.

"Though it's not quite true that there's no one about," said Holo, her tone slightly different now and her tail switching restlessly underneath her robe.

Then she sighed, bored.

So far, Holo had tended to her tail without alarming the merchants they passed on the road. When Lawrence saw her now deliberately hide it away, he wondered why — and soon had his answer.

"I smell sheep. There will be a shepherd ahead — I so hate shepherds."

If there were sheep on the plains ahead, there would be shepherds as well. Shepherds were legendary for their ability to detect wolves, and Holo must have known this.

Her small nose wrinkled when she spoke of them, making her distaste entirely evident.

Shepherds and wolves were natural enemies.

But as merchants and wolves were also basically antagonistic, Lawrence kept silent on that point.

"Shall we detour?"

"Nay, it's them who should run from us. There's no need for us to move aside."

Lawrence found himself chuckling at Holo's displeasure. She

glared at him, but he pretended not to notice and looked elsewhere.

"Well, if you say so, we'll stay the course. The fields suit our wagon quite well."

Holo nodded silently as Lawrence took up the reins.

The wagon traveled along the thin road through the plains, and at length, white dots that might have been sheep became visible in the distance. Holo's irritated expression remained.

Lawrence noticed when he stole a glance at her, and the sharp-eyed wolf girl seemed to notice.

She sniffed, twisting her lip. "I've despised shepherds longer than you've been alive. Getting along with them now is impossible," she said, sighing as she looked down. "There's all that delicious meat just walking about, but imagine just having to look at it, never tasting it — you'd hate them, too, would you not?"

Her somber tone was amusing, but it was clear that she was in fact very serious, so Lawrence made an effort to keep a straight face as he looked ahead.

They had now gotten close enough to the flock of sheep that Lawrence could tell one from another.

The sheep were grouped closely together, so it was hard to be sure of the precise number, but it was a score, certainly, that roamed lazily across the grass, chewing away placidly.

Of course, it was not only sheep on the plains. Holo's nemesis, the shepherd, was there as well, accompanied by a sheepdog.

The shepherd wore a robe the color of dry grass, and he had a horn fixed at the waist with a mist-gray sash. He also carried a staff longer than he was tall, with a palm-sized bell affixed to the top.

A black-furred sheepdog paced to and fro about its master, as if keeping guard. Its long fur made it seem like a tongue of black flame as it sprinted across the plains.

It was said that there were two things travelers needed to be careful of when encountering a shepherd on their travels.

The first was not to offend the shepherd. The second was to make sure the shepherd robes did not conceal a demon.

The shepherds, who wandered the vast plains with naught but sheepdogs for company, evoked such strange warnings because their lives were even lonelier than those of traveling merchants — they were often seen as nearly inhuman.

Leading their flocks across the plains alone, controlling the animals with nothing but staff and horn in hand — it was easy to imagine shepherds as some kind of pagan sorcerers.

Some said that meeting a shepherd while traveling ensured protection from accidents for a week, thanks to the spirits of the land — others said that shepherds were demons in disguise, and if you let your guard down, they would imprison your soul within one of the sheep they tended.

For his part, Lawrence found nothing strange in these beliefs. Shepherds were mysterious enough to warrant such ideas.

He raised his hand and waved it thrice in the way that had become ritual for greeting shepherds, and he was relieved to see the shepherd raise and lower his staff four times in the traditional fashion. At the very least, this shepherd was not a ghost.

This first barrier had been cleared, but the real test would come when he got closer and could ascertain whether or not the shepherd was a demon in disguise.

"I am Lawrence, a traveling merchant. This is my companion, Holo," declared Lawrence by way of introduction once he got close enough to make out the patchwork on the shepherd's cloak and brought his horse to a stop. The shepherd was rather small of stature, only a bit taller than Holo. While Lawrence talked, the dog that had been rounding up the sheep came trotting over to its master, sitting beside the shepherd like a faithful knight.

Gray eyes tinged with blue steadily scrutinized Lawrence and Holo.

The shepherd was silent.

"I have come by this road and met you by the grace of God, and if you are a good shepherd and true, you'll be well met."

A true shepherd would be able to prove himself with the traditional hymn and dance of his kind.

The shepherd nodded slowly and planted his staff directly in front of him.

Lawrence found himself surprised at the shepherd's small, slender hand, but he was even more surprised at what came next.

"By the blessing of God in the heavens..."

The voice that intoned the shepherd's hymn was that of a young girl's.

"By the protection of the spirits of the land..."

Moving her staff with skill, the shepherdess drew an arrow in the dirt with practiced ease and then, starting from the tip of the arrow, inscribed a circle around herself counterclockwise.

"The word of God is carried on the wind, and the blessings of the spirits of the land inhabit the very grass eaten by the lamb."

Once her circle reached the tip of the arrow, she began to stamp her feet in the earth.

"The lambs are led by the shepherd, and the shepherd by God."

Finally, she held her staff still, aligned with the tip of the arrow in the earth.

"By the grace of God, the shepherd follows the path of righteousness."

No matter the country, the shepherd's hymn was always the same. It was not the habit of shepherds to associate the way craftsmen or merchants did, but it was no exaggeration to say that the hymn and its dance were universal.

It was enough to lend credence to the idea that shepherds could converse across great distances by sending their words on the wind.

"My apologies for doubting you. You surely are a shepherdess," said Lawrence as he climbed down from the wagon. The shepherd girl's mouth quirked in a smile. Her hood still obscured much of her face, so it was difficult to be sure, but based on what was visible, she was a beauty.

Even as he remained gentlemanly, Lawrence was filled with curiosity.

Female merchants were rare, but shepherdesses were rarer still. Given that she was also a fetching young lass, a curious merchant could hardly fail to be interested.

However, merchants are completely hopeless at anything outside of the mercantile world.

Lawrence was a fine example of this. Unable to find a topic of conversation beyond their encounter on the road, he suppressed his curiosity and stuck only to the most standard of greetings.

"Having met you by the grace of God, I would have you pray for our safe travels, shepherdess."

"With pleasure."

At the sound of the girl's voice, calm as a grazing sheep, Lawrence's curiosity grew larger than a summer cloud. He didn't show it, but it was only with effort that he kept his inquisitiveness hidden. It was not his nature to ask shamelessly personal questions — nor did his nature grant him any gift for smooth talk. As he approached the shepherdess to receive her prayer, he thought of Weiz, the money changer in Pazzio, and envied him his easy way with women.

Added to that was Holo sitting in the wagon — Holo who hated all shepherds.

Somehow, that last fact was the weightiest reason for stifling his curiosity.

As Lawrence considered this, the shepherdess held her staff high to give the prayer for safe travel that had been requested of her.

"*Palti, mis, tuero. Le, spinzio, tiratto, cul.*"

The ancient words from scripture, used by shepherds in every country no matter what the language, retained their mysterious quality no matter how many times Lawrence heard them.

Shepherds did not know the true meaning of the words, but when praying for safe travels, they always used the same ones as if by some ancient agreement.

The way in which the shepherdess lowered her staff and blew a long note on her horn was also thus.

Lawrence gave his thanks for the prayer of safety and produced a brown copper coin. Copper, rather than gold or silver, was customary as a token of thanks for a shepherd, and it was also traditional for the shepherd not to refuse the token. The girl extended her hand, just slightly larger than Holo's, and Lawrence thanked her again as he placed the coin in her palm.

Unable to find any reason to continue his conversation with her, Lawrence reluctantly gave up.

"Well, then," he said, taking his leave — though his feet were slow to move as he tried to return to the wagon.

Unexpectedly, it was the shepherdess who spoke next.

"Er, are you perchance bound for Ruvinheigen?"

Her clear voice was different from Holo's, and it was hard to imagine that she could be counted among those who chose the harsh life of the shepherd. Lawrence glanced over his shoulder at Holo, who looked off in a different direction. She seemed quite bored.

"Yes, we're on our way there from Poroson."

"How did you come to hear of this path?"

"It's the pilgrimage road of Saint Metrogius. We heard of it just the other day."

"I see...Er, have you heard about the wolves, then?"

With these words, Lawrence understood why the girl had gone to the trouble of starting a conversation.

She no doubt took Lawrence for a simple merchant who had chosen this route without any information.

"I have indeed," he replied. "But I'm in a hurry, so I decided to take the risk."

There was no need to explain about Holo. For enough profit, any merchant would risk a wolf-infested road so there was no reason for suspicion.

But the shepherdess's reaction was strange.

She seemed almost disappointed.

"I see...," she muttered quietly, her shoulders slumping. She had clearly been hoping for something — but what?

Lawrence mulled the conversation over — there were not many possibilities.

Either she had hoped he didn't know about the wolves or she was in no hurry.

That was all he could guess from their brief exchange.

"Is something the matter?" he asked.

Were he not to ask the girl what her troubles were, it would be his failing not as a merchant, but as a man. He put on his most gentlemanly manner and gave her a businesslike smile.

Behind him, Holo was probably quite irritated by now, but he put the thought out of his mind.

"Er, well, um...that is..."

"Anything at all — is there something you need?"

When it came to negotiating, Lawrence was in his element. Selling her something would let him find out more about this rare female shepherd — even fairies were more common. Of course, behind his smile he was trying to work out exactly what he could sell her.

But with her next words, such thoughts evaporated.

"Well, I…I was wondering if you mightn't…hire me."

Faced with this shepherdess looking up at him as she held, no, *clung* to her staff, Lawrence's mind raced.

When a shepherd asked to be hired, it was equivalent to being asked if you would leave your sheep in their care.

But Lawrence had no sheep. What he did have was a single clever, cheeky wolf.

"Ah, well, as you can see, I'm a merchant, and I don't trade in sheep. I'm sorry, but…"

"Oh, no, not that —"

Flustered, the girl waved her hands hastily, then glanced from side to side as if to buy herself some time.

Her head was deep enough in the hood that her gaze wasn't visible, but it was clear that she was looking for something.

Perhaps that something was a tool that would help her explain her request.

Soon it seemed as if she had found it — from underneath her hood, she somehow communicated a sense of relief, almost as if she had expressive ears hidden under there, like Holo.

What the shepherd girl was looking for sat alertly beside her, a four-legged portrait of a faithful knight executed in black fur — her sheepdog.

"I'm a shepherd. Um, I tend my flock, but I can also drive off wolves."

As she spoke, she waved her right hand slightly, and the black dog stood at attention.

"If you'll be so good as to hire me, I can protect you and your companion from wolves. Would you consider it?"

As if to punctuate his mistress's clumsy sales pitch, the dog barked once, then dashed off to round up the flock, which was beginning to disperse.

Though knights or mercenaries were often hired as protection on dangerous roads, Lawrence had never heard of hiring a shepherd to drive off wolves, but now that he thought about it, having a shepherd at your side would give you a keen set of eyes and ears. He'd never heard of such an arrangement, though, because shepherds that would propose such a thing were nonexistent.

Lawrence looked at the dog as it rounded up sheep, as if practicing for possible wolf attacks, then turned back toward the girl.

Living the lonely life of a shepherd, she probably had no occasion to give a fake, ingratiating grin. Under the hood, she smiled awkwardly.

Lawrence thought a moment, then spoke.

"Wait a moment, if you would. I'll consult with my companion."

"Th-thank you!"

For his part, Lawrence was ready to hire the girl unconditionally, but hiring the shepherdess meant paying her money, and whenever money was involved, a merchant could think of nothing beyond the possible losses and gains.

Lawrence trotted back to the wagon bed and raised his voice to Holo who lounged there, looking bored. If he wanted to know about a shepherd's ability to repel wolves, he thought his best bet would be to ask the nearest wolf.

"What do you think of that shepherdess?"

"Hm? Mm…" Holo rubbed her eyes lazily and looked at the girl; Lawrence did likewise. The shepherdess did not return their gaze as she gave orders to her dog.

She didn't seem to be trying to show off her skills — she was merely rounding up the scattered sheep. Sheep, after all, tended to disperse when they stopped to graze and came closer together when forced to walk.

Holo turned away from the girl and spoke irritably. "I'm far more fetching."

The horse neighed, as if chuckling.

"Not that — I mean her skills."

"Skills?"

"What can you tell of her, as a shepherd? If she's good, she might be worth hiring. You heard us, surely."

Holo glanced at the girl, then gave Lawrence a bitter glare. "You already have me, do you not?"

"Of course. But it never occurred to me to use a shepherd to drive off wolves. There could be new business in it."

Holo the Wisewolf could tell when a person was lying. Despite the truth of Lawrence's statement, she still regarded him with suspicious eyes.

Lawrence soon understood why.

"I'm not being blinded by charm. You are the fairer, after all," he said, shrugging his shoulders as if to add, "Okay?"

"I suppose that's a passing mark" came the reply. It was a bit harsh being graded like that, but Holo smiled pleasantly, so surely it was a joke.

"So, what of her skill?" he asked.

Holo's face was instantly tense again. "I cannot say for certain without seeing her in action, but I suppose she'll be in the top half."

"Can you be a bit more concrete?"

"I could take a sheep from her. However, normal wolves would be dealt with, even if they attacked together."

It was an unexpectedly high appraisal.

"Her treatment of the sheep is very proficient. The worst shepherds are the ones with clever dogs who know how to cooperate with them. That one does both, I daresay. Her voice suggests that she's young, which makes it even worse. Before she gets any more dangerous, I've half a mind to — "

"All right, all right. Thanks."

Lawrence wasn't sure whether Holo was joking or not, but the swishing of her tail suggested she was half serious.

It was enough to know that the shepherdess was a good one. If he just provisionally hired her, it would still cost money, which would be wasted if she turned out to be clumsy. Lawrence turned to approach the girl but was stopped short by Holo speaking up.

"Hey."

"Yes?"

"Are you really going to hire that?" Holo's voice had an accusing tone.

Lawrence heard her and remembered that Holo had no love for shepherds.

"Aah. You hate her that much?"

"Well, as long as you're asking, no, I don't care for shepherds, but that's not what I mean. I'm talking about you."

This was the very definition of being caught off guard.

"...Excuse me?" asked Lawrence with all sincerity, having no idea what Holo meant. Holo sighed in irritation and narrowed her eyes. Her red-tinged amber irises were keen, burning with a cold fire.

"If you're going to hire her, that means she will be traveling with us for a time. I'm asking you if you have no problem with that."

Holo's eyes fixed Lawrence coolly in their gaze.

She sat in the wagon bed and thus looked down on him.

That wasn't necessarily why, but Lawrence couldn't shake the feeling that she was very angry with him.

Lawrence frantically thought it through. Holo was furious at him because he was going to hire a shepherd. If it wasn't because she hated shepherds, there were not many other possibilities he could imagine. The options disappeared one after the other, leaving only one.

Perhaps Holo preferred traveling as a pair, just the two of them.

"You don't like it?" he asked.

"I didn't say that" came her quick, sulky reply.

Musing fondly on this peevish side of Holo's, Lawrence smiled slightly as he spoke. "It's about two days to Ruvinheigen. No good?"

"...Nor did I say *that*," she said, shooting him a glance that he couldn't help but find charming.

"Well, in that case, I'm sorry, but I'll have to impose upon your patience," he said. He smiled openly, unable to resist Holo's unexpected charm.

Holo knitted her brow. "What exactly am I to endure, then?" she asked.

"Mm, well...," said Lawrence, hesitating. He couldn't very well suggest that she was jealous to her face. Once Holo's contrariness was roused, her opposition would be tireless.

"I'd just like to see how effective a shepherd is against wolves. You can manage for two days, can't you?"

"...'Tis not impossible. But that is not the issue."

"Well...," Lawrence began, concerned about the shepherd-ess — but Holo took the opportunity to continue.

"If we travel carelessly with someone else, they might find out about me, might they not? And I could manage, aye, but what about you?"

In those words, Lawrence heard something that made him stiffen. It was not his imagination, nor was it some grandiose thing, and even the shepherdess some distance away cocked her head as she looked on.

Of course. That was it. That was the other possibility. How had he overlooked it? He wished the sudden cold sweat that broke out all over him would wash away his mistake.

Thinking that Holo wanted to travel alone with him had distracted him from the obvious. He'd been presumptuous.

Holo's gaze bored into the back of his head.

The change in Lawrence's demeanor was obvious even from a distance, and the ancient wisewolf sitting next to him surely discerned his inner workings.

"Oh ho. I see how it is."

Lawrence reddened.

"You wanted me to say something like this, mm?"

He turned slowly back to her, facing the wolf girl with an expression that was downright desolate.

Holo put a closed hand to her mouth and spoke with a hesitant, modest tone. "I...I wanted to travel with just you..."

She twisted her body away fetchingly, averting her gaze with mock bashfulness, then looked back at him suddenly. In that brief interval, her expression shifted from demure to cold as she delivered the final blow.

"I jest."

Lawrence had no reply, and whether from frustration or embarrassment, it was doubtful if he would even be able to remain standing.

Wanting in any case to put some distance between himself and Holo, he turned and began to walk away before he was stopped by her call.

Lawrence looked over his shoulder, wondering if she hadn't had her fill of tormenting him, and saw Holo smiling there in the wagon bed.

It was an exasperated sort of grin.

He felt better as soon as he saw it.

"Honestly," he said with a sigh, giving her a rueful smile.

"I doubt I'll be exposed in two days. Do as you will," said Holo with a yawn and looked away as if to say, "This conversation is over."

Lawrence nodded, then trotted over to the shepherdess.

He had the feeling he'd grown a bit closer to Holo.

"Sorry to keep you waiting."

"Oh, n-not at all. So —"

"How does forty *trie* for the trip to Ruvinheigen sound? With a bonus if wolves attack and we make it through safely."

Lawrence wondered if she would refuse, since the conversation with Holo had wasted some time. The shepherdess's mouth hung open for a moment, but eventually Lawrence's words seemed to sink in, and she nodded hastily.

"Y-yes, please!"

"It's a deal, then," said Lawrence. He was about to extend his hand to shake, thereby sealing the contract, when he realized he hadn't asked the girl her name.

"Might I inquire as to your name, miss?"

"Oh, um, my apologies," said the girl. She seemed not to have realized that her hood was up, and now she hurried to pull it back.

Lawrence had spent a lot of time being humbled in front of Holo lately, and this was a sight for sore eyes.

The face that emerged was soft and meek, not unlike the sheep she tended, with faded, obviously uncombed blond hair tied back into a ponytail. She was slightly bedraggled and underfed, but her eyes were a beautiful dark brown, and on the whole she gave off an honorably impoverished impression.

"It's N-Norah. Norah Arendt."

"Again, I'm Kraft Lawrence. I go by Lawrence in business."

He took Norah's timidly offered hand and noticed that it — which was just slightly larger that Holo's — was shaking a

74

bit. Soon, though, she calmed herself and gripped Lawrence's hand lightly. Though her hand was small, its roughness marked her unmistakably as a shepherd.

"I'll be counting on you 'til Ruvinheigen!"

"My thanks," said Norah.

Her smile was like soft summer grass.

Lawrence had assumed they would only be able to go as fast as the sheep could walk, but he was mistaken.

The sheep were deceptively quick, and when climbing hills, the wagon was easily left behind.

Their *baaing* was as pastoral as ever, and the flock was like a white thread as it flowed quickly along the land.

Norah, of course, kept up with no difficulty. At the moment the sheep led the way, followed by Norah, who in turn was followed by Lawrence's wagon.

"Enek!" Norah called out, and like a bolt of black flame, the dark-furred dog came streaking back to his master, leaping into the air, barely able to wait for his next order. No sooner had the bell on Norah's staff rung than Enek charged off to the head of the group of sheep.

Lawrence didn't know much about shepherds, but he could tell that Norah's sheepdog handling was clearly excellent. The rapport she enjoyed with Enek was not gained in a single day.

But Enek did not seem like a young dog. Norah couldn't have been more than seventeen or eighteen herself, so perhaps her parents had been shepherds and the sheepdog was her inheritance.

His merchant curiosity was obvious.

"So, Norah, you..."

"Yes?"

"Have you been a shepherd long?"

After hearing Lawrence's question, Norah gave her bell one long ring, then slowed her pace, and came up along the wagon's right side.

Holo napped along the left edge of the wagon bed.

"Just four years now."

Since the profession required only that one memorize the hymn, dance, and phrases for blessing travelers who requested it, it was not uncommon to find even young shepherds with ten years' experience.

Even without a proper staff or sheepdog, one could guide a flock with a piece of dead wood and still be a fine shepherd.

"So your sheepdog — er, Enek, I mean — you trained him yourself?"

"No, I found him."

It was an unusual answer. A competent sheepdog was a prized possession — it was unthinkable that a shepherd would just let one go.

Lawrence could think of but one scenario. Its former master must have retired, leaving the dog to another.

"I became a shepherd after I found him."

"And before that?" Lawrence asked without thinking.

"I helped at an almshouse attached to an abbey and in return was allowed to live there."

It wasn't polite to pry into someone's past, but Norah answered smoothly, her feelings apparently unhurt. As a rare female shepherd, perhaps she was used to such questions.

If she had once lived at an almshouse, that suggested she had neither relatives nor inheritance, but now she was a fine shepherdess — the gods did still bless some with luck, it seemed.

"When I was relying on the almshouse, I thought I would never leave such work. It was good fortune meeting Enek."

"The result of daily prayer, surely."

"Yes, I can't help but think that I have God to thank for our meeting."

Her bell rang out again, and Enek came streaking back to her side.

As the dry sound of Enek's footfalls reached Lawrence's ears, Holo stirred, leaning lightly against the inside of the wagon. It seemed true, surely, that she could detect the approach of a wolf even while sleeping.

"I met him after the almshouse had lost its land to a swindling merchant," said Norah.

It pained Lawrence to hear of a fellow merchant's misdeeds, but the fact was such things were common.

"When I found him, he was in a sad state, covered in wounds," continued Norah.

"From wolves?"

Holo seemed to twitch. Perhaps she was only feigning sleep.

"No, I think it was brigands or mercenaries...There weren't wolves in the area. He was wandering about at the base of a hill with this staff in his mouth."

"I see."

Enek barked his pleasure at having his head petted.

Undoubtedly the dog hadn't been the only one wandering half dead at the foot of that hill. Most of those who were driven from an almshouse would have likely died from hunger. The bond between the girl and dog—they had suffered great hardship together—was no superficial thing.

And the life of a shepherd was lonely and mean. Enek was surely a welcome companion.

Certainly better than the goods Lawrence found himself transporting. Horses, too, were poor conversationalists.

"Still, this is the first time I've had a shepherd offer their services as an escort."

"Hm?"

"Normally they'd refuse such a request, to say nothing of offering work," he said with a laugh. A flustered Norah looked hastily at the ground.

"Um...," she began.

"What's that?"

"I just...wanted to talk to someone..."

Apparently her way of clinging to her staff—which was taller than she—was something of a habit.

Still, Lawrence certainly understood her feelings.

Outside of townspeople, those who did not find themselves stricken by loneliness were few.

"Although there is one other thing," the girl continued. Her demeanor brightened as she looked up. "I'd like to become a dressmaker."

"Ah, so it's the guild membership dues you need."

Norah again seemed embarrassed by Lawrence's words. Not being a merchant, it appeared she was unused to frank talk about money.

"They're high nearly everywhere. Though not necessarily so in a new town."

"Really? Is that true?" Her pretty brown eyes lit up with a frank anticipation that was entirely charming.

It was the fondest wish of most who lived by travel to settle in a town. Such a life was difficult even for an adult man, so the shepherdess must have felt the hardship still more keenly.

"Sometimes the guild dues are free, in newly founded towns."

"F-free...," whispered Norah with a countenance that betrayed her disbelief.

After days of enduring Holo's japes, seeing such a guileless face put Lawrence's heart at ease.

"If we meet any other merchants on the road, you should ask

them if they know of any plans to found new towns in the area. If they know, they'll probably be happy to tell you."

Norah nodded, her face shining with good cheer, as if she had been told the whereabouts of some grand treasure.

If such news made her this happy, there was clearly value in telling her.

And there was something about the girl that made him want to help her — something clearly conveyed in the way she worked so hard with her slender arms.

He found himself wishing that the wolf nearby — who could make a sly old merchant into her plaything with a single word — would take a page out of the shepherdess's book.

She'd be more likable that way, he thought to himself after a moment's hesitation.

"Fewer towns have been founded recently, though, so you'd do well to save steadily as you pray for good fortune, of course," said Lawrence.

"Yes. God can become angry if you rely on him too much."

He'd thought the girl was serious, so her joking tone took him by surprise.

If Holo hadn't been sleeping behind him, he would have invited her to sit in the driver's seat.

The moment the thought crossed his mind, though, Holo stirred; Lawrence spoke up hastily. "Uh, er, so, speaking strictly from the standpoint of a merchant, you might make more money escorting my kind like this than you do tending sheep. Surely the territory disputes are difficult."

"...They are," said Norah with a pained smile after a short pause. "The safest places already have shepherds occupying them."

"So all that's left are wolf-strewn fields."

"Yes."

"Wolves certainly can be troublesome — ow!"

79

Lawrence felt a sudden pain in his buttock and rose involuntarily from the driver's seat. Norah looked at him, puzzled, and he forced a smile before sitting back down.

Holo's sleep was evidently feigned. She had pinched him soundly.

"I'm sure the wolves are only looking for food, but sometimes they take lives in the process...A safer place would be nice," said Norah.

"Well, wolves are sly and treacherous creatures," said Lawrence, partially to get even for the pinch.

"If I speak ill of them, they may hear, so I won't."

Norah's humble manner was very charming, but Lawrence's reply, "Indeed," was mostly for the benefit of the wolf behind him.

"Still," he continued, "if you've skill enough to defend your flock even through wolf-infested fields, shouldn't your services be in great demand and your flock huge?"

"No, no, it's only by the grace of God that I remain safe... and I'm thankful to have any work at all. A huge flock, I just couldn't..."

Perhaps she was just being modest, but it seemed as though there was something else behind her sad smile. Lawrence couldn't think of many possibilities. Was she dissatisfied with her employer?

Though he knew it wasn't healthy, Lawrence's inquisitive nature voiced itself again. "Well, then your employer has no eye for skill," he said. "Mayhap it's time for a change."

Shepherds, after all, were merchants, too. It was only natural they should seek more favorable conditions.

"Oh, I couldn't possibly!" gasped Norah, taken aback.

It didn't seem like she was protesting out of fear of being heard, either. She was sincere.

"My apologies. I am sorry. As a merchant, I am always thinking of gains and losses."

"N-no, it's all right," said Norah, as if surprised at her own outspokenness. "...Um," she began.

"Yes?"

"I, I was wondering...do people change their employers... often?"

It was a strange question.

"Well, yes, I think it's normal if one is unsatisfied with one's terms of employment."

"I see..."

When she talked like this, it sounded as if she was somehow dissatisfied.

Yet Norah's total shock at the suggestion of changing those terms implied that she found the very idea outrageous. If that was the case, one might deduce the identity of her employer.

She had no relatives, so finding someone who would entrust his sheep to her would be difficult. Even the stoutest shepherd could expect to lose two sheep for every ten they herded — and such was an acceptable loss. It would be normal for someone to worry about a seemingly frail girl being able to bring back even half the flock.

Given that, whoever hired Norah had to be someone motivated by charity rather than self-interest.

In other words...

"If you don't mind my asking, is your employer by any chance the Church?"

Norah's expression was so stunned that Lawrence was glad he'd seen it. "How did you — "

"Call it a merchant's secret," said Lawrence with a laugh. Holo stomped her foot lightly. "Don't get cocky," she seemed to be saying.

"Er, well…yes. I receive my flock from a priest of the Church, but…"

"If it's the Church, you should have no troubles with your work. You've found a good employer."

Her employer was probably a priest connected with the alms-house she'd mentioned earlier. Personal connections were overwhelmingly more useful than either good fortune or strength.

"Yes, I was truly blessed," answered Norah with a smile.

But to Lawrence, whose very livelihood was based on discerning the truth among flattery and lies, her smile was obviously false.

As Norah turned aside to work with Enek, Lawrence looked at Holo, who had been feigning sleep. Holo returned his gaze, then she sniffed and turned away, shutting her eyes.

If she'd spoken, she would likely have said something like, "I've no sympathy at all."

"They've entrusted me with a flock," said Norah, "and they've aided me in many other ways."

She spoke as if to remind herself of the fact — it was pitiable to see.

The reason for Norah's downcast expression was clear. The Church was not employing her. It was watching her.

Of course, at first it probably had been out of charity that they'd entrusted her with a flock — which is precisely why she never thought of changing employers.

Shepherds were often thought of as being vaguely heretical. They weathered constant accusations of being "the devil's hands," so it was far from strange that the ever-suspicious Church would come to doubt a falsely accused woman who took such a job — all the more so when she excelled at it. It was just more evidence of pagan magic.

Even the most oblivious person would eventually notice such suspicion.

At the same time, the shepherdess's wages could not be high. She was worked hard for meager pay — there would certainly not be enough to set any aside. Lawrence guessed that was the reason she offered her services as an escort.

But Lawrence's merchant sense told him not to get any more deeply involved in the issue.

His curiosity was sated. Pursuing it any further would make him responsible for further developments.

"I see," he said. "I daresay you need not worry about finding a different employer."

"Do you think so?" asked Norah.

"Yes — with the Church's insistence on honorable poverty, your pay will always be a bit low, but so long as God doesn't abandon us, the Church will always exist. You'll not want for work. As long as you have work, you'll eat. Isn't that something to be thankful for?"

Having roused her concerns and suggested changing employers, Lawrence knew that the hard fact was nobody would hire a shepherd who'd caught the eye of the Church. It wouldn't do for his actions to rob a lone girl of her livelihood.

Lawrence wasn't lying, in any case, and Norah seemed to accept it. She nodded several times, slowly. "I suppose so," she agreed.

It was true that having a job — any job — was good, but hope was important, too. Lawrence cleared his throat and spoke as cheerfully as he could manage.

"Anyway, I've many acquaintances in Ruvinheigen, so we'll try asking there after any merchants that might need protection from wolves. After all, God never said anything about having a nice little sideline, eh?"

"Truly? Oh, thank you!"

Norah's face lit up so brilliantly that Lawrence couldn't help but be a bit smitten.

At such times, he was unable to muster his usual disdain for Weiz, the womanizing money changer in the port town of Pazzio.

But Norah was not a town girl nor was she an artisan girl or a shopgirl. She had a unique freshness to her. Part of it was a serious demeanor likely inherited from nuns at the almshouse, who had a slightly negative way of thinking, as if trying to suppress their feelings.

Norah seemed to have taken that unpleasant tendency and replaced it with something else.

It didn't take a womanizer to notice it. Lawrence was willing to bet that Enek, who even now wagged his tail at Norah, was a male.

"Settling in a town is the dream of all who live by travel, after all."

These words were still true.

Norah nodded and raised her staff high.

Her bell rang out and Enek bolted, turning the sheep neatly along the road.

They began to talk about food for traveling, becoming excited at the prospect.

Stretching across the wide plain, the road ahead was clear and easy.

Shepherds' nights come early. They decide where to camp well before the sun sets and are already curled up and sleeping by the time its red disc is low in the sky and the peasants are heading home from the fields. They then rise once the sun is down and the roads free of traffic, and they pass the night with their dogs, watching over the flock.

When dawn begins to break, shepherds sleep on alternate shifts with their dogs. There is little time for sleep in the life of a shepherd — one reason why the profession is such a hard one. The life of a merchant, who can count on a good night's sleep, is easy by comparison.

"Hard work, this," Lawrence muttered to no one in particular as he lay in the wagon bed, holding a piece of dried meat in his mouth. It wasn't yet cold enough to bother with a fire.

He glanced frequently at Norah's form, curled up like a stone by the roadside. He'd offered her the wagon bed, but she had begged off, saying this was how she always slept, before laying down in the meager padding afforded by the grass.

When he looked away from her, his eyes landed on Holo, who was at his right. Finally free from the prying eyes of humans, she had her tail out and had begun grooming it.

She never tires of that, thought Lawrence to himself as he looked at the busily grooming Holo, her profile the very image of seriousness. Suddenly she spoke, quietly.

"Daily care of one's tail is important."

For a moment Lawrence didn't understand, but then he remembered what he'd just said a moment age to himself; she was merely responding. He chuckled soundlessly, and Holo glanced at him, a question in her eyes.

"Oh, you meant the child," she said.

"Her name's Norah Arendt," explained Lawrence, amused at Holo's derisive use of *child* to refer to the girl.

Holo looked past Lawrence at Norah, then back. Just as Lawrence opened his mouth, she snatched the jerky from it. Lawrence was stunned into silence for a moment. When he came to his senses and tried to take the meat back, he received such an evil eye from Holo that he withdrew his hand.

It wasn't necessarily because of his teasing, but she was clearly in a foul temper.

She had gone out of her way to sit next to Lawrence as

she groomed her tail, so presumably the object of her anger wasn't him.

The source of her bad mood was obvious, really.

"Look, I *did* ask you," said Lawrence.

It sounded like an excuse. Holo sniffed in irritation.

"Can't even groom my tail in peace."

"Why don't you do it in the wagon bed?"

"Hmph. If I do it there…"

"If you do it there, what?" Lawrence pressed the suddenly silent Holo, who sneered at him, the jerky still held between her teeth. Evidently she didn't want to discuss the matter.

Lawrence wanted to know what she was going to say, but if he pushed any further, she would become genuinely angry.

He looked away from Holo, whose wounded-horse mood made her entirely too difficult to deal with, and put a leather flask filled with water to his lips.

Lawrence had just managed to stop thinking of her, and as the sun set, he considered starting a fire when Holo snapped at him. "You certainly seemed to enjoy your little chat with her," she said.

"Hm? With Norah?"

Holo still had the stolen jerky in her mouth as she looked down at her tail — but her proud tail was obviously not what was on her mind.

"She wanted to talk. I didn't have any reason to refuse, did I?"

Apparently the indulgence of a wisewolf was not so broad as to forgive pleasant conversation with a hated shepherd.

Holo had pretended to sleep the entire time. Norah had glanced at Holo and seemed inclined to engage the girl — who after all appeared to be roughly her age — in conversation but had stopped at asking her name. If Holo had wanted to speak to Norah, there had been opportunities aplenty.

"Also, I haven't spoken to a normal girl in some time," said Lawrence jokingly as he looked back to Holo — and faltered at what he saw.

Holo's expression had completely changed.

But it was nothing like the tears of jealousy he'd hoped to see.

She looked at him with nothing less than pity.

"You couldn't even tell that she hated speaking with you?"

"Huh...?" said Lawrence, casting a look back in Norah's direction, but stopped himself after a moment. As a merchant, he couldn't keep falling for the same trick twice.

Pretending he hadn't looked back at all, he calmed himself and remembered the words of a minstrel he'd once heard.

"Well, if she fell in love with me at first sight, she'd miss the fun of falling for me over weeks and months, eh?" he said.

Lawrence hadn't been convinced by this statement when he'd first heard it, but saying it now lent it a kind of conviction. Perhaps it really was more fun to fall in love gradually, rather than all at once.

But apparently, it was too much for Holo.

Her mouth dropped open in shock, and the piece of jerky fell to the floor.

"I've some wit myself, eh?" said Lawrence.

He'd said it to get a laugh out of Holo, but he was also half-serious.

As soon as she heard it, the wave that hit Holo became a tsunami on its way back, and she exploded with laughter.

"Mmph...bu-ha-ha-ha! Oh, oh, that's too good! Oh! Ha-ha-ha-ha!" Holo was doubled over, clutching her stomach, as she laughed, trying occasionally to stifle it only to dissolve into giggles yet again. Eventually her face turned red and she pitched forward into the pile of armor in the wagon bed, her pained laughter continuing.

Lawrence joined in at first, but as he saw more of Holo's reaction, his expression darkened.

Her tail, fluffier than normal thanks to its recent grooming, slapped against the wagon bed, almost as if begging for help.

"Okay, that's too much laughing."

It was no longer funny.

"...Ye gods," Lawrence muttered, taking another drink from the water flask, as if to wash down both the irritation at being laughed at, as well as the embarrassment he now felt for quoting a minstrel of all things.

"Haah. Whew. Oh...oh my. That was amusing."

"Are you quite done?" inquired Lawrence with a sigh, looking off to the sun that now sank into the horizon. He didn't much feel like looking at Holo, mistake or not.

"Mm. That was quite a trump card you had there."

Out of the corner of his eye, Lawrence saw Holo nestled atop the pile of armor, her laughter-fatigued face angled toward him.

It was as though she was exhausted after an all-out sprint.

"Well, as long as you're happy now."

No matter how much she hated shepherds, Holo's foul temper had been a bit *too* foul, Lawrence felt. It was hard to imagine that she was actually jealous of the conversation he'd had with the girl, nor was it true that she'd had absolutely no opportunity to groom her tail.

For a moment he wondered if it was simply shyness, but then he recalled their first meeting and decided that was entirely impossible.

"Hm? Happy?"

The wolf ears of the individual in question — which had become uncovered when she collapsed in laughter — now pricked up curiously as she regarded him with tear-blurred eyes, as though he had said something quite strange.

"You were in a foul temper earlier — because you couldn't tend to your tail, you said."

She seemed to remember something.

"Oh, quite," she said, her face calm.

She hauled herself up off of the cargo, then plopped herself back down, wiping the tears from the corners of her eyes.

Looking at her now, Lawrence thought she could not care less about whether or not she had sufficient opportunity for tail grooming. Had that just been an excuse to vent her irritation about something else entirely?

"Can't be helped," she said.

The tip of her tail slapped lightly against the floor of the wagon.

"Anyway, your trump card made me laugh so hard I turned giddy," said Holo, chuckling at the memory. She then looked outside the wagon. "Is the child not cold, I wonder?"

Her observation brought Lawrence back to the present. The sun was mostly down, and the sky was a darkening blue. He had best build a fire.

He had heard that shepherds didn't generally build fires, though that was because they had to watch over and chase down their sheep, not out of any particular resistance to cold.

Lawrence mused on this as he looked at Norah, curled up on the grass's paltry cushion.

He felt a sudden movement near his mouth and turned to find Holo thrusting a piece of jerky in his direction.

"Payment for your services as a jester."

"Only one piece of jerky for such laugher?"

"Oh, you don't want it?" taunted Holo, amused. Despite his embarrassment, Lawrence decided to accept the offering.

— but his teeth closed on air. Holo had drawn her hand back at the last moment.

The wisewolf snickered; Lawrence realized that going up against her was a fool's errand. If she decided to be so childish, he could only ignore her.

If he didn't build a fire soon, then they would all be eating dinner in the cold. Lawrence moved to get off the wagon, but Holo grabbed his sleeve and drew near.

Lawrence's heart skipped a beat.

Her eyelashes still had traces of tears in them, which caught the red light of the setting sun.

"I do think, from time to time, that some raw mutton would be nice — what say you?"

With the mournful bleating of the sheep echoing through the twilight air, Holo's words — spoken through her ever-keen fangs — could not have been entirely in jest.

After all, she *was* a wolf.

Lawrence patted Holo's head as if chiding her for making a bad joke, then hopped off the wagon.

Holo's lip curled in a brief snarl, but she soon smiled slightly and passed Lawrence the bundle of straw, tinder, and firewood.

CHAPTER THREE

Entering Ruvinheigen required passing through two separate checkpoints. One controlled passage through the city walls, and the other was situated out on the main road, which encircled the sprawl of greater Ruvinheigen.

Owing to the heavy traffic in and out of a city this size, one had to obtain a passage document at the outer checkpoint in order to pass through the station at the city walls. Legitimate travelers would use the legal routes into the city, obtain proper documents, and pass through the walls — any who lacked the passage document would be turned away on the spot.

The checkpoints also provided some degree of control over the inevitable smuggling and counterfeiting that large cities attracted.

The road that Lawrence and his companions took was evidently less traveled as their checkpoint — while not exactly crude — was rather simpler than checkpoints on more common routes, and the guard there seemed to know Norah. Using some strange power, she guided her sheep through the purposefully narrow checkpoint gate, and Lawrence followed after having his wares inspected.

The plain checkpoint stood in sharp contrast to the grand, august walls of Ruvinheigen.

It would be completely impossible to breach Ruvinheigen's walls without control of the surrounding areas. Walls of earth and timber were spoken of with pride in other areas, but here a barrier of stone surrounded the city with lookout towers positioned at regular intervals. Ruvinheigen was nearer a castle than a city, and Holo let out an involuntary gasp of wonder as they regarded it from a convenient hill just past the first inspection point.

Just outside the walls were cultivated fields, and between the fields, roads stretched radially out from the city.

Here a group of pigs was driven by a farmer; there a long merchant caravan was visible. Farther in the distance, a white carpet moved slowly over the ground — probably a flock of sheep some shepherd had brought to pasture. Shepherds with flocks numbering over one hundred were not rare, but this shepherd was likely biding his time before finally bringing his sheep into Ruvinheigen to support the city's consumption of meat.

Everything about the place was extraordinary.

Lawrence and his companions descended the hill and took one of the roads that ran between the fields.

The city was so large that from the hill it had seemed close, but traversing the distance took some time. Norah had to be careful that her sheep didn't eat the crops growing at either side of the road. At length, the group was close enough to make out the designs on the city walls.

At this point, Lawrence carefully produced two silver coins and held them out to Norah.

"Right, then, here's your forty *trie*."

Trie were simple copper coins. However, that many coins would be unwieldy, and Lawrence reckoned that the two silver coins he gave her could be exchanged for forty-five *trie*.

He had paid Norah extra because he felt indebted to her. He and Holo had been fortunate not to encounter any wolves, but Lawrence was still impressed by the girl's skill. Even Holo would concede it, and it was easy for Lawrence to see Norah distinguishing herself in the future. The extra money was just an investment to that end.

"Er, but, if I exchange this, won't it come to more than…?"

"Call it an investment," said Lawrence.

"An…investment?"

"Now that I know such a skilled shepherd, I might be able to turn a surprising profit on wool," said Lawrence in a purposefully greedy tone. Norah laughed and grudgingly accepted the two silver coins.

"We'll be at the Rowan Trade Guild for a while. If you've plans to take your flock afield again, come by there first. I might be able to introduce you to a merchant in need of escort."

"I shall."

"Oh, one last thing. The area where you can provide escort — is it just the route we took?"

"Er, I can go as far as Kaslata and Poroson. Oh, and also to Lamtra."

Kaslata was a remote town with little to recommend it, and Lawrence was surprised to hear Norah mention Lamtra. Lamtra was one of the few places in the area not under the influence of Ruvinheigen, which controlled the rest of the region. It was not so very far north from the great city — Lawrence and his party could have gotten there by heading north from the midpoint of the road they had just taken. However, to reach Lamtra required passing through a dark and eerie forest, which even knights blanched at, so it had long resisted invasion from Ruvinheigen and was the only city where significant numbers of pagans still lived.

All the legitimate routes to Lamtra were incredibly round-about, so Norah must not be suggesting she could provide escort along them. She clearly had confidence in her ability to navigate the forest.

If that was true, there were many merchants who would want to go with her.

"Lamtra, eh? I daresay you'll have some business," said Lawrence.

Norah's face lit up. "Thank you very much!" she said, bowing low as if she was still living in an almshouse.

"My pleasure. Well, then, I'll be entering from the southeast gate, so here's where we part ways."

"Certainly. I hope we meet again," said Norah.

Lawrence nodded and reined his horse to the left as Norah rang her bell. Ruvinheigen was large enough to have no less than seventeen great gates. Between those were smaller gates used for large groups of sheep and other livestock, which Norah would have to use.

Also, given the city's labyrinthine interior, it was common sense to enter via the gate nearest one's destination — the city was just that big.

As they parted, Lawrence looked back over his shoulder at the girl and saw that Norah was still watching him and Holo. When she saw Lawrence turn, Norah waved wistfully to them.

He couldn't very well not wave back, but he was afraid of being mocked by Holo. Lawrence stole a sideways glance at her, which the wolf girl noticed.

"You think me so ill-natured?"

Lawrence grinned, pained, then faced forward after returning Norah's wave.

"Hmph. Well, now we'll see how those honeyed peach preserves taste! I am surely looking forward to that."

"Hm. So you remembered that, did you?" Lawrence said. As

they approached the gate, he considered how much of his load of armor he would lose to the entrance tax.

"Surely you're not saying you won't buy any!" Holo was intimidating, despite her sweet smile and modestly tilted head.

Lawrence averted his eyes and muttered almost as if he were praying. "We can't buy any if they aren't selling any."

"Well, naturally," said Holo, as if entirely confident that the preserves would be for sale.

"Oh, and you probably know this already, but try to act a little more nunlike at the next checkpoint. They'll be more lenient on a nun."

"Hmph. I'm not so foolish as to stir up trouble in a city such as this. But do I even resemble a nun?"

"There's no trouble on that count."

As soon as he said it, Lawrence regretted it. Holo had endured much suffering at the hands of the Church. Saying she looked like a nun might make her angry.

"Heh, is that so?" Holo said, giggling. She seemed happy — surprisingly so.

"... What, you're not angry?"

"Hm? Why would I be?"

"Well, I mean . . . the Church is your enemy, more or less."

"Not necessarily. 'Tis the same as having someone like you around. Nuns are all fundamentally kind, and even a wolf like me can tell that most of them are quite lovely. Beauty transcends species."

For his part, Lawrence understood well enough but was mostly glad she wasn't cross.

And it was true that many nuns were beautiful. This may well have been partially because they were so assiduously meek, pure, and ascetic, but there was also the fact that the illegitimate child of many a noble became a nun.

Many a beautiful woman contrived to use her beauty to become the mistress of a wealthy noble, and many a fetching noble daughter was seduced by a rake, who wielded poetry and art like a weapon.

Often the children resulting from such liaisons were more hale and healthy than their legitimate siblings — most likely because the men and women able to seduce nobility were formidable themselves.

Such children were the cause of a fair share of succession struggles, but most of them would enter an abbey — thus many of the abbey's brothers and sisters were handsome indeed.

"I don't think I could suffer the constant fasting, though," said Holo.

Lawrence laughed openly.

As they progressed down the road that ran alongside the great wall, a lively group of people became visible at its end.

It was the southeast entrance.

The huge gate was flung open, and while some people entered the city, others left, setting out on their travels.

The inspections of people and goods were conducted as one passed through the walls, and despite the volume of travelers, there was little waiting since so many inspectors were on duty.

However, unlike Poroson, not a single person bothered to form a line, so unless one was familiar with the protocol, it was possible to wind up standing outside the gate for hours. Lawrence knew the procedure, though, and he guided his horse forward, trying his best to avoid colliding with anyone; threading his way past less-knowledgeable folk; and finally arriving at the road that passed under the archway, carved out of the stone wall, which led into the city. In times of war, this was an important point to defend, so the walls here were very thick. Lawrence glanced up to see a thickly timbered gate suspended above the crowds, and with a chill, he wondered what would happen if it were to fall—though he'd never heard of such an accident. Just past the gate, there was an opening in the roof through which boiling oil could be poured on invading enemies should they breach the wall. The stone around the opening was discolored, perhaps due to frequency of use.

Just past the walls was the inspection checkpoint, and beyond that, Lawrence could see the streets of Ruvinheigen.

Any large city hemmed in by walls—not just Ruvinheigen—had to expand upward, rather than outward, owing to limited space. Ruvinheigen was particularly challenged in this regard, and the city which greeted Lawrence was reminiscent of a ship's hold piled high with goods. Several buildings looked ready to overflow at any moment. Still beyond those, he could see the high, high roof of Ruvinheigen's great cathedral.

"You there, merchant!" a voice called out.

Lawrence shifted his attention to a guard wearing thin leather armor who pointed at him.

"Staring at the city will get you in an accident!" chided the guard.

"My apologies."

There was a titter at Lawrence's side.

"Next! Uh, you there! The merchant that just got scolded!"

It was difficult to navigate without a proper line. Lawrence choked down the embarrassing brand and guided his horse toward the inspector, bowing in greeting.

"Passage papers," demanded the inspector impatiently.

"Right here."

"Hm. Out of Poroson, eh? Your goods?"

"Twenty sets of armor."

Commerce was prohibited outside the walls, so it was required that a merchant's load match the travel document.

The inspector blinked rapidly. He seemed surprised.

"Armor? From Poroson?"

"Ah, yes. I bought them from the Latparron Company in Poroson. Is there a problem?"

Ruvinheigen had been founded when knights' companies tasked with suppressing the pagans had set up fortifications, and to this day, the city remained an important supply depot for soldiers heading north. Weapons and armor from surrounding areas were imported here and flew off shelves immediately.

Lawrence was thus puzzled by the inspector's reaction, but the official just shook his head and turned his attention to the wagon bed. The cart contained twenty sets of helms, gauntlets, breastplates, and greaves — all fashioned out of leather and chain mail. The wine had not been merchandise for sale but would still have been taxed. However, it had long since been drunk dry.

There was nothing suspicious, and the inspector seemed satisfied. He climbed atop the wagon to verify that no taxable items like gold or jewels were hidden within the armor; then, appeased, he climbed back down. He gave the bundle of firewood a cursory check, but hiding anything within it would have been impossible.

"This does seem like Poroson armor. Will you be paying in coin or stock?"

The armor was worth one hundred *lumione* total, so the 10 percent tax would amount to ten *lumione*.

Ten *lumione* itself came to more than three hundred pieces of *trenni* silver, and no merchant would travel carrying so much coin. It would have been inconvenient for the inspector to count out three hundred pieces even if Lawrence had them.

Handing over some of the armor itself as tax solved all these problems.

"Stock," said Lawrence.

"Good answer," replied the inspector, which elicited a sigh of relief from Lawrence. "Turn in two sets of armor over there," he said, recording something with a quill on a piece of paper, which he handed to Lawrence.

Two suits of armor out of twenty satisfied the 10 percent tax.

Lawrence nodded after confirming the accuracy of the receipt.

For Holo's part, she was every inch a nun and thus went unquestioned. This was a city of the Church, and suspicion of priests or nuns was likely more trouble than it was worth.

In any case, relieved that he'd gotten through the checkpoint smoothly, Lawrence descended from the wagon, then took hold of the reins, and walked on. It would only become more crowded — and thus dangerous — ahead.

The area around the tax collection point was like a war, a din of colliding languages and clothing. Lawrence could hear the same haggling and begging one heard at any site where taxes were remitted.

Naturally, he didn't engage in anything so foolish as haggling over taxes and obediently handed over the required two suits of armor.

However, the clerk took a look at the receipt Lawrence received from the inspector and knitted his brow.

Lawrence was suddenly nervous — had there been some impropriety? But no, it seemed everything was in order.

Unclear as to what had just happened, Lawrence passed through the checkpoint and into the city, climbing back atop the wagon.

The reaction of the inspector on seeing the cargo of armor was a mystery, but Lawrence had made it through, so there no more cause for concern.

He muttered reassurances to himself, but a certain uneasiness remained.

"Hey, merchant," said Holo.

Lawrence was suddenly unsettled at the sound of Holo's voice, as though he was about to hear something unpleasant. "What?"

Holo spoke slowly in response to Lawrence's question. "Mm. I am hungry."

"..."

Lawrence looked ahead again, ignoring both Holo's complaint and his own lingering unease.

The great cathedral of Ruvinheigen is so massive that it is visible from anywhere in the city. The metropolis spreads out around the cathedral — the district closest to it is known as the old city, hemmed in by the old city walls, and surrounding those walls, in turn, is the rest of Ruvinheigen.

In the southern part of the roughly circular municipality was its biggest gate, and passing through the structure — which was large enough to allow siege engines through — there was a plaza so wide as to be the envy of any foreign king, with a fountain created using the latest craftsmanship available in the south and a permanent marketplace.

Around the edges of the plaza sat the great trading firms of the region, the homes of true power and influence in the city, all linked at the eaves. Beyond them were smaller trading companies and the homes and shops of a wide variety of craftsmen.

The great cathedral stood in the middle of another of Ruvinheigen's plazas, which were arranged as a great pentagon with the southern gate at its peak. Each plaza had its own characteristics, almost like a city within a city.

Lawrence and Holo passed through the southeast entrance, and though the square they entered could hardly be compared to the great southern plaza, it was still sizable.

In the center of the square stood striking statues of knights, who had accomplished some memorable deed in the war against the pagans, and saints, who had made some important contribution to the faith.

Scores of stalls were lined up in the plaza with people on straw mats hawking their wares within the structures.

There were no stalls around the bronze statues, though. Instead, an ensemble traded musical phrases with a minstrel playing a plain wooden flute while a famous troupe of comedic actors plied their trade. Mingling with the entertainers were pilgrim priests, clad in rags and wielding tattered books of scripture as they preached; their rapturously attentive disciples wore even worse clothing.

It seemed like the order of the day in the district was getting a light snack at one of the booths, watching the performers, and taking in a sermon after you had your fun.

After Lawrence and Holo arranged for a room at an inn and stabled the horse, they started for the trading house to begin their business arrangements when they found themselves drawn toward the commotion of happy voices and delicious scents.

They held some fried lamprey eel, which seemed to be a popular snack. The sweetness of the oil masked the earthy smell of the stuff, and no sooner had you finished a piece than you wanted another, which seemed to be human nature. The next thing Lawrence knew, he and Holo had stopped in front of a drink stand, taking in the comedy show over some beer.

"Mmm, that's tasty," said Holo after she drained one cup, and with foam still clinging to the corners of her mouth, she ordered another round. The barman was only too happy to serve such a profitable customer.

Having snacked on fried eel and beer all afternoon, Holo no longer looked anything like a nun.

The outfit she used upon entering the city would have been less convincing because of Lawrence's presence — nothing was fishier than a person of faith traveling with a merchant, after all.

So Holo had switched her robe for a rabbit-skin cape, but she folded the robe up and wrapped it about her waist, using the resulting makeshift skirt to hide her tail. Her perpetually troublesome ears were concealed under a triangular kerchief.

Thus had Holo transformed from nun to town lass. The square was packed with girls who had abandoned work for an afternoon of fun, so she hardly stood out. The way she drank, with no regard for her coin purse, made it easy to think she was parting some guileless merchant from his money.

Actually, as Lawrence paid in advance, the barman seemed to think it was he who had been tripped up by this casually expensive girl.

Lawrence gave the man a pained smile to deflect the issue, but the barman wasn't necessarily wrong, either.

"The liquor is good and the people lively — 'tis a good city, no?"

"The liveliness comes at a price — we have to watch ourselves, especially around any knights or mercenaries. A quarrel with their ilk will be more trouble than we need."

"You can count on me," said Holo.

Lawrence sighed instead of voicing his thoughts on the matter. "Right, well, we should be moving on."

He had finished his second beer while Holo had downed four in the same amount of time, so it seemed an opportune moment to leave.

"Mm? Already? I've not yet begun to drink."

"You can drink more tonight. Let's go."

Looking back and forth from Lawrence to her cup, Holo finally seemed to give up and backed away from the stall. The barman called out "come again!" and his voice disappeared into the crowd alongside Lawrence and Holo.

"So, then, where do we go?"

"To the trading house — and at least wipe your mouth, hm?"

Only now aware of the foam at the corners of her mouth, Holo brought her sleeve to her lips as if to wipe them.

However, thinking better of this at the last second, she instead grabbed Lawrence's sleeve and wiped her mouth on it.

"Why, you — I'll remember that."

"And yet you've already hit me," said Holo, holding his head off with one hand and glaring at him, her other hand firmly clamped around Lawrence's. Her anger at being poked lasted but a moment.

"Still," she continued.

"Hm?"

"Why must you drag me along to this trading house? I'd just as soon drink my fill in the square."

"It's too dangerous to leave you alone," warned Lawrence.

Holo looked blank for a moment, then giggled bashfully — perhaps she'd misunderstood.

"Mm, 'tis true. I am a bit too lovely to be left alone!"

It was true that Holo, with the fall of her red-brown hair swaying, tended to attract attention, and some of those who looked on must have envied Lawrence, who held her hand.

It wasn't that he didn't take a bit of pride in walking around with Holo, but the fact was that there was no telling what trouble she would get into if left on her own.

The square was a fun, lively place, but fun, lively places seemed to attract more than their share of trouble. If by some fluke her true form was exposed there, it would be disastrous.

"No amount of loveliness will put Church guards or temple knights off your tail," said Lawrence. "What if you get drunk and let your ears or tail show?"

"Why, I'll just turn on them. I'll grab you in my jaws, and we'll dash from the city. I can surely leap over those walls. Isn't there some old story about a knight and a princess like that?"

"What, the one where the knight rescues the captured princess?"

"That's the one!" said Holo, amused. For Lawrence, there wasn't a trace of romance in the idea of Holo assuming her wolf form and escaping with him between her teeth.

Quite the contrary, just the thought of being clamped between those great jaws made Lawrence want to shudder.

"Well, don't do *that*," he said.

"Mm. If you're the one that's captured, there's little gain in rescuing you."

Lawrence made a pained expression and looked at Holo, who eyed him mischievously.

The two of them passed around the swirl of people and headed north on a narrow lane where storefronts stood under the sparkling, sunlit eaves that lined the block. There were no trading companies here, but rather buildings with merchant unions and trading houses. Some were economic associations created by mixed groups of merchants from different areas; others were buildings for craft unions created by textile merchants who cooperated regardless of their origin.

The world offered no protection for merchants who met with danger or accidents. Just as knights wore helms and breastplates, merchants banded together to assure their own safety. The largest economic alliances were a match for even a merchant's worst enemy: a nation bent on abusing its power.

One famous story had eighteen regions and twenty-three guilds coming together in the most powerful economic alliance ever created, matching forces with an army fourteen thousand strong and claiming victory almost instantly. The union that was formed to preserve profits transcended borders and was a good example of the solidarity to which such groups could give rise.

For that reason, the buildings these unions and associations made use of were somehow quite orderly, and those that frequented them conducted themselves politely.

Without civility, a long-standing rivalry between (for example) a fishmonger and a butcher might escalate into violence and overflow into the town.

Such manners generally sprung from an aversion to sullying one's organization's good name, but they were still very important to merchants. Commerce depended on trust and reputation, after all.

"Right then, I've got business to take care of, so just wait here," instructed Lawrence once they arrived at the trading house with which he was associated. He saw the building painted in the local style and could not help but feel a certain nostalgia. He kept it to himself, though, out of consideration for Holo, whose homeland was still far away.

Holo regarded him as he feigned indifference. "What, are you not going to bring me in and show me off to your old village mates?"

It seemed she had spotted the bit of pride he'd mustered along the way, but that wasn't enough to bother him anymore.

"That would basically amount to a preamble to marriage. My town's marriage ceremonies are quite rowdy — are you sure you're up for that?"

This sort of thing was quite universal. Holo's knowledge of the human world seemed to give her some idea.

She shook her head in distaste.

"I'll be done soon. If you wait nicely, I'll buy you some sweetbread," said Lawrence.

"I'll thank you not to treat me like a child."

"Oh, you don't want any?"

"I do."

Lawrence couldn't help but laugh at Holo's serious reply, and leaving her there, he ascended the steps to the building and rapped on the door of the trading company. The door had no knocker, which was a sign that only members should knock.

After waiting some time, however, there was still no answer.

Lawrence ventured to open the door on his own. Given the time of day, it was possible that everyone was out in the market-place — and as he expected, the interior was silent. The first floor was a spacious lobby set up as a drinking hall in which the members could relax, but the chairs were set atop the round tables, and a mop leaned against one wall. Evidently the room was being cleaned.

Nothing had changed in the year Lawrence had been away, save the hairline of the guild master who tended the front counter — which had receded. He imagined the master's already large belly had grown larger, but unfortunately the man seemed to find it difficult to stand, so Lawrence couldn't be sure.

The master lifted his gaze from the counter and with a friendly smile began his usual ribbing. "Well, now, what a poor merchant is this! Wandering around a trading house at this hour — cares not a whit for making money. You'd do better changing into a thief's clothes and getting yourself to an alehouse!"

"The greatest merchants make money without dirtying their shoes with so much as a speck of dust; their only stain is the ink upon their fingers. Running around the marketplace all day is the sign of the third-rate merchant. Am I wrong?"

Every time they met like this, Lawrence used to get angry recalling the master's inexplicable habit of jesting at him when he was a young apprentice. Somewhere along the line, he had learned to spar right back without getting flustered.

Lawrence easily returned the master's jape, then straightened and brought his heels together smartly, squaring himself to the counter as he approached it.

The man ensconced behind the counter was squarely built and stout and slapped his forehead at Lawrence's reply, grinning. "You've gotten clever, boy. Welcome home, my son!"

"Stop the 'my son' nonsense."

"What are you saying? All in the Rowen Trade Guild are my sons and daughters."

The two shook hands over the familiar exchanges.

"And yet I know of all the times you wet your bedroll after we made camp — and is it not the teaching of God that a good father knows well his son? Or should I mention the time you stole the cash box and snuck off with your friends, trembling, to the whorehouse?"

"All right, all right. I'm Kraft Lawrence, then, son of the great Jakob Tarantino."

"So, Kraft my boy. You're back in Ruvinheigen after a year gone. How fares our family in other towns?"

Jakob's manner was as overbearing as always, and it hit Lawrence with all the harsh edge and warmth of liquor. The trading house was truly his homeland in a foreign city.

This was the kind of harsh hospitality he only tasted at home.

"They're all doing well by the grace of the saints."

"Good, good. Well, now, if you've gone the rounds among family, you must be fairly brimming with profit! If your purse is heavy, your trousers sag. If your trousers sag, the ladies won't like you. And you, lad, are a vain one. Am I wrong?"

Lawrence had no comeback. Laughing at the master's heavy-handed way of seeking a contribution, he replied, "I've heard that the ability to handle figures gets bad with age, but old Jakob's eyes are still sharp, I see."

Lawrence seamlessly withdrew ten silver pieces from the purse fixed at his waist and slapped them down on the counter with a flourish.

If he'd grudgingly handed over two or three copper coins, he would have gotten an earful.

He wanted to show the old man up, and in any case, his profit from the spice had been sizable. The generous donation was a kind of report that he was doing business on this scale now — and Jakob broke into a grin at it.

"Ha-ha-ha, the little bed wetter's bringing in real silver now! How lovely."

"Enough about the bed-wetting."

"You still are one to me, boy."

Lawrence shrugged, at which point Jakob's laugh rang out again.

"Well, then, you've come all the way out here in the middle of the day, so you must be here on business. You need a certificate?"

"Yes."

"I surely look forward to the day when you're a famous enough merchant that people flinch at the mention of your name," said Jakob.

"You're telling me," agreed Lawrence — then remembered he had something else to mention. "Oh, right. Do you know of any traders in the guild that're headed to Lamtra?"

Jakob placed a pen and ink pot on the desk, then looked up, and raised his eyebrows at Lawrence. "Now that's a strange question," he remarked.

"I was just thinking of providing a shortcut to Lamtra in exchange for a consideration..."

Jakob's gaze swung around for a moment before settling again on Lawrence. He wore a meaningful smile.

"Oh ho. Have you met a certain young shepherdess?"

Lawrence was taken so off guard that his breath momentarily

caught in his throat, but when he stopped to consider it, he found it was far from surprising that merchants in Ruvinheigen would know of Norah the shepherd girl.

Which meant that Lawrence's radical idea had already occurred to others.

"You're far from the first to have that idea, boy. Especially after the road that went through the area she wanders was finished. But nobody makes a business of that now, and nobody asks that girl for escort. Do you know why?" Jakob spoke smoothly as he wrote out the certificate.

Lawrence answered with a sigh, "Because there's no business in it?"

Jakob nodded and looked up. "That girl's the only one who wanders that area unscathed. Sure, Norah the Nymph's pretty popular with her charm and skill, but I don't have to tell you what the Church thinks about that. Nobody wants to get tangled up with those sons of bitches."

He dipped the tip of his quill in the ink pot and continued, a malicious leer on his face. "I know Norah the Nymph is the type of girl you like, but here's some free advice: Give it up."

It was just everyday morning conversation, but it cut a little too close to the quick, and Lawrence could only offer a pained sort of smile in reply.

"So, who do I make the certificate out to? Or should I leave it blank?"

"No, make it out to the Remelio Company, please."

Jakob paused again for a moment.

He looked back at Lawrence with the appraising eyes of a merchant.

"Remelio, eh? If you already know who you're selling to . . . , you must be selling on margin, then, hmm?"

"Yes. Out of Poroson. Is there something I should know?" asked

Lawrence, only to be hit by a sudden, severe look that surfaced like a fish from the depths of a pond.

"Mm. Well, you'll see when you get there. Here, your certificate."

When a merchant first sold goods to a trading house, the worst problem he might encounter was if a competing merchant forced their prices down. Such things didn't happen too often in smaller towns like Pazzio and Poroson, but Ruvinheigen was large, and because of the connections between the many trading firms and associations, it happened often. Ruvinheigen was an obvious place for large transactions, and the smaller transactions of individual merchants were like grains of sand.

Thus, Lawrence would state which trading guild he was associated with and make it clear that he could not be trifled with. With the name of a guild behind him, he wouldn't be treated badly.

"The Rowen Trade Guild is under the protection of Saint Lambardos. I'll pray for your good fortune," said Jakob.

"My thanks…"

Lawrence took the certificate that proved his affiliation with the Rowen Trade Guild, vaguely thanking Jakob, who clearly knew more than he was saying.

Lawrence knew from experience that if he asked for more information, he would not get it.

However, in such situations, it was likely that he would come to the answer after either further thought or investigation.

What could it possibly be? he wondered.

"Yes, yes, you'll see when you go. It's you we're talking about here, so I'm sure you'll turn it to your advantage." Jakob's words only served to further confuse Lawrence, but if going to the trading house would lead to understanding, he had no choice but to advance. In all likelihood, some commodity's price had destabilized, and the Remelio Company was in some kind of chaos.

Lawrence put the thought out of his mind, gave Jakob his

thanks, and turned to leave. He had come here to sell his goods, and getting distracted before he did that accomplished nothing.

The moment he put his hand to the door, he was stopped short by Jakob's voice.

Lawrence looked back and saw Jakob smiling pleasantly.

"Oh, and just you wait before getting involved with any girls, you hear? Even a mild one like Norah's too much for you to handle — a city girl would take up all your profits just like that!"

There were windows in the guild house's walls, but they were not made of glass like the great trading companies' — instead oil-soaked sheets of linen cloth served as the panes. This let a bit of light in, but one could hardly see through them.

Yet it seemed Jakob had spotted Holo just beyond the door.

It was proof the man possessed the cunning to run a trade guild in a foreign land; his was far beyond that of a normal person.

"You can't invest without capital."

"Ha-ha! Well met, you bed wetter!"

Lawrence grinned sheepishly and opened the door; Jakob was still laughing when he closed it behind him.

He remembered his days as an apprentice. When faced with people like Jakob, he had been in such a hurry to grow up, to surpass them. It was nostalgic, but bitter and biting at the same time.

Lawrence reflected on how young he still was as he looked toward the base of the stone steps. Just at that moment, Holo glanced over her shoulder at him.

"Oh, there he is. That's my companion," said Holo.

She was sitting at the base of the steps as she pointed rudely at him. In front of her were two boys, probably apprentices to some tradesman. They looked to be around fifteen or sixteen, about the same age Holo appeared. They were carrying packages, perhaps out on an errand for their parents.

The boys, just barely old enough to shave, regarded Lawrence with animosity after hearing Holo's words. Dealing with them could have been a hassle, but they flinched slightly when Lawrence sighed.

There was a world of difference in the social position of a craftsman's apprentice and a guild merchant. The boys had probably approached the obviously bored Holo, but now, confronted with Lawrence, they realized there was nothing they could do, so looking to each other, the two apprentices scampered off.

Holo giggled. "They were precious. Called me a beautiful rose, they did," she said, laughing as she watched the boys dash off, but Lawrence's face showed his distress.

"Don't mess around with them. Apprentice boys are like wild dogs. You could get taken."

"And in that case, you could come rescue me again. Am I wrong?"

Faced with her unexpectedly guileless response, Lawrence couldn't help but feel a bit happy, but his face remained stern. "Sure, I'd rescue you."

Holo grinned and stood. "Of course, in the end, *I* was the one who rescued *you*."

She had him there.

Lawrence covered his eyes out of irritation and descended the steps. She took his right arm, snickering.

"I don't know what kind of return you're expecting, but I'll take that investment," she said.

"...You heard all that?"

"My precious little ears can tell when you so much as twitch an eyebrow. So you have a thing for fair hair, do you?"

Lawrence only managed a confused "Huh?" at Holo's utterly inexplicable reasoning before she continued.

"And so scrawny, too. Or do you like the careworn look? Or do you just have a thing for shepherdesses?"

Her rapid-fire interrogation made Lawrence think of a

suspension bridge with its ropes being cut one after another. He stared at Holo, alarmed, but she just smiled back.

Her smile was the most frightening thing yet.

"Now wait just a minute — that's just Master Jakob's way of saying hello. If he's got an opportunity, it's like a game for him to say stuff like that. I'm not — "

"Not what?" Lawrence saw in Holo's eyes that she wouldn't tolerate a lie.

He had no choice but to tell the truth. "W-well, sure, I thought Norah was nice. I can't say our conversation wasn't nice. But... that doesn't mean I'm not thinking of you, or... well, it doesn't mean that."

He got flustered halfway through, and it was suddenly very hard to face Holo. He'd never had to say anything like this in his entire life.

Having gotten it out, he took a deep breath. After composing himself a bit, he glanced over at his companion, who regarded him with a measure of surprise on her face.

"I was just teasing..."

The embarrassment and anger Lawrence felt at these words was sliced clean through by the smile Holo gave him.

"I didn't think you'd take me at my word, there... it's nice."

She looked down and squeezed his arm just slightly.

For Lawrence, it hadn't been the dissembling or prevarication of a business negotiation, but a way of seeing how close they could become.

Mostly unconscious of and unconcerned with how it might look, Lawrence moved to put his left arm around Holo but embraced only air.

She had soundlessly slipped from his grasp.

"Still, males are ever thus. They'll say anything."

Looking at her sad, serious manner, even Lawrence could easily imagine that sometime in Holo's past, someone had said something careless and hurtful, something that she still felt resentment over.

But Lawrence was a merchant. He was always careful with his words.

"So — you'll need to show me something. Do knights not entrust their swords and shields as proof of their good faith? You're a merchant, so what will you show me?"

Lawrence had also heard the tales of knights who would hand over their swords and shields — said to be their very souls — when swearing oaths of loyalty.

So what, then, of a merchant? The answer was obvious: money.

Lawrence could just imagine Holo's unamused expression if he handed her a purse full of coins.

He needed to buy something for her, something that would both make her happy and stand for the money — his merchant's soul — that he would unhesitatingly use for her sake.

The item that sprang immediately to mind was the ultimate luxury: honeyed peach preserves.

"Fine," said Lawrence. "I'll show you I don't say such things lightly."

Her eyes filled with a mixture of suspicion and anticipation. If he could somehow answer the question in those red-brown pupils of hers, well — than honeyed peach preserves would be a bargain.

"I'll buy you some honeyed peach..."

That was as far as Lawrence got before a strange feeling came over him, specifically regarding the triangular kerchief on Holo's head.

Holo cocked her head curiously at the frozen Lawrence.

Then, with a quick "Oh," she hastily put her hands to her head.

"Don't tell me you —," Lawrence started.

"Wh-what? What's wrong? You were about to say you would buy me something?"

He had to give her credit for staying shameless, but Lawrence wasn't going to simply laugh this off.

Looking at the kerchief on her head made it obvious. Beneath it, her ears had been twitching strangely, vigorously. That was the proof.

This was all part of her plan.

"You know, there are some things you just can't do!" he said.

Holo seemed to realize that her plan had failed, and now suddenly sullen, she stuck her lower lip out in a pout. "You said I should ask more charmingly!"

For a moment Lawrence didn't follow her, but then he remembered their conversation on the outskirts of Poroson. Exasperated, he looked up to the heavens.

"No, I said you should ask *nicely*. I never said anything about feminine wiles!"

"But I was charming, was I not?"

Lawrence hated himself for not having a ready reply, and hated himself still more for not becoming angrier with her.

"Though I must say," continued Holo, "you were twice as charming. That was far more exciting than if my plan had gone as I meant it to."

Finally, at a loss for words, Lawrence simply walked down the road.

Holo laughed and followed him.

"Come now, don't be angry!"

When he gave her a look that said "whose fault is that?" she just laughed at him harder.

"I *was* happy, though, truly. Are you still angry?"

Lawrence found his expression softened by the way Holo's swaying, chestnut-brown hair complemented her smile.

He suddenly very much wanted to share a drink with his reliably silent horse — who was male.

"Fine, I'm not mad. I'm not mad — okay?"

Holo let slip a private smile as if enjoying her victory, exhaling before she spoke again.

"It won't do to get separated. May I take your hand?"

To return to their lodgings, they would have to reenter the crowded streets, but even separated from Lawrence, Holo would have no trouble finding her way.

So it was an obvious pretense.

She was a canny old wolf, indeed. Lawrence relented. "Yes, we mustn't get separated," he agreed.

Holo smiled, and her hand slipped into his.

All Lawrence could do was tighten his grip ever so slightly on that hand.

"So, what about my honeyed peach preserves?"

The cathedral bells rang out to signal noontime — and the beginning of a new battle.

The Remelio Company was a wholesaler that operated a shop in the Church city of Ruvinheigen.

Lawrence, betting that he would be able to turn a profit, had half threatened the Latparron Company into letting him buy up more armor than he had assets to secure. In order to pay them back, he planned to sell to the Remelio Company, which Latparron often dealt with — and there would be no need to return all the way to Poroson to repay his debt. He'd just have them record it in their ledgers and that would be that.

He entered a street one block removed from a crowded main road and arrived at the Remelio Company.

It was the rear entrance, where a large area was reserved for loading and unloading goods.

In a city the size of Ruvinheigen, unloading goods through a shop's front entrance was considered uncivilized. If you tried it on a street with heavy traffic, you'd be laughed at, at best, and at worst, you would not be able to sell your goods at all. In fact, in many places, merchants weren't even supposed to take their wagons on streets with heavy traffic.

This was why, on the side streets running parallel to the main street, horses pulling wagons often outnumbered pedestrians. Lawrence knit his brows.

The area around the Remelio Company seemed oddly quiet.

"Is this company managed by monks?" Holo asked.

"With monks, I'd at least expect to hear prayers. But I don't hear a thing."

Holo, munching on a bread roll, lightly took off her kerchief and started to prick up her ears, but Lawrence had no time for such roundabout methods. He got off the driver's seat, crossed the slope for wagons to pass through, and entered the loading dock.

Buildings were densely packed, and maintaining a loading dock in Ruvinheigen — a city where people constantly joked that buildings were so close together that "poor people can sleep between them standing up" — was not easy. Yet the Remelio Company's dock could accommodate at least three wagons with space for easily a hundred sacks of wheat. There was a table for conducting negotiations and an exchange stand in the corner, and the walls were decorated with parchment on which blessings for good commerce had been written.

It was a magnificent dock.

But livestock feed was scattered everywhere, along with pieces of horse dung and the remains of this and that cargo. Clearly, no one was tending to its upkeep, and there was not a dockmaster in sight.

Business comes and goes, so it would not be outlandish to have times when there are simply no customers. But it was still common sense to keep your shop neat and tidy.

It was as if the company had been destroyed. Lawrence withdrew and got back in the wagon's seat. Holo appeared to have finished her bread and now rummaged around for her meat pie, which, if Lawrence remembered correctly, was supposed to be his.

"If you eat that much, the sound of your chewing is going to wreck that hearing you're so proud of."

"Nicely put—but for the sake of my reputation, I should tell you I can hear the sound of someone in the building."

Holo then bit down enthusiastically on the meat pie. She was clearly not going to have just a bit.

"There's someone there?"

"Mm…mmph…mrgh. Seems dangerous, though. At the very least, it's nothing pleasant."

Hearing this, the five wooden stories of the Remelio Company, given the state of its loading dock, started to seem downright sinister. Nothing was so cursed as a trading company that had gone bankrupt. When that happened, the local church usually found itself very busy conducting funerals for the newly deceased.

"Well, there's no point wandering around here. We can't make money if we can't sell the goods."

"A meat pie's no good until you eat it," agreed Holo.

"I was saving that!"

Lawrence shot Holo a glare before moving the wagon and got an equally sour look for his trouble.

But perhaps eating the whole thing would have been a bit too much guilt—Holo split the pie and offered one half to Lawrence. It was about a quarter of what he had originally planned to eat, but as complaining might have cost him what little was left, he snatched the piece up.

Normally meat pies were made with ground beef that was approaching the expiration date set by the butchers guild, but here in Ruvinheigen, the meat pies were as noble as the city itself.

121

The meat was entirely tasty, and Lawrence ate his pie in two bites as he drove the wagon up to the deserted loading dock.

The horse's hooves clopped against the ground, and it seemed as though their familiar sound reached the ears of the people within. Lawrence drove the wagon up, climbing down from the driver's seat just as the dockmaster finally emerged.

"I daresay there are a few hours left before the sabbath — so what is the matter?" said Lawrence.

"Er, well, that is … did sir come to the city today … ?" The middle-aged dockmaster slurred his words initially, but his faculties seemed to return to him as he appraised Lawrence.

Those eyes were like a thief eyeing his mark's coin purse, and Lawrence's merchant instinct sensed danger. The dockmaster seemed ragged now that Lawrence got a look at him. This was a place of physical labor, so he would hardly be standing ramrod straight, but even so, Lawrence could tell if someone was filled with vigor.

This was not good. This was clearly not good.

"No, I came a few days ago. You know how it goes. Well, you seem busy, so I'll come by later. I'm in no special hurry."

Lawrence avoided making eye contact, and without waiting for the dockmaster's reply, he turned back to the wagon.

Holo seemed to sense something off as well. She looked to Lawrence questioningly but soon nodded. Despite her appearance as a normal town girl, her wits were extraordinary. She didn't boast of being a wisewolf for nothing.

But the dockmaster did not give up so easily.

"Well, now, do wait just a moment, sir. I can tell sir is a trader of some repute. It would be rude of me to let sir leave empty-handed."

If Lawrence just refused the man, there was no telling how his reputation might spread around the city.

But the merchant blood fairly frothed in his veins.

Run, it said. *This is dangerous.*

"Not at all," replied Lawrence. "I'm a merchant with little besides complaints to sell."

It was only a third-rate merchant who was so clumsily self-effacing when selling. Humility was a virtue for men of the cloth, but for traders, it was like sticking one's head in a noose.

But Lawrence had judged that escape was the best plan. Holo's frozen posture reinforced this decision.

"Sir shouldn't sell himself so cheaply! Even a blind beggar could tell sir is a man of stature!"

"Flattery will get you nowhere," said Lawrence, sitting in the wagon seat and grabbing the reins. The dockmaster seemed to be able to tell that it was time to relent. He had been leaning forward so earnestly that he almost stumbled, but now he righted himself.

It seemed like Lawrence was off the hook, so he spoke briefly to the dockmaster. "Well, then, I'll take my leave..."

"Yes...most unfortunate. I await sir's return," said the dockmaster with an ingratiating smile. Lawrence took that as his cue to exit, so he started to move the wagon.

The dockmaster, however, took advantage of this small gap in Lawrence's defense. "I believe I forgot to ask sir's name," he said.

"Lawrence. From the Rowen Trade Guild."

Lawrence gave his name without thinking, then suddenly, he wondered if giving his name to someone he didn't know, in a situation he didn't understand, was a mistake — but he could think of no reason why it would matter.

Most likely, the dockmaster simply hadn't known what Lawrence had come to this place to do.

However —

"Lawrence, you say. Indeed. From the Latparron Company."

The dockmaster grinned unpleasantly.

The jolt that ran through Lawrence's spine was impossible to describe.

There was no reason he could think of for the dockmaster to know his name.

"You were bringing some armor to our company, yes?"

Lawrence was suddenly nauseated as he sensed he had fallen into some kind of trap. His instinct screamed it at him.

He looked slowly over to the dockmaster.

It can't be. It can't be. It can't be.

"Actually, last night a messenger on a fast horse came to us. The Latparron Company has had their obligations assigned to our company. So, you see, you have a debt to us, Mr. Lawrence."

With those words, everything changed.

Normally, obligation transfers did not take place over messenger horse. But the abnormality made the transfer all the more believable — for example, if two companies were engaging in fraud.

If Lawrence hadn't been sitting in the wagon, he would have collapsed.

Even sitting, he lurched over from the force of the words.

Holo, surprised, caught Lawrence as he toppled.

"What is wrong?" she asked.

He didn't want to consider it.

The dockmaster answered for him.

"The merchant beside you has failed at business — just like us." His happiness was clearly no more than schadenfreude.

"What?" asked Holo.

Lawrence wished desperately for this all to be a dream.

"The price of armor must have plunged some time ago. The old fox at Latparron shifted his dead stock onto us."

The future was dark.

"We've been had…"

Lawrence's hoarse voice was all that tied him to reality.

CHAPTER FOUR

"We both live by such agreements. You understand, right?"

These were the words every merchant feared.

And every merchant would lament his fate upon such a collapse.

"Of course I do. I'm a merchant, after all." It was all Lawrence could do to say even that much.

"It's simple. Of the exactly one hundred *lumione* worth of armor you bought from the Latparron Company, you will need to remit to us the amount recorded in the obligation deed, to wit — forty-seven and three-quarters *lumione*. You are aware of what this amounts to, correct?"

Remelio looked as stricken as Lawrence felt.

The man's eyes and cheeks were sunken, his shirt hadn't been changed in several days, and his eyes glittered strangely. He was not a big man to begin with, but Remelio's weary, thin features made him look like a wounded bear cub.

He didn't just seem wounded — he *was* wounded, nearly fatally.

Hans Remelio, the master of the Remelio Company, unconsciously ran his hand through his slightly graying hair as he continued to press Lawrence.

"We'd like you to settle your debt immediately. Otherwise..."

Lawrence thought about how much he would rather be threatened at knifepoint than hear this.

"...We'll have to demand that the Rowen Trade Guild assume the debt in your place."

It was the threat every merchant who was attached to a trading house feared.

The guild was a merchant's second home, but it could turn into an angry debt collector in the blink of an eye.

In that moment, merchants who go about their work, prepared to half abandon their homes, have nowhere to go for respite.

"Well, the term of the loan was through the day after tomorrow, so give me two days. I'll pay back the forty-seven and three-quarters *lumione* by then," said Lawrence.

It was not an amount he could hope to collect in two days. Even if he were to call in all the credit from every conceivable source he had, the money wouldn't amount to half of what he owed.

A person could live for three months on a single *lumione*. Even a child knew that forty-seven *lumione* was a huge amount of money.

As did the bearlike master of the company, Remelio.

Ruin.

The word seemed to hang before Lawrence's eyes.

"What do you wish to do with the armor you brought, Mr. Lawrence? It will only sell for a pittance if it even sells at all, regardless of where you go."

Remelio's thin, derisive smile was not meant to mock Lawrence.

After all, Remelio himself had been brought to the edge of ruin by the same plunge in armor prices that now threatened Lawrence.

Ruvinheigen served as a supply depot for knights, mercenaries, and missionaries heading north to suppress the pagans. Thus, armor and scriptures were reliable sources of profit.

Every winter there was a major campaign. The march was timed to coincide with the birthday of Saint Ruvinheigen, and in order to equip the mercenaries and knight brigades that amassed from surrounding nations, goods like armor, scriptures, rations, cold-weather clothes, horses, and medicine all flew off the shelves.

This year the march had been hastily canceled. There was political unrest in the nation that stretched out between the pagan territories and the Ruvinheigen-controlled land where the battles normally occurred, and that nation's disposition toward Ruvinheigen had suddenly soured. If it had been a normal nation that would have been one thing, but this particular nation bordered the pagan lands, and even within its borders, there were here and there pagan villages. One of the closest was Lamtra. Those who had to fight the pagans could cross into the other nation, but if they marched through it like they would any other year, there was no telling when the pagans, who silently watched them, might attack. The archbishop that controlled the grand diocese was in attendance, as were members of the imperial family from the south. They could not let the unthinkable happen.

Thus, the campaign was canceled.

As to how stricken the city's merchants were because of this decision, one had to look no further than the predicament of the Remelio Company, which had operated in Ruvinheigen for many years. Even so, Lawrence should have realized something was awry while he was traveling — if the mercenaries that fought in the battlegrounds of the north were wandering around Ruvinheigen, there had clearly been some kind of change in the battlefield.

What's more, given the drop in armor prices and the way Lawrence had learned of it, he had to assume that when he'd gotten the armor in Poroson, the master of the Latparron Company had already known.

In other words, when he'd thought he was taking advantage of a weakness in order to force favorable terms for himself, he had actually been used.

Having sold devalued armor to Lawrence at such a price, the Latparron Company master was probably still laughing to himself. And because the price of armor had dropped so much, he knew that it would be either impossible for Lawrence to pay him back or would take a significant effort. Thus, he had sold the obligation to the long-standing Remelio Company, perhaps judging that it would salvage his position.

In the middle of all of this, Lawrence had drawn the worst lot.

It was a failure that made Lawrence want to tear his own limbs off.

And yet, Lawrence found some strength.

"I'll sell it high somewhere. You'll see. We'll settle the debt in two days. Will that do?"

"Yes, we'll be waiting."

You could have put out a fire with the cold sweat that both men were bathed in, but somehow they managed to preserve the decency of a business negotiation.

They were both people, after all.

However, they were also both merchants.

Lawrence stood, and Remelio gave him some parting words.

"I should say," he began, "that our company's stalls are near the city gates. If you plan to use them, do let us know."

In other words, don't try to run away.

"I expect I'll be busy with negotiations, so although I appreciate your informing me, I doubt I will use them." If Holo had been there, Lawrence would have had to laugh at the battle of wills, but as both he and Remelio were on edge, he had to be honest.

Bankruptcy meant death in society. It would be better to be a beggar, shivering from cold and hunger. If creditors caught up with you, they would sell off everything you owned. Even your

hair would be cut off and sold for wigs — and if you had good teeth, they would be pulled and used for someone's dentures. Your very freedom could be sold, and you could be made to toil as a slave in a mine or aboard a ship. And even that wasn't the worst that could happen. If a nobleman or wealthy person demanded it, you might even pay with your very life — but you would have no grave, and none would mourn your passing.

That was the inevitable reality of bankruptcy.

"I'll take my leave, then," said Lawrence.

"We look forward to seeing you in two days. May God's protection go with you."

The weak devour the still weaker; it was the way of the world.

Nonetheless, Lawrence clenched his fists until his knuckles were white from the rage he felt.

But half of that anger was at himself. He could not undo this error.

Unescorted, he walked down from the negotiation room on the third floor to the loading dock on the first floor.

Holo was dressed as a town girl and was thus unable to be present for the negotiation; she waited in the driver's seat of the wagon, watched over by someone from the trading company. The moment Lawrence emerged onto the dock, Holo turned around with a start.

Lawrence wondered how terrible he must look.

"Sorry to keep you waiting," he said, climbing onto the wagon. Holo gave a vague nod, peering at Lawrence curiously.

"Let's go."

Lawrence took the reins and ignored the dockmaster, heading the horse away from the loading dock. The dockmaster had apparently been informed of the situation in advance, so he silently watched Lawrence and Holo leave.

As they descended the slope from the dock down onto the cobbled street, Lawrence let slip a great sigh.

It escaped with all the anger, frustration, and regret piled up within him.

There was so much sheer defeat in the sigh that if a rabbit had been nearby, it might have died on the spot.

But it was not as though the sigh had taken Lawrence's merchant sense from him.

This was no time for despair. His mind swirled with cold fury as he began to calculate how he might raise the funds.

"...Hey."

A timid voice cut through his trance.

"Hm?"

"What...what happened?" Holo asked with an awkward, anxious smile—Holo, whose true wolf form Lawrence had fully accepted. She had surely overheard the conversation with Remelio, so her question must have some other intent.

Lawrence imagined what he looked like to Holo.

Image was a merchant's life. He took his hands off the reins and forced himself to relax his tense facial muscles.

"If you want to know what happened, the load behind us is worthless."

"Mmph. Then I suppose I didn't hear wrong."

"Incidentally, this could mean bankruptcy for me."

Holo's face twisted, pained—perhaps she understood the sad fate that awaited the bankrupt, like a lamb being led to the slaughter. Then her expression changed.

Her cool wolf's eyes regarded Lawrence evenly.

"Will you run?"

"If I run once, I'll be on the run forever. The information networks of the trade guilds and companies are like the very eyes of God. No matter where I went, if I tried to do business, I'd be found out immediately. I'd never be able to be a merchant again."

"But the going rate for an injured animal to free itself is gnawing through its own limb. You won't content yourself with that?"

"Impossible," answered Lawrence flatly.

Holo turned away, as if thinking.

"If I pay back the equivalent of forty-seven *lumione* gold pieces, that'll be enough. I still have my goods on hand. I can settle my debts here and sell the armor somewhere far away, where it'll fetch a decent price. It's not impossible," said Lawrence, as if it were simple. In reality, the ease with which he explained it was equivalent to the impossibility of the task.

But he had no other choice. His merchant's spirit was part of it — if he tried to run, his life as a merchant was over. His only option was to struggle until the end.

After averting her gaze for a while, Holo turned back to Lawrence.

As if weary of looking at his stricken face, she smiled thinly. "I'm Holo the Wisewolf. I'm sure I can be of some help."

"This is rather different from covering your meals."

Holo jabbed Lawrence in his side with her fist. "I said all along I'd pay for my own food."

"I know, I know," replied Lawrence as he brushed her fist away.

Holo's eyebrows were raised as she sniffed slightly, her anger dissolved.

She looked expressionlessly at the horse. When she spoke, it was as though she was uttering a grave oath.

"If it becomes necessary, I swear on my honor to free you — even if I must use the power within this wheat."

Within the pouch that hung from Holo's neck was the wheat that contained her essence. If she used it, she could easily return to her true form.

Yet Holo loathed above all else the terrified gazes of those who saw that form. Those reactions were a prison that condemned her to loneliness. She had once returned to that shape deep in the underground canals beneath the port city of Pazzio, but that had been because Holo herself was in danger.

This was different. The danger now confronted Lawrence alone.

He was meekly gratified that Holo was prepared to go to such lengths for his sake.

"You promised to accompany me back to the northlands. I can't have you getting tripped up here."

"I'll keep that promise, and — "

Lawrence closed his eyes and took a deep breath.

" — if it comes to it, I may need saving."

Lawrence felt a new sense of relief, knowing that there was someone he could rely on.

Holo grinned. "Count on it," she said.

Holo would come to his rescue.

That option *did* exist.

But it wasn't something he wanted to resort to. If the situation got that bad, it meant Lawrence's place in the world was entirely gone.

That was what it meant to have to leave your home, to desert your native soil. Failure left nothing behind.

"So, what will you do now?" asked Holo in front of the inn after they had left the wagon with the innkeeper.

It was exactly what Lawrence himself wanted to ask, but he had no time for such weakness.

The inn had been paid for up front, so they didn't have to immediately worry about where to sleep and stable the horse. He had a fair amount of cash on hand. It was fortune within misfortune that they wouldn't immediately lack for food and shelter.

But the remaining options were few and time in short supply.

"We'll go to the guild house first. That's all we can do."

"Mm. If they're truly your comrades they'll come to your aid."

She meant it as encouragement, but Lawrence knew all too well that the world was not so simple. In his ten years spent in the world of merchants, he had seen any number of people whose support would disappear as soon as you found yourself in a predicament.

"Right, I'm heading out for a moment, so you just wait here — "

Holo stamped her foot before Lawrence could finish his sentence.

"Do I look like the kind of ungrateful wolf that lets her companion face a crisis alone?"

"No, but — "

"Do I?!"

She looked up at him, feet planted.

"You don't, but that's not the issue."

"What *is* the issue, then?"

She moved aside for the moment, but the look in her eyes made it clear that she would block him again depending on his answer.

"The guild house is like home for merchants like me. You understand what bringing a girl home means, right?"

"It is not as though I'm playing at ignorance of the situation."

"Explaining our situation is impossible! How am I supposed to account for my relationship to you?"

Holo would be burned at the stake as a demon if the Church was to find her. Although Jakob, who ran the guild house in this city, was an even more understanding man than himself, Lawrence knew that it would be a disaster if he for some reason decided to turn Holo in to the Church. And besides, many merchants from the Rowen area came through the guild — and not all of them were so understanding. He couldn't risk it.

Lawrence would have to engage in at least a bit of deception in order to explain his connection to Holo. But could he pull it off? Jakob could spot a lie a hundred leagues away.

"Just claim we're lovers, then. 'Tis better by far than being left here," said Holo.

It was clear she was worried about him.

Lawrence knew that if their positions were reversed, he would be angry if she tried to go off and solve her problems alone. He knew he would feel betrayed if she told him to "stay at the inn."

Holo averted her eyes.

He would just have to pray.

"Fine. Come along. You're the smart one, anyway."

"Mm. You can rely on me."

"However — " Lawrence stepped aside to allow a traveler to enter the inn "— this is a business meeting. Don't do anything crazy. That lot can give a rough welcome." Lawrence said this with a tone that made it clear he would brook no argument on the matter — his colleagues' idea of a welcome could be a real baptism by fire.

But Holo seemed happy as long as he was taking her with him. She nodded agreeably.

"Right then, let's go."

"Let's!"

The two walked off briskly and soon disappeared into the crowds.

Just as Lawrence was about to knock on the door of the guild house, someone came out.

It was obvious at a glance that he was a town merchant, but no sooner had he spotted Lawrence with surprise than his face soured and he looked away — he was clearly a messenger from the Remelio Company. The most likely scenario was that he had come to inform the guild of Lawrence's position and the possibility that the Remelio Company would turn to them to guarantee Lawrence's debt.

Lawrence said nothing, simply giving way to the man as though he was no one in particular.

The merchant himself would probably never have deigned to undertake such a role if his own company were not in such dire straits. As it was, though the Remelio Company was trying to force Lawrence to pay up, the man practically scurried away from Lawrence.

A person who liked bringing others to ruin was actually rare among merchants, who spent their days trying to outwit their competitors. Destruction and competition were totally different things.

"I daresay I thought he was going to take a swing at you." Holo seemed to have noticed that the man was from Remelio, but Lawrence only gave a pained grin at her joke.

"At least he spared us the trouble of explaining the worst of the news. I should thank him."

"I suppose it depends on perspective."

Finally able to smile, Lawrence entered the guild house.

The merchants that dealt with fish, vegetables, and other perishable goods had mostly concluded their work for the day. Unlike the morning when Lawrence had come, the guild was now filled with men sitting at the tables, drinking wine, and having a grand time. Lawrence could put a name to each face. Some raised a hand in greeting to him as soon as they noticed him.

However, when Holo entered just behind him, the activity came to a sudden stop, and a strange commotion rippled through the assemblage. It was like a sigh. And the look — calling it "envy" or "jealousy" didn't do it justice. Holo was entirely indifferent to the situation, but Lawrence found it almost painful.

"Oh ho, this must be God's will."

Jakob was the first to speak — the smile he displayed failed to reach his eyes.

"You've caught a rare jewel here, Lawrence."

Holo ignored the myriad eyes fixed on her and walked smoothly toward Jakob, leading Lawrence by the hand.

The fact that Jakob had called him Lawrence rather than Kraft stabbed at him.

It meant that Jakob would no longer treat him as a member of the guild, but only as a merchant like any other.

"I didn't catch her — I was caught *by* her, Chief Tarantino."

Jakob grinned so widely his face became distorted, then he rose laboriously and patted Lawrence heavily on the shoulder, gesturing inside. "Let's talk."

The sharp-eyed merchants in the room had noticed the unusual mood of the exchange. None spoke.

Past the lobby was an enclosed courtyard. Looking out over the courtyard with its sparse seasonal decoration as he led them in, the giant Jakob spoke.

"Didn't you pass the fellow from the Remelio Company?"

"I did. At the front door."

"Ah. I thought you'd be lucky and miss him."

"...Why is that?" Lawrence didn't understand what Jakob was getting at, but he could see Jakob's shoulders shaking with mirth.

"Because there was no noise when we came to blows."

Holo smirked slightly, and Lawrence relaxed.

Jakob opened the door to a room on the right side of the hallway they were in and motioned for the two to enter.

"This is where I work. There'll be nobody to listen to our conversation here, so you can relax on that count," said Jakob.

It was not a large room, but it gave the impression of housing limitless knowledge.

Looking through the open door, they could see the walls were almost entirely covered with shelves, upon which rested care-lessly stacked bundles of documents.

There was a small table in the middle of the room wedged between two simple couches of wood and leather construction.

Also facing the door was a desk piled high with a mountain of documents. Though paper was becoming less expensive with each passing year, there were still fine varieties to be had. It was proof that Jakob spared little expense in the preservation of knowledge. Even a well-regarded theologian might not have collected so much.

"Well, then, where shall we begin?"

Jakob faced the table and sat on one of the couches, which heaved a creaky sigh under his significant weight. Normally that was the seed from which a friendly chat would bloom, but in these circum-stances, it was only the authority that bore down on Lawrence.

Lawrence was glad Holo was beside him.

If he had been alone, his mind might simply have gone blank.

"First, I'd sure like to know who and what that beauty of yours is." Jakob's gaze fixed steadily on Lawrence.

It was admittedly preposterous for a merchant facing bank-ruptcy to be walking around with a town girl. Were Jakob a less-patient man, he would have given Lawrence the boot as soon as he had shown up with Holo in tow.

"She's a business partner. We're traveling together."

"Ho, a business partner?" Jakob looked at Holo for the first time, seeming to think this was a grand joke. Holo smiled and inclined her head.

"The Milone Company in Pazzio offered me one hundred forty *trenni* for the furs I was selling, but in the end, they bought them for a full two hundred *trenni*. She's the one who made it happen."

Holo's face betrayed a certain amount of pride in opposition to Jakob's doubtful expression.

His doubt was understandable. If someone had told Lawrence

a similar story, he would have assumed it to be a lie. The Milone Company was known in many nations, and those who worked for it were first-rate traders — bargaining them higher in price was not something that happened easily.

"I said it this morning when I was here. 'You can't invest without capital.'" Since the story of the furs was true, Lawrence spoke without fear.

He had not thought about whether Holo would be angry at him for talking about it, but she seemed to understand that it was for expediency's sake.

Jakob closed his eyes, and strangely, his expression shifted.

"I don't need to know the details. Your like does show up every once in a while, after all."

"Huh?"

"One day they just show up at the guild, stunning beauty in tow, everything going well in business and life. And they never want to give details about the woman. So I don't ask anymore. The scriptures say not to open strange boxes, after all."

Lawrence wondered if it was a trick to make him tell the truth, but he didn't know what purpose it would serve. He tried to rethink his position.

Perhaps the story of the cart horse turning into the goddess of fortune and traveling with a merchant was true.

Lawrence himself was traveling with a wolf spirit who had taken the form of a girl. Merchants like him were too realistic to assume they were somehow special.

"'Tis a prudent decision," said Holo, which elicited a hearty laugh from Jakob.

"Well, then, let's speak frankly then, shall we? If you two were a couple, I'd have tried to convince you to head straight to the church and make it official. But if you're in business together, well, that's different. You'll hang together or hang separately — your partner's fall is your own misfortune. The bonds of gold run thicker than blood!"

Jakob's couch creaked.

"Let me get the story straight. The fellow from Remelio that just left told it like this: Kraft Lawrence, attached to the Rowen Trade Guild, bought one hundred *lumione* worth of armor from the Latparron Company in Poroson. We're liable for roughly half. Now the Remelio Company holds the debt. Is that it?"

Lawrence nodded painfully.

"I didn't hear what kind of armor it was, but the armor is going for about one-tenth what it previously was, so even if you sell it for that price, you've still got to make up about forty *lumione*. That comes out to fifteen hundred pieces of *trenni* silver."

After all was said and done, Lawrence had come away with about a thousand pieces of silver from the Pazzio affair. Even if he were able to repeat the stunt, there would be debt left over.

"It looks like you were completely taken in by the Latparron Company. I won't ask the details. From what I've heard, that won't change the situation. No matter what anyone thinks, you got greedy and made a mistake. Is that right?"

"It is, exactly."

Lawrence didn't try to make excuses. Saying he had become greedy and failed summed up his predicament precisely.

"If you understand that, this will be a simple conversation. You must pay back on your own the debt that the guild will, in all likelihood, shoulder. When you meet with fraud or extortion, when you become sick or injured and suffer losses, we in the trade guild put our credit on the line to save you. But not this time. The only ones to come to your aid now will be the gods —"

Jakob pointed a finger at Holo, who glanced at Lawrence.

" — or that beauty."

"I understand."

Unlike craft guilds, a regional trade guild was built around assurances of mutual assistance. It ran on contributions from its members, and as Jakob said, it gave aid to merchants who had suffered misfortune and would otherwise be unable to get by. Members would also assemble in foreign lands to protest unfair treatment.

The guild had not been created to guarantee the debts of merchants whose greed led them to ruin.

In such cases, even if the guild temporarily assumed the liability, it would pursue repayment relentlessly. The other guild members wouldn't stand for the loss, and it served as a lesson in the restraint of greed.

Jakob's eyes were like bows drawn tight.

"Unfortunately, I'm not in a position where I can show you any compassion — and the reason why I must be so strict is just outside in the lobby. It is guild law. If it became known that this trade house goes easy on its members, it would be a target for riffraff from all around."

"Of course. I myself would be angry if I heard some other member had been saved from his own failure."

Lawrence put on a brave face, for if he didn't, he would have collapsed.

"Also, you surely know this, but guild members are forbidden from lending money to each other. Neither can the guild lend you money. It would set a bad example."

"I understand."

Lawrence's second home was barring its doors to him.

"Based on what the Remelio Company messenger told me, your obligation comes due in two days. Their own investments in armor have failed, so they're feeling the heat as well. They won't hesitate in demanding repayment. In other words, your failure will become public the day after tomorrow, and I'll have to detain you. What have you concluded from this?"

"If I do not collect forty-seven *lumione* in two days and pay the Remelio Company back, there is no future for me," said Lawrence.

Jakob shook his head slowly, then looked down at the table. "That's not quite true."

There was a slight rustling sound next to Lawrence; probably Holo's tail.

"You future will come," continued Jakob. "But it will be black, bitter, and heavy."

The implicit message was that suicide in the face of this bankruptcy would not be acceptable.

"Forty-seven *lumione* could be paid off in ten years of rowing on a trade ship — or working in a mine. Of course, you'd have to avoid injury and sickness."

Anyone who had ever seen correspondence between a ship's captain and its owner knew that was pure fantasy. Nine-tenths of such correspondence was devoted to the captain requesting fresh rowers and the owner trying to make them last a little longer.

About 80 percent of rowers on long-distance ships were worthless after two years, another 10 percent were finished after two more years, and the remaining 10 percent — unbelievably strong-bodied men — wound up on antipirate vessels and never returned. And even that was preferable to mine labor. Most miners died of lung disease within a year, and the lucky few who avoided such a fate died in collapsed tunnels.

In contrast, some who encountered misfortune might have their trade house cover their debts and then gradually repay their creditors at low interest — far better treatment.

Those who failed as a consequence of greed had to understand the seriousness of their crime.

"But it is not as though I wish death on you. Don't forget that. A sin must be punished — and it is my duty to enforce that simple principle."

"I understand."

Lawrence looked into Jakob's eyes. For the first time, a flicker of empathy appeared there.

"There's nothing I can do besides wish you luck over the next two days, but if there is anything I *can* do, I will. Standard business assistance is no problem. Also, I trust you. I ought to tie you up for the next two days, but you can go free."

The word *trust* weighed heavily on Lawrence's shoulders.

Holo had promised to rescue him if it came to that.

But taking her up on that offer meant betraying the trust Jakob was showing him.

Lawrence wondered if he could do that.

He unconsciously muttered the problem to himself before speaking up.

"I thank you for your consideration. I'll try to find the money in the next two days, somehow."

"There are always possibilities in business — and some you can only see when you are in true danger."

Lawrence's heart thudded at the statement. It could be interpreted as suggesting illegal activity.

As the master of the Ruvinheigen branch of the Rowen Trade Guild, Jakob had to confront Lawrence with harsh reality, but he was also worried about the young merchant. A person who was capable only of severity would be unfit to be the master of the merchants' second home.

"Have you anything you want to ask or say?"

Lawrence shook his head, but then spoke as something suddenly occurred to him.

"I want you to think of what you'll say when I repay the money."

Jakob blinked, then laughed loudly. The inappropriate timing of the joke made it all the funnier.

"I'll think of something, don't you worry! And you, my dear, have you anything to say?"

Lawrence was sure she would say something, but Holo — surprisingly — shook her head wordlessly.

"Right, that should wrap things up. We shouldn't talk too long. They're a suspicious lot out there, you know. If rumors get around, it'll be harder for you to act."

Jakob stood from the couch, which creaked again. Lawrence and Holo did likewise.

Jakob and Lawrence knew it was a bad idea for merchants to wear dark expressions, so they made every effort to appear normal, as if the business they had just discussed was nothing more than a bit of small talk.

When the reached the lobby, Jakob returned to his usual spot and waved Lawrence off lightly.

Yet the people drinking wine in the lobby said nothing to him, as if they had sensed something was amiss.

Lawrence felt the weight of eyes on his back; he closed the door behind him and Holo as if to seal the guild members away.

They might even have been thinking about restraining him. He couldn't help but feel grateful at Jakob's generosity in letting him go free.

"Well, we've got two days of freedom. We've no choice but to see what we can do with it," murmured Lawrence to himself, but the notion of raising forty-seven *lumione* without any capital was delusional at best.

If there were any such method, the beggars of the world would all be rich men.

Yet he had to think of something.

If he didn't, his future wasn't worth contemplating.

His dream of having a shop would collapse; his recovery as a merchant would be hopeless; and his life would end either in the gloom of a mine shaft or the bowels of a ship, where the cries of anguish were said to drown out the crashing of the waves.

He tried to buck himself up, to put on a brave face, but the more he tried to reassure himself, the more the impossibility of his situation closed in around him.

Jakob trusted Lawrence enough to give him his freedom for two days.

But now Lawrence began to wonder if it was just Jakob giving a doomed man his last days of freedom. As he thought about it realistically, raising forty-seven *lumione* in two days seemed impossible.

He noticed his hand was trembling.

Shamed, Lawrence made a fist to stop the shaking. Then a small hand rested atop his.

It was Holo — he suddenly remembered she was there.

He wasn't alone.

Coming to that realization, Lawrence found the composure to take a deep breath.

At this rate, he would break his promise to accompany Holo to the northlands.

His frozen mind began to turn. Holo noticed this and spoke.

"So. What will you do?"

"First, before we do any more thinking, we need to test something."

"And that is?" Holo asked, looking up to Lawrence.

"Debt for debt."

None can feel at ease when lending large amounts of money unless they are very wealthy or generous indeed.

On the other hand, one does not nag for repayment of a trivial loan unless they are especially petty or especially strapped for cash.

Debt was like a looming mud slide. Even if it were impossible to stop, if one could manage to divert it into other rivers, it could be managed.

One way to manage a debt of forty-seven *lumione* would be to borrow small amounts from many different people to pay it off and then gradually pay each lender off in turn.

However.

"Well, well, Lawrence! It's been a while. What's your angle today?"

Every merchant Lawrence knew greeted him roughly the same upon seeing his face again, but when the talk came of lending their expressions grew grim.

"Five *lumione*? Sorry, friend, times are tough for me at the moment. It's the end of the year, prices of wheat and meat are up, and I've got to lay in stock for spring. Sorry, I just…"

Everyone gave the same answer, as if their responses had been prearranged. They were merchants just like him, sensitive to exactly what he was trying. If traveling merchants could just head to a company and borrow money instead of borrowing from their guild, that would put the trade companies in the same position that forced guilds to have rules against lending.

And no one wanted to load their goods aboard a sinking ship.

When Lawrence pressed them for even a single *lumione*, they regarded him as if he was especially foul smelling.

With no island to cling to, he was often just kicked out or sent off.

One who came not for commerce or negotiation but simply to borrow was little more than a thief.

That was common sense in the world of merchants.

"We'll try another one."

After Lawrence met back up with Holo, who waited outside the row of companies and mansions, he didn't bother with a fifth rendition of that same line.

He had only put on a brave face for the first three stops, and Holo stopped asking him how it had gone after four.

As a "by the way" to his request for a short-term loan, Lawrence had asked after any opportunities for profit, but that, too, had withered into silence. After all, merchants used capital to turn a profit. It was obvious that without money on hand, there was nothing to be done.

Lawrence unconsciously quickened his pace as he walked, opening a bit of distance between himself and Holo.

When he noticed, he told himself to calm down, but the words merely echoed in his empty mind, and he began to find Holo's words of encouragement irritating.

He was in a bad way.

Despite the chilly air that descended as night drew near, Lawrence's forehead and throat were slick with sweat.

Though he had thought himself prepared, the reality of his circumstances affected him more than he'd anticipated. The seriousness of the situation seemed to spill out of him like water from an overtaxed ceramic cup.

Why had he made that deal in Poroson? The feelings of regret warred with the uselessness of such recriminations within him.

Again, Holo's voice reminded Lawrence that he had put too much distance between them. He was assailed by an exhaustion that made him wonder if he would ever be able to walk again were he to stop.

But he had no time for exhaustion.

"Excuse me," Lawrence asked at yet another door.

The bell signaling the close of the market rang; all the companies would soon be closing their doors for the day.

The ninth location Lawrence visited was already tidying up its loading dock, and a wooden sign was posted on the entrance, indicating that the day's trading was over.

A trading company was home to the master and men working there, so it wasn't as if no one was about. Lawrence used the knocker and took a deep breath.

He hadn't many acquaintances left. The merchant *had* to get someone to lend him money.

"Who is there?" asked the woman who opened the door. She was well built, and Lawrence remembered her face.

Just as Lawrence steeled himself to ask after the master, the woman looked back over her shoulder. Flustered, she went back into the house.

In her place appeared the master of the company.

"It has been a while, Mr. Lawrence."

"It has. I'm very sorry to trouble you after the market's closed, but I have a favor to ask…"

The first couple of stops Lawrence made, he had had the luxury of beginning with small talk, feigning normal business.

But he no longer possessed such a luxury. As he plunged into his request, the master regarded him scornfully.

"I happened to hear that you've been making the rounds with your request."

"Er, yes… though it embarrasses me to say so…"

The ties between merchant companies in a city were strong. The master had clearly heard from one of the companies Lawrence visited earlier.

"And it's a sizable amount. Is this because of the drop in armor prices, I wonder?"

"Yes. I was naive and made a mistake."

Even if he had to grovel and throw himself on the mercy of others, Lawrence had to borrow the money. Starting penniless and raising forty-seven *lumione* in two days was simply impossible.

And if he was refused here, he would be turned away at the gates everywhere else.

If even one of the other companies had lent to him, Lawrence felt that others would have too. But the fact that none had offered him aid made him wonder if they all thought his recovery so impossible that they wouldn't bother lending.

Merchant companies were closely connected. Once a piece of information escaped, the news would be all over town in an instant.

The master's tone was unchanged and cold.

"A naive mistake? I suppose it was at that."

This was something that it didn't take the skill of a merchant used to discerning others' feelings to grasp.

This was not the tone of a man prepared to lend money.

The master furrowed his brow and let slip an exasperated sigh. It seemed as if he might have known that Lawrence had gotten greedy and amassed an oppressive debt by buying armor on margin.

Trustworthiness was a merchant's life. If you couldn't be trusted, none would extend their hand to aid you.

And your debt was your own responsibility — if you couldn't pay it back, it was your own fault.

Lawrence hung his head, feeling the strength drain from him like so much water.

The master continued speaking.

"Yet only the gods can predict a sudden fall in price. It's unfair to rebuke you for being unable to do so."

Lawrence looked up in spite of himself. He saw a glimmer of hope. If he could get a loan here, it would be easier to get loans from others, and his skill as a traveling merchant would be acknowledged to a degree. If he promised to pay it back with interest, he might yet save himself.

Hope, he thought, dangled now before his eyes.

But when he looked at the master, the face that greeted him held only scorn in its eyes.

"If you're in trouble, Mr. Lawrence, I thought that I might be able to be of some help to you. You've helped me turn a profit many a time. But while I'm a merchant, I also live by the teachings of God, and I need to know your sincerity."

Lawrence did not understand what he was hearing, but nonetheless, he frantically began to formulate an excuse when he was cut off by the particularly mercantile form of the master's speech.

"You've got a woman in tow even as you make the rounds, depending on the compassion of others to lend you money? Preposterous. How far the Rowen Trade Guild has fallen!"

The words froze Lawrence cold as the master slammed the door in his face.

He could neither move forward nor backward.

It was as though he'd forgotten to breathe.

The closed door was so quiet it seemed painted on stone. It was surely as cold and heavy as stone. The door would not open again; Lawrence's connections with the merchants of the city had been cut.

They would lend him no money.

He backed away unsteadily from the door, not of his own volition, but rather because his body seemed to move on its own. When he finally noticed his surroundings, he was standing in the middle of the street.

"Don't just stand in the middle of the road!" the driver of a horse-drawn cart shouted at him, and like a stray dog, Lawrence moved to the edge of the lane.

What should I do? What should I do? What should I do?

The words passed endlessly before his eyes.

"Hey there. Are you all right?"

At the sound of the voice, Lawrence started.

"Your face is quite pale. Let's hie to the inn —"

Holo extended her hand by way of comfort, but Lawrence slapped it away.

"If only you hadn't — ," he shouted. But by the time he realized his error, he was too late.

Holo looked at him as though she had been stabbed though the heart. Having nowhere to go, her hand hovered there in midair for a moment before she slowly lowered it.

She looked down, her face blank with neither anger or sadness on it.

"I'm ... sorry ...," she managed in a strangled voice, but she did not offer her hand again.

Lawrence could do nothing but curse himself.

The sound of the appalling thing he had done pressed in on him.

"... I'm going back to the inn," announced Holo quietly, walking off without a second look at Lawrence.

Holo could hear conversations within the next building, so she had certainly heard Lawrence's exchange with the master.

Of course, she would feel responsible and want to get away — she had been worried enough about him to accompany him, after all.

Yet just because her actions had backfired, she hadn't lightly apologized or acted confused; instead, she had been genuinely concerned for Lawrence. He knew it was the most appropriate response. He knew that, which made his treatment of her all the more reprehensible.

He couldn't find the words to speak to Holo, whose back was disappearing into the crowds — and he didn't have the courage, either.

Lawrence cursed himself again.

If the goddess of fortune existed, Lawrence wanted to punch her square in the face.

Lawrence finally returned to the inn only after the stalls that had permission to conduct business past sunset had closed their doors for the day.

He wanted to drown himself in wine, but he had no money and sensed that it would be a kind of betrayal.

Standing drunkenly before Holo — that was something he simply could not do.

It was his visits to the various trade companies that had kept him out so late.

If he abandoned pride and dignity altogether, he reasoned they would give him a bit of money simply to be rid of him.

In the end he'd gotten three *lumione* from four people. Three of them had told him he didn't need to bother returning it. They knew who was borrowing, after all.

His goal of forty-seven *lumione* was still clearly distant. He had to take this small amount and multiply it significantly in the little time that remained. It was not as if his situation had improved. The relationships he had destroyed in order to raise even this much money were important, even necessary, for doing business.

There were essentially no legitimate opportunities that remained for making more money.

And in any case, there was something that had to be considered before that — something that had to be regained before he could even think of making more money — which is why he had gone thither and yon asking after loans with no care for the consequences.

The memory of how Holo's hand felt when he unwittingly drove her away came back to him. Pain swirled in his chest, seeming to pierce his very heart.

When Lawrence entered the inn's lobby, the sleepy innkeeper stood behind his counter, enduring a large yawn. The city required that the innkeeper remain awake until all the guests had returned to the inn. If a guest hadn't returned by the next day, the town guard had to be notified.

It was a precaution against thieves and criminals entering the city and perpetrating foul deeds.

"Well, you're back early" came the sarcastic greeting from the innkeeper. Lawrence waved it off and headed to his room.

It was a single room on the third floor. Lawrence didn't want to consider the possibility that Holo had simply gone off somewhere else.

For the second time that day, he took a deep breath and opened the door.

Whether he opened the door slowly or quickly, the creaking would have been the same, so he did it briskly and entered.

Between the terrible building conditions and the huge number of travelers who passed through Ruvinheigen, a room with a bed was already fairly luxurious. This room, with its crude bed in the center, had a simple table by the window and still cost a pretty penny.

But now Lawrence was grateful it was so small.

If it had been even a little bit bigger, he probably would have hesitated to speak.

Holo was curled up on the bed, illuminated faintly by the moonlight that entered through a crack in the shuttered window.

"Holo."

The brief utterance diffused in the small, dark room, and Lawrence was beset by the illusion that he had never said anything at all.

On the bed, Holo did not so much as move.

If she had never wanted to see his face again, she would not have come back to the inn. The fact that she was curled up there on the bed soothed him that much at least.

"I'm sorry."

Those were the only words he had, all he could think of to say, but Holo remained still.

He could not imagine that she was sleeping, so he took one step toward the bed and gulped.

Instantly, he felt a sharp sensation at his feet. He stepped back quickly as a sweaty chill ran up his spine, and the frightening feeling vanished.

He looked back and forth between Holo and his feet.

When someone is truly angry, Lawrence thought, just getting close to them can almost feel like being burned. Disbelieving, he slowly reached his hand out; it was met by an overwhelming aura. Her anger was literally palpable. There was a distinct layer of air that felt strangely hot and cold at the same time.

Lawrence steeled himself and reached his hand out again. It felt as if he were plunging his fist into burning sand laced with blades. His senses told him that his flesh was charring and being cut into pieces.

He remembered his first glimpse of Holo's true form in the underground passageways.

He willed himself to take a step forward.

And in that moment.

" — !"

There was a rustling sound, and just as Lawrence thought he saw Holo's blanket move slightly, his hand was deflected by something hard. He saw her bristling tail had been flicked away, but a pain lingered in his hand, distinctly enough so that he didn't have time to wonder whether it was illusory or not.

Then he realized that Holo had felt the same pain when he struck her hand. Lawrence had been prepared for this reaction, whereas his rejection of Holo came utterly without warning. The surprise alone must have hurt her.

156

Again, he cursed his own mistake.

Lawrence took a leather pouch out from underneath his shirt and tossed it onto the bed.

It was all the money he had spent the day burning bridges to acquire.

He had cashed in all the relationships he'd built up in this city.

"This is all the money I was able to get on my own. Three *lumione*. I still have to raise over forty more, but I've no way to do it. I can think of no way to use that as capital to raise what I need."

It was like he was talking to a cobblestone, so complete was Holo's lack of reaction. Still, Lawrence cleared his throat slightly and continued.

"All I can think of to do is take the money to a gambling house and hope for luck. But if I give it to the person who really should have it, I feel it may yet increase. So I entrust it to you."

Drunken singing could be heard from the street outside the window.

"And if everything goes bad, well, adding three *lumione* won't make a difference anyway."

Lawrence had sacrificed possibilities for cash half in the hopes that Holo would be able to use her wits to find a way to increase their funds and half because he wanted to leave her some money in the event that the worst happened.

Though it was only a verbal contract, Lawrence had promised to take her to the northlands, and parting on such bad terms would leave a bad taste in his mouth.

He felt that the least he could do for Holo, as a merchant, was to give her some coin.

Still, there was no response.

He backed up a step, then turned, and pulled the door open, going into the hall.

He couldn't stay in the room when it was like that.

Lawrence descended the dark stairs and went outside, ignoring the rebuking voice of the innkeeper.

Off to his right, he heard the drunken singing that previously had filtered through the room's window.

The town guard would soon be making the rounds. Having no particular place to go, Lawrence thought of going to see Jakob, who was quite involved with his problems at the moment. Since Lawrence had gone around practically forcing his request on every merchant in the vicinity, Jakob had undoubtedly received a flood of complaints.

But he stopped after taking a step.

The realization that tonight could well be his last opportunity to walk around as a free man seized his heart.

He looked up unconsciously. He started to angle his sights toward the room on the third floor where Holo was. Holo, who surely had some terrible knowledge that could help him now; Holo, who he couldn't possibly ask a favor of now.

His gaze didn't even reach the third floor before he stopped and lowered it.

Just as he resigned himself to go to the guild house, something hit him on the head.

Lawrence's field of vision swam from the sudden shock, and he fell to his knees. The word *robbery* came to mind, and he reached for the dagger at his waist, but there was no assailant. Instead came the distinctive clinking of coins jingling against one another...

He searched around and saw the bag containing the three precious *lumione* he had left on the bed.

"You fool" came the words above his head.

He looked up to be met with Holo's scowl, as cold as moonlight.

"Get back in here, then," she said and immediately disappeared into the room. Just as she did, the innkeeper opened his door and emerged.

If a traveler staying at an inn were to perpetrate any misdeeds, the innkeeper could also be held responsible. As someone going out in the middle of the night had to be up to no good, the innkeeper had come to bring Lawrence back in.

But Lawrence no longer had any reason to stay out.

He calmed himself and picked the purse up, holding it up lightly to the innkeeper.

"My companion threw it out the window, you see," he said with a rueful smile.

The innkeeper made a put-upon face. "Try to keep it down, please," he chided, opening the door.

Lawrence nodded cursorily and headed back up the stairs to the room.

In his hand was the purse with the three *lumione*.

He stood before the door to the first room on the third floor and opened it without much hesitation.

Holo had taken off her robe and sat cross-legged on a chair by the window.

"You *fool*" was the first thing she said.

"Sorry."

Lawrence could think of no better reply. It accurately reflected what was in his heart but was too brief.

Yet no other words came.

"The money...," said Holo with equally short words, a displeased expression on her face. "How did you collect it?"

"You want to know?"

Holo looked away, as though presented with her least favorite food. "What was I to do, run off with your precious money?"

"That's half the reason I collected it. If my failure means I can't

159

fulfill my end of the bargain, the least I could do is leave you some travel money — "

He swallowed the rest of the sentence.

Holo still averted her gaze, her lips tight — but tears welled up in her eyes.

It was as if the emotion within her was overflowing, and she was trying desperately to hold it back.

Then a single tear sparkled as it fell. The dam had broken.

"'Travel...money'...?"

"Well, yes..."

"Of all the absurd..."

Defiantly, Holo wiped her tears with both her sleeves, then stood, glaring at Lawrence, her eyes still blurry.

"It is *my* fault, is it not? If I were not here, you'd shoulder no debt! Why aren't you angrier? If I were...if I were...!"

Her small fists quivered as the words within her became tears, overflowed, and fell.

Yet Lawrence did not understand.

Holo had come with Lawrence to the trade guild because she was worried about him. She certainly had not known that he would be turned down for loans because he had a woman with him.

And though it had been but a moment's passion, he had slapped her hand away.

No matter how he considered it, he was the one at fault. He couldn't find a reason to be angry with Holo.

"But I was the one at fault. You came along because you were worried about me. I can't be angry at you for — "

She looked at him sharply. The moment he started speaking, Holo turned and grabbed the back of the chair.

"You — "

She picked the chair up —

" — *fool!*"

Alarmed, Lawrence winced, but Holo did not throw the largish chair.

Soon he realized it took all her strength to lift the chair, and she couldn't throw it.

"Urgh...damn this...," she said, perhaps cursing the heavier than expected chair — or perhaps Lawrence.

But there was one thing he knew. Holo's thin arms could not hurl the chair by force of emotion alone. Her moonlit body leaned toward the window, hands still on the chair, eyes still glaring at Lawrence.

"Look out!"

Just as the chair leg clattered against the window frame, Lawrence sprang forward, grabbing the chair with his left hand and Holo's thin wrist with his right.

Despite the fact that she had nearly fallen out the window, chair and all, Holo continued glaring at Lawrence.

Unable to bear that gaze, he looked away.

Not knowing what else to say, he pulled the chair away from her to set it back on the floor and Holo relinquished it unexpectedly readily.

Then, as if that chair had been the entirety of her anger, the strength drained from her small body.

"...You..."

Her eyes dropped as tears hit the floor; her voice was low.

"You're so naive..."

Lawrence put the chair down as she said it.

"I'm...naive?" he asked reflexively, so unexpected was her statement.

Holo nodded, childlike, her hands still balled up into fists.

"But...you *are*...are you not? No one would loan you money because I was with you, yet...yet..."

"I hit your hand away! I was mad at you — unjustifiably mad!"

Holo shook her head and hit Lawrence's chest with her free hand.

Her face looked like she wanted to be angry, but she had forgotten how.

"I...I...I followed you because I was selfish. When it went awry, of course you were angry. But I never thought you'd hit my hand away like that, so I wanted to be angry—I wanted to, but..."

Lawrence started to understand now.

"H-how could I be angry at you when you looked at me like that?"

Holo wiped her tears again with her free hand.

"I became so foolishly vexed..."

She had been angry when he slapped her hand away, but looking at Lawrence's face once he realized what he'd done had caused that anger to subside.

Lawrence thought he must have looked quite pathetic.

But that didn't mean the rage inside Holo had entirely vanished. She had still been irritated at having her hand slapped.

And wanting to be truly furious but not being able to—that was only more frustrating.

She hadn't responded to him when he returned to the inn because she had not known what to say. Her mind worked far faster than Lawrence's, yet it had been thrown into confusion without a clear object for her anger.

Then, completely misunderstanding her, Lawrence left her at the inn with the three precious *lumione*.

That was like throwing oil on a fire.

Holo was already upset at herself for not being able to be properly indignant, and him leaving the coin with her only made it harder to be angry.

"I'm sorry...No, what I mean is, when I hit your hand away, I thought I'd done something I'd never be able to take back, no matter how much I apologized," said Lawrence slowly.

162

Holo looked at him with eyes that seemed tired of fighting.

She probably *was* tired. Despite her quick mind and quicker tongue, she had been angry enough to try to pick up and throw a heavy chair. Her wolf form notwithstanding, Lawrence did not think that her small body could sustain such ferocity for long.

"Anyway, I...I just wanted to undo what I'd done. And if it didn't come across, well...I'm sorry."

Lawrence inwardly cursed his limited eloquence. Holo lightly hit his chest again with her raised right hand.

"...Right, you."

"Hm?"

"Just answer me one thing."

Lawrence had no reason to refuse, so he nodded at Holo, whose hand clutched his shirt.

But Holo did not say anything immediately. She hesitated several times before finally speaking.

"Why...why are you so..."

She glanced up at him only for a moment.

"...softhearted?" she finished and then looked immediately away, as if to escape.

Nonetheless, the whole of her attention was focused on Lawrence and Lawrence alone.

It felt like she was anticipating something.

Her wolf ears, which until a moment ago drooped dejectedly, now pricked up slightly, and her tail swished just a bit.

Her small body was illuminated by the moonlight that fell through the open window.

The truth was the reason he had been so stunned by his own actions when he hit her and the reason he had so frantically gathered travel money for her were one and the same: Holo was very special to him.

And that was surely the answer she wanted to hear.

Lawrence looked down at her and tried to answer.

When he opened his mouth to speak, he realized that what emerged was something other than what was in his heart.

"Just my personality, I guess."

He was afraid of the reaction he would get if he answered honestly.

There was no telling what would come of a frontal assault on the unassailable Holo.

He feared her response, hence his answer. It seemed unfair.

It seemed a consequence of his own weakness.

However.

"Y-you..."

Just as he realized her hand was shaking, Holo smoothly slipped her wrist from his grasp, delivering a punch to his gut as she spoke.

"...Fool!"

Staggering back at the surprisingly forceful impact, he saw Holo glaring at him, still holding on to his clothes as if to prevent his escape.

"Y-your personality? Your *personality*? At least be a man and tell a lie worth falling for, you dunce!"

Lawrence winced in spite of himself. Holo could see through that much.

"S-sorry. The truth is —"

But that's as far as he got.

Still grabbing his collar, Holo grinned.

"Hear this, you. There are times when I want you to tell me something even if it's a lie, and times when if you lie to me it makes me want to give your face a sound beating. Which of these do you think we now face?"

He was so stunned by her malicious smile that he barely

managed to say, "The latter," whereupon Holo gave a long-suffering sigh and shoved him away.

Her ears and tail twitched her displeasure. Her anger was easy to understand.

"Oh, you're a rare dunce indeed! How many males are there in the world, do you think, who would not have managed to say, 'I'm in love with you,' or 'You're precious to me,' or any other line to get a female to fall for him? I can see quite clearly what you are thinking, but I simply cannot believe it — I cannot believe you are *such* a soft touch!"

Her eyes had gone past amazement and into disdain, but she didn't seem too irked.

Thinking about it the other way, Holo had wanted him to say it.

"But I suppose 'tis that same quality that lets me travel with you so easily. One can't have everything one wants."

Her comments were scattered, but Lawrence had no real rebuttal.

What had Holo really wanted him to feel when he delivered this supposed line?

Had she just been acting spoiled, teasing him? Or perhaps...

As soon as it occurred to Lawrence, Holo reached her hand smoothly over to him and drew him near.

Lawrence was immediately on guard for whatever she was planning, but she soon made her motive clear.

"Still, I did want to hear you say it. So come now, try again."

All he could think of to say was "Give me a break, please," but he knew doing so would call down a fiery wrath upon him.

Holo gave a slight cough and looked at him entirely expectant; Lawrence took a deep breath, preparing himself. The way she looked at him couldn't possibly be an act.

"Why are you so softhearted?" she asked again.

She looked even more serious than before, her sad eyes glistening and her lip trembling slightly.

He could feel the blood rising to his face, but Lawrence steeled himself and spoke anyway.

"Because you're very special to me."

She looked happy — so happy that it couldn't be an act — and bowed her head, resting it against his chest.

The unexpected gesture took Lawrence by surprise. Holo looked up at him, pouting, then took his arms and guided them around her back.

Apparently he was supposed to hold her.

It was so absurd and oddly endearing that he was stunned for a moment. Her tail swished as he embraced her slim body. It made him so happy, he dared to squeeze a bit tighter.

It was not long, but somehow the moment seemed to last.

Holo moved in his arms, which brought Lawrence back to himself — at which point, she laughed.

"Ha-ha-ha, what *are* we doing?"

"You made me do it!" said Lawrence, releasing her.

"Hee-hee. I suppose it was a good rehearsal for you," said Holo mischievously.

Lawrence was in no mood to give her a serious reply.

When he slumped, she laughed hugely.

"Still, I must say —," she said, apparently not finished. "Next time, just make me angry, yes? 'Tis nice you were so thoughtful, but sometimes it is quicker to have a nice loud row and solve our problems that way."

It was a strange thing to say, but Lawrence couldn't bring himself to disagree.

It was not an idea he would ever have come up with himself, But it seemed fresh and somehow warm to him.

"Right, then. Looking at your face I can imagine how you got the money together — how much?"

"Three *lumione* and two-sevenths."

Her ears twitching, Holo again put her forehead against Lawrence's chest. If she tried to blow her nose against him, he was going to push her away, but as she was just wiping her tears, he let her be.

When she finally looked up, she was back to her old self.

With a proud smile, she began to speak.

"You were right to count on my wit. I have a cunning plan."

"Wha...what is it?"

Lawrence leaned forward unconsciously out of a mix of curiosity and surprise; Holo made a face and pulled away.

"Don't look *too* forward to it, or else I'll worry about not being able to do it," prefaced Holo, and then she launched into a very brief description of her scheme.

It was simplicity and straightforwardness itself. It was so simple, in fact, that Lawrence's eyes bulged.

"What think you? Can it be done?"

"I'm sure everyone's thought the same thing, but it's actually impossible. I'm sure there are those who've tried it and been caught."

"Oh, surely, if you have to get a bunch of different people to cooperate. You'd never make it past the first gate."

Holo had suggested smuggling in gold, using an incredibly simple, straightforward method.

Lawrence would never have imagined Holo the Wisewolf could make such a dangerous, hopeless proposal.

Unsurprisingly, she then made the case for why the plan was, in fact, possible.

"I swear on my own ears and tail, I happen to know exactly who we can count on to turn this plan into reality. From what I saw, she can certainly do it. In truth, I'm reluctant to ask her.

Even I can jump over the city walls if need be. But with your pre-dicament, we don't have that luxury."

Lawrence, of course, soon understood who Holo was talking about.

Holo was almost certainly right as far as this person's ability was concerned.

But smuggling gold into Ruvinheigen wasn't simply a matter of getting it through the checkpoints. Being caught meant death, so everyone involved had to understand the risks and be willing to trust each other with their very lives.

There were many other problems, as well. There was no question that persuading the carrier was a daunting task. No matter how great the potential reward, you were still placing your life in the hands of another.

However, if smuggling gold in were a possibility, Lawrence could not afford to ignore it. It couldn't be dismissed out of hand.

"So if help can be secured, you think it's possible?" asked Lawrence.

"I should think so, as long as nothing extraordinary happens."

"I see…"

Lawrence's mind was already thinking about what would be necessary to smuggle in gold.

To even propose it, he and Holo would need to offer the carrier enough money to offset the danger and ensure his or her silence. The amount they could make by smuggling in gold bought in some other town with the three *lumione* they had on hand wouldn't be enough. They would lose all the potential profit just by compensating their partner. And compensation aside, it was doubtful that the gain made on three *lumione* could even approach the amount of Lawrence's debt. They had to pull in more capital. Holo, who said she could get past each checkpoint, realized this and suggested an alternate plan. Even if they proposed this plan to a potential investor, explaining the smuggling part would be a problem. Even more, they had to trust that the person lending them this money and aiding in the smuggling would not betray them. And those weren't even the biggest problems. The biggest problem of all was that Lawrence had no time.

He was deep in thought when he felt a tug on his hand, bringing him out of his reverie.

He soon realized that nothing had pulled him — rather Holo had extricated her intertwined fingers from his and had withdrawn her hand.

"Right, I'll leave you to work out the little details," she said. "I'm going to sleep."

She yawned, and then her tail flicked once in a sort of sigh as she walked slowly over to the bed.

"What, now?" Lawrence had planned on borrowing her intelligence again, but she had crawled under the plain blanket on the bed and popped out only her head to regard him.

"I know nothing of the city. I've nothing to offer save the fact that it is possible to get gold into the city."

Lawrence internally conceded the point, at which Holo smiled.

"Or, what, do you want me to stay beside you there?"

Unfazed, Lawrence remembered the "rehearsal." "I certainly do."

"It's cold, so no."

Holo's head disappeared beneath the blanket, but her tail — which seemed much warmer than the blanket — waved happily.

Lawrence took a deep breath, smiling at this, the sort of pleasant exchange that never happened when one traveled alone.

If he didn't figure something out between the sun rising and setting tomorrow, everything pleasant in his life would wind up sacrificed as an offering at the feet of the gods.

However, there was hope. He had no choice but to make that seed of hope bloom into a flower of success.

He sat in the chair Holo had lifted earlier and picked up the leather coin purse from the floor.

The familiar sound of jingling coins echoed in the quiet room.

A wagon clattered noisily along the cobblestone road, and Lawrence looked out the window to see the wagon's bed piled high with produce — probably a merchant heading to the marketplace first thing in the morning. Other people started to emerge here and there as well.

Just as Lawrence thought that it was about time for the morning sermon bell, the great cathedral bells echoed out through the whitening morning sky. Despite the considerable distance, the weighty sound carried quite well.

Then, before the echo of the great bells had faded, the bells from the many smaller churches that dotted the city answered the call; a little riot of sound to start the morning.

The townspeople were used to this, but for travelers used to dawn breaking with naught but birdsong, it was a bit raucous. And to a wolf whose hearing far surpassed that of any human, the noise was more than a bit raucous. She moaned her displeasure before rolling out of bed.

"..."

"Good morning."

Holo said nothing, only nodding glumly.

"I'm hungry" were finally the first words from her mouth.

"If we head to the plaza, the stalls should be opening soon."

"Mm," said Holo, stretching almost catlike, then combing her silky hair. "So, having thought about it for a night, what do you think?"

"We can do it."

It was such a short, blunt answer that Holo, who had finished with her hair and was now combing her much more important tail, looked up, surprised.

"That's an awfully quick answer for you," she said.

"What do you mean?"

Holo looked away purposely. Lawrence continued, ignoring her.

"Although, in any case, there are two barriers we have to overcome."

"Two?"

"In addition to whoever's carrying the gold, we have to find an investor who will help us buy up our supply. The three *lumione* I have on hand won't even be enough to compensate the carrier."

Holo thought for a moment, then looked at Lawrence doubtfully. "There is one more problem, is there not? You only have today. Can you bring the gold into the city so quickly?"

The self-proclaimed wisewolf's thinking was quick as usual.

But he'd had all night to think, and his mind had reached a place the wisewolf's had yet to settle.

"Naturally I've thought of that. It seemed like the biggest problem to me, as well. Call it strange, call it a miracle, but there is a key to solving all of those problems."

"Oh ho."

Lawrence smiled proudly at Holo, who regarded him as a master would a student about to be tested.

"We'll get the Remelio Company to invest."

Holo tilted her head slightly.

The Remelio Company was in the process of failing, just as Lawrence was. But it was hard to imagine that they were so stone broke that they would need to do the same kind of naive door knocking as Lawrence. They would probably have enough capital to fund one last attempt at a grand comeback, and those last precious funds would support the gold smuggling. Since the Remelio Company itself was on the verge of ruin, they would have every reason to be interested in a reliable plan to move gold.

Such smuggling was extremely susceptible to betrayal. In other words, once the smuggling was proposed to them and they were on board, it would be bad for them if Lawrence preceded them on the road to ruin. There was no need for discretion on the part of those already headed for death. Lawrence would have only to say, "The Remelio Company is planning to smuggle gold," and their plans for a comeback would be destroyed.

Thus, they would have no choice but to postpone the repayment of Lawrence's debt, and in order to protect against betrayal, Lawrence had no choice but to make them his accomplice.

This was his conclusion the previous night.

"But, in any case, we still lack time."

This was the biggest problem that faced them.

"Mm. Shall we then go right after breakfast?"

"Breakfast?"

"One can hardly fight on an empty stomach."

Now that Holo mentioned it, Lawrence thought back and realized he had not had a bite since lunch the previous day, but either because of the all-nighter he had pulled or because of the intense work that was left to do, he did not have much appetite.

But Holo was entirely cheerful as she hopped off the bed, fastened her robe and skirt snugly around her waist, and put her kerchief on her head.

"Some meat would be nice!"

Even if he had been fit as a fiddle, Lawrence would have found the idea of meat first thing in the morning entirely distasteful.

After taking breakfast at a stall, Lawrence and Holo headed on foot to the Remelio Company. Since they weren't arriving on a cart and horse, they called this time at the front door entrance.

As one might expect given that the entrance faced the street, it did not seem much different from normal, but once they opened the door, which bore no sign reading either OPEN or CLOSED, the unmistakable odor of financial troubles filled Lawrence's nose.

It was clearly a different atmosphere from outside, where hope bloomed in the morning air. Here, despair lurked in every nook and cranny, and there was a hungry impatience, a feverish aura scattered throughout the place. The simple presence or absence of money could change the very atmosphere.

"Er, might I ask who is there?"

The middle-aged man who greeted them wore a hard expression; it was early for a sudden visit. Nonetheless, he was relatively calm and his voice polite. He was thin and probably always had been.

"My name is Lawrence. I visited yesterday. There is something I would very much like to speak with Mr. Remelio about…"

"Is that so? This way, please…Oh, I'm terribly sorry, your companion —"

"She's my apprentice. It's convenient for her to be dressed as a town girl at the moment, but I look forward to her becoming a fine merchant woman in the near future. I'd like her to sit in on the meeting."

Lawrence spun the great lie without any hesitation, and the man seemed to accept it. Female merchants were uncommon, and girls aiming to become one were even less so.

"If you'll follow me, then…"

Lawrence followed the man into the building, Holo trailing after him. The workers on the first-floor office sported bloodshot, dark-circled eyes. Just like Lawrence's previous days, they had been working frantically through the nights on ways to raise money most likely.

"Please wait here."

They were led to a room on the third floor. This was probably the room normally used for negotiations about jewels, spices, and other high-priced items. Lawrence sat not on a plain cloth chair, but on an overstuffed couch with leather cushions.

"May I convey what your business with us is today, Mr. Lawrence?"

"I'd like to discuss a way to settle my debt with this company, and possibly for this company to settle its own debts as well," said Lawrence smoothly and evenly, looking straight into the man's eyes.

The man straightened as if struck by lightning, his eyes widening. He considered Lawrence with obvious doubt in his eyes, probably wondering if this visit to a struggling company was the last-ditch effort of a thief.

"Your doubt is entirely understandable. That is why I'd like to speak with Mr. Remelio as soon as possible."

The man appeared flustered at having been seen through. "I will take the message to the master," he said, taking his leave.

Eight or nine times out of ten, Remelio would have taken the bait — nothing Lawrence said was a lie. The only people who called on a company whose bankruptcy was near were those proposing liquidation arrangements. Merchants trying to salvage as much money as possible from a sinking ship would gather like ravenous ghosts. They could not possibly ignore someone coming along with even the flickering possibility of turning their fortunes around.

Holo's gold-smuggling proposal would potentially yield enough profit to wipe out the Remelio Company's vast debt, to say nothing of Lawrence's relatively meager liability.

However, the plan would never succeed unless the Remelio Company was fully involved.

Additionally, if people in the company were caught, they

wouldn't be spared execution. The Remelio Company's employees and their families would never be able to live in this city again. The danger was very real.

However, sitting and waiting would bring much the same outcome. Given that, the company would certainly take the chance. Then once Lawrence had repaid his debt, they would be able to lend on an absurd scale.

The greater the risk, the larger the potential gain.

It was the same as in Poroson when Lawrence had seen through the Latparron Company master's cheat and forced him into a deal.

Lawrence chuckled ruefully to himself at the memory, but the past was done; there was only the future now.

He had to convince the Remelio Company to take the risk. That was the first mountain to climb. He took a deep breath and straightened himself, then felt eyes on his face. There was no one else in the room; it was Holo.

"I'm with you. Don't worry." Holo gave him a lopsided smirk, exposing one sharp fang. It was a fearless smile.

"Yeah."

Lawrence's reply was short. His brevity was proportional to his trust in her. The closer a relationship, the less the need for lengthy contracts; the more a simple handshake suffices.

There was a knock at the door.

It opened, and there stood Hans Remelio, looking every bit as careworn as Lawrence.

"You said you have something important to discuss?"

The first step in the plan had been taken.

CHAPTER FIVE

There was no need for elaborate tricks. First, Lawrence explained the objective.

Unsurprisingly, Remelio's eyes became wide. "You don't mean —," he said.

"I mean exactly that," said Lawrence, but soon the common sense he would expect from a merchant running a trading company in Ruvinheigen showed on Remelio's face. It turned scornful as the master sat in a chair.

"I understand that your debt is a difficult one to repay, but I can't have you making such ridiculous chatter."

He began to stand, as if unwilling to waste any more time, when Lawrence stopped him.

"I'm sure there have been those who tried to smuggle gold this way before and were caught."

"Well, if you understand that, this will go quickly. It's easy for someone on the brink of ruin to mistake a reckless plan for a perfect one."

It occurred to Lawrence that this statement was half aimed at Remelio himself, but he continued undaunted.

"What if you could entrust it to someone especially talented at smuggling?"

Remelio looked at Lawrence gravely and sat back down. "What you propose is not possible. Someone so skilled as to be able to smuggle gold in would already be making plenty of money on his own. He wouldn't cooperate. If you plan to bring in someone from outside, you might as well give up now. There's no end to gold-smuggling plots like this, so inspections of anybody not registered with the city are especially thorough."

Remelio's objections were exactly the arguments Lawrence had been expecting.

"What if there were someone who was highly skilled but not making good money?"

"If he is so skilled, finding work in this city is not difficult. There's already a shortage of labor."

Remelio sat and waited for Lawrence's reply.

His expression was faintly reminiscent of Holo's the previous night.

He'd given his objection and waited for Lawrence's counterobjection. He wanted to give up but couldn't.

Lawrence took a deep breath.

"What if this skilled person had only ill-paying work in the city and a need for money? More importantly, what if this person's current employer left something to be desired? I'm referring to the Church. Importing gold flies directly in the face of the Church. We'll offer not only the opportunity for profit, but to exact some small revenge against the Church—it will be irresistible and the probability of betrayal very low, owing to a fair distaste for the employer."

"Th-that's far too convenient a tale."

"That's when business is most profitable. Am I wrong?"

Procuring produce when the crop has been bad, buying fashions that go out of style only to find them booming in another city — the biggest profits are realized from the most improbable coincidences.

Remelio's face twisted.

He wanted to believe but couldn't quite manage it.

"If I tell you this person's name, I think you will be able to accept it."

"I-in that case, why would you go to the trouble of coming to me and having another party demanding a share?"

Having established smuggling as the topic, Lawrence proceeded to this tangential problem, setting aside issues of possibility or impossibility.

"There are two reasons. The first is that the debt I owe this company comes due today, and at sundown I will surely be taken into custody in lieu of payment. The second is that this is all the coin I have on hand."

Lawrence produced the coin purse, untied its drawstring, and emptied its contents onto the table.

It was a mixture of silver and copper coins totaling three *lumione.*

The coins glittered in Remelio's eyes — Remelio, who faced bankruptcy, just as Lawrence did.

"It's three *lumione.* If you want to know how I raised it, just ask around among the merchant houses; you'll soon find out."

Hearing this, Remelio took a deep breath.

Given the situation, he surely knew how Lawrence had collected the money.

"This is truly everything I have. I want you to take it as collateral and trust what I am saying."

Lawrence leaned forward and looked straight into Remelio's eyes.

"I also want you to suspend the repayment of my debt and for your company to finance the purchase of gold for us to smuggle."

Remelio's haggard face was covered in a cold sweat, wrinkles gathering at his chin.

The only reason he didn't deny Lawrence and Holo on the spot was that he had just enough funds to finance the plan.

— And just enough hope to want to believe them.

All it would take was one more push, but if Lawrence pushed too hard, it would only make Remelio more doubtful.

Gold smuggling could yield enormous profit, but it came with terrible risk. And given the current condition of the Remelio Company, the deal to finance the smuggling could itself be seen as fraud.

There were plenty of people willing to destroy a struggling company in order to make a quick profit, so these doubts were hardly strange.

Lawrence had to choose his words carefully.

But before he could —

"Listen, you," said Holo.

Surprised, Remelio looked at Holo, blinking, as if only just now realizing that there was somebody else.

Lawrence, too, turned to Holo. Holo herself regarded the floor.

"Do you think you have the luxury of wavering?"

"Wha — " Remelio was tongue-tied at the provocative, threatening question.

Thinking this an unwise approach, Lawrence was about to stop her. However —

"Another person left just now. Can you keep dillydallying like this?"

Transfixed by Holo's sharp look, Remelio froze, as if he had swallowed a stone. "E-er…"

"I've excellent hearing. Shall I tell you about your workers and their plans being hatched downstairs right now? Their plans to escape while they can?"

"Uh — "

"Whoops, there goes another one. At this rate the shop will be — "

"Stop!" cried Remelio, clutching his head.

Holo regarded the man, her expression entirely unperturbed.

Lawrence half agreed with her. A company was like a boat. If there is a hole in the hull and no hope of patching it, the crew ignored the captain and abandoned ship.

But it was clear enough that Holo had chosen that line of attack for a reason. She knew better than anyone the meaning of the word *loneliness*.

She certainly understood Remelio's distress.

"Mr. Remelio," began Lawrence mildly, having understood Holo's angle. "I propose that you take these three *lumione*—everything I have—as a deposit and invest in gold. We know someone who will make the smuggling possible. If this person is paid well enough, trustworthiness is assured. And given your company, I'm sure you have a means to move the smuggled gold. What say you? If you'll postpone my loan and give me a fair portion, I want to conduct this operation with no unfavorable conditions placed on you."

A moment passed.

"What say you?"

Remelio looked down, head in hands.

Lawrence's words, more seductive than wine, were surely filtering through the man's mind now. He still hadn't looked back up.

Time silently passed.

It was quiet, as if the entire company was focused on Remelio's decision.

Just as Lawrence began to say, "Mr. Remelio," the master finally spoke.

"All right." He lifted his head, his face exhausted, a flame burning in his eyes. "Let's do it."

Lawrence stood up without thinking and extended his hand.

183

The two men, both of whom faced bankruptcy, shook.

"May God forgive us."

After settling the arrangements regarding roles and compensation with the Remelio Company, Lawrence and Holo found themselves in front of a smallish church in the eastern part of Ruvinheigen. The level of ornamentation, the size of the bells, and so on were decided based on the chapel's standing within the Church's organization—the reasoning being that the higher the abbey, the closer to God it was.

The church Lawrence and Holo visited was in the bottom middle of that hierarchy. Its adornment was not at all poor, but for Ruvinheigen, the church was rather subdued.

It was just after noontime, and the midday service was in progress within the parish.

"Now, then," said Holo abruptly, sitting on the stone steps as a hymn praising the holy mother wafted out of the chapel. "Think you can really pull one over on the girl?"

"Such things you say."

"Am I wrong, then?" asked Holo, amused.

Lawrence made a stern face and stared straight ahead as he answered. "You don't change."

He and Holo waited at the entrance of this house of worship because they had business with Norah the shepherdess. They did not know which church in particular she was affiliated with, but there weren't many that housed a female shepherd. Their search had been quick.

And having gone to all the trouble of searching, they weren't here to make idle gossip.

They had come to ask her to play a crucial role in the gold-smuggling operation—the carrier.

However, Norah was not facing financial ruin the way that Lawrence and the Remelio Company were. Still, proposing the gold-smuggling plan would certainly involve deception because they would need to make the profit that would come in with the plan's success seem equal to the danger.

Any who smuggled gold bet their life on it — and nothing could compensate for loss of life. Yes, some fudging of the details would be necessary.

Yet both Norah's skill as a shepherdess and her standing in the city were indispensable to their scheme.

And the merchant had faith that she would be their accomplice.

Lawrence felt a pang of conscience at treating someone's heart as a commodity in the marketplace. If Norah had been a merchant, he would have no such compunctions, but she was an innocent shepherdess. Nonetheless, the fact was not lost on Lawrence's keen merchant insight.

In addition to being a shepherd — and thus already regarded as vaguely heretical — she was a woman, which made her all the more likely to be a tool of demons. It was simple to conclude that the Church was not sheltering her out of some sense of charity, but rather to keep an eye on her. That was probably the root of her unease, which he had picked up on when talking to her about the shepherding work she did for the Church.

Also, though Norah had expressed her desire to save up enough money to become a dressmaker, it was not in the girl's personality to be avaricious — and the extra income afforded by doing escort work did not give her that luxury. He could understand if she didn't want to be exposed to a rather harsh work environment.

Toiling the day away doing the difficult work of a shepherd, yet never quite making ends meet — it would make it impossible to greet the morning with any joy. The future would stretch out endlessly ahead, holding only bitterness and suffering.

In contrast to that, Lawrence would propose the gold-smuggling stratagem to her: Rather than scraping tiny amounts of money together, she would make enough in one fell swoop to not only pay her guild membership dues, but also to end any worries about making ends meet. Sure, there was danger, but how could she let this opportunity pass? This was how he would persuade her.

Lawrence would hardly force her, so in that sense he wasn't doing anything wrong, but he still had misgivings about using her adverse circumstances in this fashion.

Nonetheless, it had to be Norah.

The fact that she was a skilled shepherdess who could lead her small flock through wolf-infested areas, where few humans ventured; the fact that she was unsatisfied with her employer, the Church; the fact that she needed money to fulfill her dream — it truly seemed like every condition was divinely arranged specifically to help Lawrence succeed in smuggling gold into Ruvinheigen. It was impossible to imagine anyone better positioned to help them.

Yet Lawrence heaved a sigh. Convincing her still weighed on him.

While he was absorbed in thinking about it, Lawrence grew conscious of Holo's eyes on him. He looked over and saw her grinning at him resignedly.

"You really are just too softhearted by half."

It was what she had said yesterday. It was true that Lawrence was quite sentimental for a merchant. There were plenty of merchants who would happily bring misfortune to their families if it meant making money in the process.

"Still, though," said Holo, standing and looking out over the ever-lively city street. "It's thanks to that softheartedness that I've been able to travel so easily," she announced casually, descending a couple of the stone steps to stand next to Lawrence. "I suppose I'll have to talk her into it. I need to be of some use, after all."

She gave a thin smile, but her words lacked a certain spark, Lawrence thought.

He studied her and sure enough, her eyes were downcast.

Maybe it was because he and Holo were close to the boisterous, busy lane, but she seemed smaller than usual.

"What, are you still thinking about yesterday?" he asked.

Holo shook her head but said nothing. It was an easy lie to see through.

"There's no telling what would've happened back there if you hadn't leaned on Remelio. I'd say you were plenty useful."

Holo nodded; perhaps she accepted the truth of the statement, but her face remained crestfallen.

Lawrence patted her head lightly. "I'll talk to her myself. It was my eyes that were blinded by greed and got us into this mess, after all. It'd be absurd to make you do all the talking because of my reluctance."

Though he was half trying to cheer up Holo and half being self-derisive, everything he said was certainly true.

"And anyway, if I let you help me too much, there's no telling how much I'll be taken advantage of later," he said with a shrug.

After a moment, Holo looked up and smiled with a soft sigh. "And here I was thinking I'd be able to call in some favors later."

"I certainly avoided quite a trap there," joked Lawrence.

Holo casually put her arm to her forehead. "Indeed, you did, but you're backing into a still larger trap. I don't hunt a rabbit caught in a trap. 'Twould be too feeble."

"Do you know the sort of wolf snare that uses a trapped rabbit as bait?"

"Make sure not to cower at the wolf howls when you set the trap. You'll foul the snare else."

It was the empty banter of familiarity.

Lawrence shook his head at the ridiculousness of it. Holo couldn't contain herself anymore and started laughing.

"Anyway, merchants are like sabers — they're no good if they're not straight. They break otherwise," said Lawrence mostly to himself, and then he cast his eyes to the sky, as if searching for the sound of the bells.

It was a beautiful blue sky with a scattering of clouds. He shifted his gaze to the east and spied a few more white clouds.

It was a fine day — and fine weather meant good business.

As Lawrence considered that, he heard a quiet knocking sound behind him — the chapel doors were opening. Lawrence and Holo backed away to the sides of the stone steps. Soon the congregation began to filter out of the church, their faces full of post-prayer serenity as they descended the steps. The crowd divided into smaller groups as they dispersed to finish the day's work — a scene that repeated itself daily.

At length, the exodus subsided.

There was once a time when it was groundlessly believed that the longer one remained in the church, the deeper one's faith — until priests started becoming angry with anyone who lingered in the chapel. Now such things did not happen.

That said, it was not good to leave a church too quickly, lest it seem like one is trying to escape.

As a result, butchers, tanners, and other craftsmen likely to attract the Church's baleful attention tended to leave the sanctuary more slowly.

As shepherds were counted among those suspicious professions, the shepherdess was last to leave. Her downcast eyes and reserved posture were no doubt due to the fact that the church was not a place of rest for her.

"Good day," declared Lawrence as he stopped in front of Norah, smiling as pleasantly as he could manage. A good smile was an important part of negotiation.

"Er, L-Lawrence and…Holo, yes?" said Norah, reddening slightly and looking over at Holo, then back to Lawrence.

"It is clear that us happening to meet in front of a church is the will of God," said Lawrence with a slightly grandiose gesture. Norah seemed to notice something and giggled in amusement.

"I won't be fooled, Mr. Lawrence."

"And thank heavens for that. I have heard that lately there are those at services who have drunk a bit too much of the holy blood."

Lawrence was referring to wine. Were she drunk, he might be able to convince her to join him, but she might also lose her nerve or turn him down. He was glad for her sobriety.

"I cannot drink much wine, so I mostly avoid it," she said with a shy smile, then looked around nervously. Perhaps she had been contacted with an offer of escort work.

Lawrence did not hesitate to use that expectation. "Actually, I am here about some work for you."

Norah's face lit up so quickly you could nearly hear it.

"This place being what it is, perhaps we should away to a stall somewhere…"

The reason Lawrence didn't suggest a bar was because nothing would be more conspicuous given the hour. Secret negotiations were best conducted in busy public spaces.

Norah nodded agreeably. Lawrence began walking with Holo at his right side and Norah to his left, trailing behind him slightly.

The three strolled along the busy, boisterous lane until they passed through the crowds and arrived at the plaza.

The plaza was as loud and festive as ever, but fortune smiled on them as the trio found a table at a beer stall where Lawrence ordered beer for the lot of them. Ale was cheaper, but as Norah was with them, he couldn't very well order any.

The service was quick but rough as the three cups arrived; Lawrence paid a pittance in silver for them, then put his hand to his mug.

"Here's to our reunion."

The tankards clacked together noisily.

"So, Norah, did you say you were able to go as far as Lamtra?"

Taken off guard by the sudden broaching of the subject of work, Norah, who hadn't touched her beer, eyed Lawrence guardedly. Holo watched the two, nursing her drink.

"Y-yes, I can go that far."

"Even bring your flock?"

"As long as it's not too large."

She answered so directly that Lawrence wondered how many times she had crossed the fields and forests on the way to Lamtra.

But just to be sure, Lawrence glanced to Holo to check the truth of the statement. Holo nodded so imperceptibly that only Lawrence could tell.

Evidently Norah was not lying.

Lawrence took a deep breath to avoid arousing Norah's suspicion. Being excessively roundabout might damage her resolve. Better to plunge straight in.

"I want to hire you for a certain job. Compensation will be twenty *lumione*. Not in a cheap banknote, of course — it will be hard coin."

Norah looked at him blankly, as though he were speaking in a foreign tongue. In fact, it took time for the words to penetrate her mind — it was as if they had been written down in some faraway land and sent to her.

To some people, twenty *lumione* was that much money.

"However, there is risk, and the compensation is only if we succeed. Failure earns us nothing."

Looking at someone's finger as it traced circles or *x* marks on a table was one way of telling if he or she was real and not a dream or hallucination.

Norah followed the movements of Lawrence's finger, and it seemed that he was quite real.

Yet still she had trouble believing, it seemed.

190

"The job will be moving sheep — then moving them back again as safely as possible. That will be all we need of your services as a shepherd."

Norah finally seemed to wrap her head around Lawrence's proposal, and realizing that the work and the compensation he had offered were far from comparable, she began to voice her skepticism. Lawrence seemed to have been waiting for that and cut her off.

"However, the work itself involves significant danger — proportional to the risk."

Having explained the unimaginable profit, he now explained the risk. Both could inspire shock, but the first detail would leave a stronger impression.

"Nevertheless, the pay is twenty *lumione*. Even the highest guild dues are but a single *lumione*. You could rent a house and take care of your daily expenses, working without worry. With that much, you could easily buy your own business. You would be the mistress of Norah Dressmakers."

Norah's face was troubled and then on the verge of tears. The enormity of the amount of money seemed to be sinking in — and with it, undoubtedly, the concern over the danger.

She had taken the bait. Now the real challenge began. If he muddled his statements at all, she would clamp a shell around her like a clam.

"Oh, that's right — had you planned to join the tailors guild in this city, Norah?"

She was waiting, prepared, to hear the bad news, but Lawrence seemed to have thrown her off the trail. Inside her head, Lawrence knew thoughts raced of both the ridiculous amount of money and the fact that she had not yet heard the risk. There wasn't much room to ponder extraneous things, so her answer should be quite honest, Lawrence thought.

"N-no, I was thinking a different town."

"I see! Do you not like the sprawling size of this city compared with others? It can be quite hard to live in an unfamiliar city with no friends, I find."

While her mind was occupied with other matters, she couldn't easily voice her thoughts — such was the plan.

Norah nodded, looking troubled, saying nothing.

That was enough for Lawrence, whose merchant intuition told him a person's heart based on the expression on their face.

The shepherdess's mind was like glass to him.

"Well, I suppose you'll want to get away from this city and its churches, won't you?"

The trap was set.

Holo gave Lawrence an obvious look, but the result was instantaneous.

"N-no, I mean, not at all... Well, but..."

"The harder you work for them, the better you protect the sheep they've entrusted you, the more they'll suspect you of witchcraft. Am I wrong?"

She froze, her head moving neither up nor down, left nor right — Lawrence was spot on the mark.

"And as they try to expose you, you'll have to venture where other shepherds would never go — because the alternatives are already taken by those selfsame shepherds, you said."

That instant, Norah's eyes snapped wide open, and she looked at Lawrence. Perhaps it was something she had vaguely considered before, since even if other shepherds had their territories, if she was willing to travel far enough, there would be safe places that remained.

"The priests will keep pushing you farther away until you're attacked by wolves or maybe mercenaries. And every day you're not, they'll suspect you of being a pagan."

Lawrence clenched his fist under the table, as if to crush his guilty conscience.

He had lit a fire under the small doubt that had always lingered within Norah's heart. There was no way to take it back. Whether it was true or not was irrelevant.

Merchants are like sabers — useless unless straight.

"I've been in a similar situation myself. Let me say it plainly."

He looked straight at Norah and spoke in a voice just low enough for people around not to hear.

"The Church here is lower than pigs."

Speaking ill of the Church was a serious crime. The shocked Norah peered around, the flames of her doubt suddenly scattered. Lawrence placed his elbows on the table and leaned forward.

"But we have a plan. We'll give the Church some trouble, make some money, and head to a different town — that kind of plan."

The flames of her doubt turned to anger and burned hotter, but once they burned out, they would leave behind the cinders of confidence. Within Norah, the seed of justified defiance would begin to flower.

Slowly, Lawrence articulated the heart of the matter.

"We will smuggle gold."

Norah's eyes widened, but she soon calmed herself. Surprise could, at best, only be felt as a slightly strong wind.

She finally spoke, her mind working again.

"But...what can I possibly do?"

It was a good question. Her skill as a shepherd wasn't her only merit.

"As I'm sure you know, gold coming into the city is heavily regulated. Every road that enters Ruvinheigen has checkpoints and two stages of examination. If you hide something in your sleeves or among your luggage, they'll find it on the spot. If you're trying to bring in a lot of something, it's even harder."

Norah nodded fervently at Lawrence's plain explanation, as though she was a devout believer listening to a sermon.

"We plan to get gold past the checkpoints by hiding it in the sheep's stomachs."

The look on Norah's face was so astonished that Lawrence could practically hear her say, "Impossible," but the notion gradually percolated through her mind, like water sinking into hard clay.

Many animals that eat grass year-round, including sheep, tend to swallow stones in the process. There was no reason not to scatter grains of gold among the grass and have the animals swallow them, though they might cough up gold during the long inspection process. And then there was Norah, who despite her skill as a shepherd, had but a small flock that she took far afield, wandering places where few humans traveled. When coming in from Poroson, the first checkpoint was a modest one; heavier traffic would mean a larger scale checkpoint.

Norah nodded slowly. "I see," she murmured.

"But gold prices are absurdly high in any city affected by Ruvinheigen policy. That makes the pagan town of Lamtra the most convenient place from which to start. If you come via the safest routes from Lamtra, there's a lot of traffic, and much of that territory has been claimed by other shepherds. This is what makes you perfect for the job. No one will find it suspicious that you're bringing your sheep through a low-traffic route — and that route is the quickest path from Lamtra to boot."

Lawrence paused, clearing his throat slightly and looking carefully at Norah before continuing.

"You've suffered at the hands of the Church in the city, Norah," he said sharply. "This is your best chance to turn the tables on them. The Church's two biggest sources of income are tithes and the gold trade, after all. But if we're caught, the punishments will be heavy, and once the job is done, we'll have to leave the city to be safe. And depending on circumstances, we may have to ask you to butcher the sheep."

There were few shepherds who had never had to butcher an animal — and still fewer who didn't find the job painful. It was a good way to measure her resolve.

"On the other hand, it's twenty *lumione*," Lawrence said.

You're being unfair, he told himself, but the more unfair her situation seemed, the more effective the result.

Finally, the girl across the table from him — who had endured heat and cold, suspicious gazes, and terrible treatment, all the while silently tending her flock — weighed the profit, risk, and nature of the job and seemed to come to a conclusion.

Lawrence could see her eyes become calm.

Strong words were uttered from a small mouth.

"Please, let me do it."

In that moment, Lawrence had convinced another person to make a bet with her own life.

Yet he swiftly aligned himself with Norah and extended his hand — it was that hand that reached out for his own future.

"I shall count on you."

"...And I on you."

Now the promise was firm. Norah and Holo shook hands as well, and now all three of their fates were inextricably linked. All three would laugh together or all three would weep.

"Right, now for the details."

Lawrence then asked Norah about when she would take the sheep, how many she would take, the specifics of the landscape around Lamtra, and how much gold she thought she could compel the sheep to swallow. He would take this information to the Remelio Company.

Midday passed in a twinkling, and by the time they finished talking, business was ending and the merchants and craftsmen

195

appeared in the streets on their way home. Having left her beer untouched, Norah stood. She had absorbed everything while entirely sober and made her decision.

If Lawrence had thought otherwise, he would have followed Norah when she left, giving her parting thanks to the man who had brought such an extraordinary opportunity. He would have tried to convince her to rethink her position.

Lawrence drained the lukewarm beer in the cup in one go. It was bitter and unpleasant.

"Come, should you not be more happy? Everything has gone well and yet!" said Holo to Lawrence with a wry grin.

But Lawrence could not be unreservedly happy. He had persuaded Norah to choose a dangerous path.

"I don't care how great the profit; nothing exists to balance out the wager of a person's life," he said.

"I suppose that's true."

"And just talking up the profit like that is the same as fraud. Merchants have always said that it's a fool who's bound by an unfair contract. But what is she? Just a shepherdess!"

Though all he had done was raise his voice, regret swirled within his chest.

If all he cared about was survival, he could have accepted Holo's help, abandoning his life as a merchant and all the people in it.

But to Lawrence that was not so very different from death.

So he had leapt at the heaven-sent chance to turn Holo's scheme into reality, tricking Norah into helping him.

He knew what he had done but couldn't help regretting it.

"Come, now," chided Holo after a time, swirling the remaining beer around in her cup as she stared at its contents.

Lawrence looked over; she kept her attention focused on the cup.

"Have you heard the terrible cry that a sheep makes when you tear out its throat?"

Lawrence's breath caught at the sudden question. Holo finally faced him.

"Sheep have no fangs, no claws, no fleet feet with which to escape when wolves come flying across the field like arrows with claws, teeth, and speed to tear at their throats. What think you of this?"

Holo spoke as if making everyday conversation — and in truth, she was.

What she talked about happened frequently — no, more than frequently.

One hunted one's food with every method available. It was simple, obvious.

"The death cry of a lamb is indescribable, yet my empty stomach complains constantly. If I must listen to one of them, I'll lend my ear to the louder of the two, will I not?"

Lawrence understood.

If having to sacrifice something in order to survive was a sin, then the only path remaining was to die while fasting as a saint.

But that didn't excuse just any behavior.

It took someone else saying what he needed to hear in order to free himself from the conflict.

"You're not so very bad."

Lawrence saw Holo smile at him helplessly and felt his black guilt melt away.

He had very much wanted to hear those words.

"Hmph. Such a spoiled boy."

Lawrence made a grim face at having been seen through so easily, but Holo just finished off her beer and stood.

"Still, neither humans nor wolves can live alone. Sometimes one needs a pack mate to curl up with. Am I wrong?"

Surely this was the definition of flexible strength.

Lawrence nodded in acknowledgment of Holo's smile and stood himself.

"Still, you're quite the dangerous one," she said.

She was probably talking about his skillful manipulation of Norah — but a fine merchant he would be if he could not do at least that much.

"You'd best believe it. Watch yourself, lest I trick you as well."

Holo giggled. "I'll look forward to that." She laughed as though she truly did anticipate it, which made Lawrence wonder if *he* was not the one being led on. He didn't say it, but as Holo let slip a private smile when they began to walk, it seemed best to assume she could see right through him.

"In any case, we've no choice but to try and make sure we all end up laughing," said Lawrence.

"That's the spirit. Still..."

Lawrence looked at Holo, who had trailed off in midsentence.

"...Would it not be even better for the two of us to have the last laugh?"

It was a seductive notion, but no — better that everyone was happy.

"You really are simply too softhearted."

"Is that so bad?"

"Far from it."

The two smiled slightly as they walked through the city.

The road ahead was far from bright, but each sensed in the other's face that the future was clear enough.

The smuggling would succeed.

The thought was unfounded, but Lawrence believed it anyway.

"My name is Marten Liebert, of the Remelio Company."

"Lawrence. And this is my companion, Holo."

"Um, I'm N-Norah. Norah Arendt."

The Church city of Ruvinheigen had many entrances and exits, and it was in a plaza just before the northeast gate that the three introductions were made.

The morning air before the market bell rang was crisp and pleasant, and the plaza, though still cluttered with litter from the previous night's commotion, was somehow beautiful.

Among the people gathered there, only Holo had the luxury of looking at the city.

The faces of the other three were all drawn tight with nerves.

The crime of smuggling gold into Ruvinheigen carried heavy punishments, up to and including being drawn and quartered. Under normal circumstances, they would have met many times to ensure there were no unpleasant surprises, but unfortunately the situation did not allow that.

There were many creditors who wanted to crush and devour the Remelio Company. Even a firm facing bankruptcy had land and houses and accounts receivable — all of which could be converted to money.

These creditors could hardly wait for the loan deadlines, so the Remelio Company was under pressure to finish the gold smuggling quickly and turn the results into coin.

Thus, Norah picked up her sheep from the church right after morning services, then headed immediately to join up with the others. Evidently, she had not expected anybody besides Lawrence to be involved and was surprised to hear the Remelio Company's name, but she kept any doubts to herself. She seemed prepared to play her part.

"Let us go, then. Business is like fresh fish in the kitchen," declared Liebert. It spoils easily was the unspoken conclusion.

Liebert was the man Hans Remelio had entrusted with the role of smuggling in the gold. Lawrence had no objection, and of course, neither Norah nor Holo seemed opposed.

Arousing only the slightest curiosity from the sleepily yawning guards at the gate, they left the city of Ruvinheigen without incident.

Lawrence wore his usual merchant's clothes; Liebert dressed in the kind of traveling clothes a city merchant might wear on a hunting trip. Holo had returned to her nun's outfit, and Norah looked as she always did.

However, neither Lawrence nor Liebert used a wagon. Liebert sat astride his own horse, and Lawrence had put Holo upon another horse, which he led by the reins as he walked. The road was likely to be poor, and traveling without a wagon was significantly faster.

With Norah leading the way as she guided her seven sheep and her sheepdog Enek, the group headed northeast to the town of Lamtra.

It was like the road from Poroson — the route was unpopular with travelers, and the group went the entire day without encountering so much as one other person.

There was nothing worth calling conversation, and the only sounds were the bell on Norah's staff and the bleating of her sheep.

The first interaction that even approached conversation came at sunset, when Norah stopped and began to make camp, which Liebert took issue with. With his almond-shaped eyes and smooth blond hair, he was every inch the spirited young employee entrusted with an important job. He advocated, in a rather high-strung fashion, for making more progress before stopping to camp.

But Liebert lacked travel experience. Once Lawrence explained things like how shepherds work and the risks of nighttime travel, Liebert was surprisingly understanding. He may have been high-strung, but he was by no means unreasonable.

Far from it, in fact, Lawrence realized Liebert was probably a good-natured man under normal circumstances once he offered a sincere apology.

"I am sorry. The pressure is getting to me, I think."

Liebert had been entrusted with the continued existence of the Remelio Company. Sealed securely in the inside of his coat was a note for buying up gold—in the amount of six hundred *lumione*. Even his master, Remelio, was probably clasping his hands in prayer back in Ruvinheigen.

"Well, unlike me, you're carrying an entire company on your back. It's to be expected," said Lawrence. Liebert looked slightly relieved and smiled.

The night passed quietly, and soon it was morning.

Among townspeople, breakfast is often regarded as a luxury, and many do not take it—but for those who live by travel, it is common sense.

Thus, they set off with all but Liebert chewing away on flat bread and jerky.

They stopped again just before noon.

It was just at the crest of a small hill; the road beneath their feet headed straight east, bending south at the summit of the next hill. All around them grew grass ideal for grazing; it stretched out in every direction.

But the road now turned away from their destination. Faintly visible to the north was the dark green line of the forest, and tracing that line west, they could see the craggy faces of the steep hills in the distance.

They would be heading between the hills and the forest, across fields where no wagon rolled and no traveler's foot trod.

The fields dividing the craggy hills, which were so rugged that they were impassable even on foot, from the thick, eerie forest (that even knights hesitated to enter) were the quickest path to Lamtra.

No one in their right mind would take that route, which despite its entirely mundane appearance was ineffably terrifying. Though Holo sniffed at rumors of pagan sorcerers summoning wolves, it was hard not to wonder at them.

Unless they navigated the pass and arrived safely in Lamtra and unless they returned with gold, none of them had a future. Their faces met, and they all nodded with unspoken understanding.

"If we encounter wolves, do not panic. We will arrive safely," said Norah with surprising resolve — it was reassuring, though Holo did not seem to find it at all amusing.

No doubt Holo the Wisewolf had something to say. When Lawrence met her eyes, she sneered slightly, but she soon regained her composure.

"God's protection be with us," Liebert prayed.

The rest followed suit.

The weather was good.

There was an occasional wind that stirred the cold air, making it brush against the travelers' cheeks, but as they were walking, it was easily ignored.

Norah headed up the group along with Liebert on horseback; behind them came the seven sheep; and trailing the sheep was Lawrence, leading the horse on which Holo rode.

The farther north through the fields that they headed, the closer the hills drew, nudging them toward the forest's edge. They kept as close to the forest as they could, since the horses might injure themselves on rockier terrain. However, as they got close enough to make out the gloomy form of the forest, its eeriness grew.

It was hard to say, but Lawrence thought he might have just heard a wolf howl.

"Hey."

"Hm?"

"Do you think wolves will be a problem?" he asked, lowering his voice.

"No good. We're already surrounded."

Even that obvious joke made his breath catch in his throat for a moment.

Holo chuckled soundlessly. "I can guarantee your safety. The others, I don't know about."

"We'll be in trouble unless everyone's okay."

"I truly do not know. The forest is downwind; if there are wolves, they've long since noticed us and started sharpening their fangs."

Lawrence suddenly got the feeling that something in the forest was watching him.

He heard the sudden patter of an animal's footfalls, and surprised, he turned to face the sound, seeing Enek run past him in a blur of black fur.

Enek chased after two stray sheep.

"Clever dog," said Lawrence.

He had not meant anything by it, but Holo still sniffed in irritation.

"Being half-clever only invites death," she said.

"...What do you mean?" he asked. It would be complicated if Liebert or Norah, ahead of them, were to overhear the conversation, so Lawrence spoke in a hushed voice.

On the horse above him, Holo wore a sour expression.

"That dog, it knows what I am."

"It does?"

"Hiding my ears and tail will fool humans but not a dog. Ever since we first met, it's been looking at me in the most irritating way."

Lawrence could tell Enek had been looking at them, but he had not realized why.

"But, here, what *really* irritates me" — Holo flicked her ears underneath her hood; she was quite angry — "is that dog's eyes. Those eyes, they say, 'Just you try touching the sheep. I'll rip your throat out.'"

Lawrence smiled awkwardly, as if to say "surely not." The flinty-eyed look he got from Holo made him wince.

"Nothing makes me so angry as a dog that doesn't know its place," said Holo, looking away.

Perhaps dogs and wolves were enemies in much the same way that crows and doves were.

"And anyway, I am Holo the Wisewolf. I won't fall for some mere dog's provocation," she complained with a scowl. It was nearly impossible not to laugh.

But since it would be a problem if Holo got angry, Lawrence stifled his chuckle. "Indeed, that dog is no match for you. You're stronger, smarter, and your tail fur is finer."

It was obvious flattery, and the last compliment seemed to work.

Holo's ears pricked up beneath her hood, and her face broke into a proud smile that no mask of composure could hope to hide.

She giggled. "Well, I see you understand the way of it, then."

It was true — Lawrence did understand by now how to handle Holo, but of course, he didn't say that and only inclined his head in a vague bow.

Eventually the grass grew sparse and the ocher soil more prominent.

The hills that spread out to the west were closer than ever and looked like an angry sea.

The group continued down the road, though it barely rated as such when they had to cross large tree roots that occasionally slowed progress.

Soon the sound of the wind through the trees reached their ears.

Yet still they pressed onward, passing the second night of the journey without incident.

According to Norah, if they left at daybreak the next morning, they would reach Lamtra by midday. Thus, they would have spent less than half the travel time that it normally would have taken to use the established route. Their route was closer to a third or a quarter of the distance. If this path was cleared, trade with Lamtra would become simple. Looking back on the distance they had covered thus far, Lawrence realized that wolves had not been a problem. It was easy to wish there was a more proper road.

Of course, a road would also make Lamtra much more susceptible to assault. Ruvinheigen would find it hard to tolerate a pagan city situated so close. That had not happened yet, which made it easy to suspect that Lamtra secretly paid Ruvinheigen specifically to prevent such a road's construction. Wherever there is power, there is also bribery, after all.

After a bland dinner, Lawrence sat deep in thought as he sipped some wine Liebert had brought. With no one to talk to, he was left to his own devices.

Holo had quickly finished her own wine and was now wrapped up in a blanket, leaning against Lawrence, fast asleep. Liebert, tired and unaccustomed to travel, dozed before the campfire.

Lawrence looked around and spotted Norah a bit farther from the campfire, stroking Enek on her lap. Evidently, if she stayed too close to the fire, her eyes would become accustomed to the light and that could cause problems if something were to happen.

Norah seemed to notice Lawrence looking at her; she glanced over at him.

She looked down at her hands, then back up, smiling pleasantly.

For a moment Lawrence didn't see why she was smiling, but then he looked down at his own hands and understood.

Holo snored away on Lawrence's lap—"the same as me," Norah's smile said.

Lawrence, though, was quite afraid to stroke Holo's hair. The wolf on his lap was far more fearsome than Enek.

As he looked at Holo, peaceful and innocent as she slept, the temptation to caress her grew keener. Surely there would be no problem if he mimicked Norah with Enek.

Liebert was asleep, and Norah minded her sheep as she tended to Enek.

Lawrence set down the roughly hewn wooden cup he held and slowly moved his hand toward Holo.

He had stroked her head many times before, but suddenly it now seemed somehow sacred.

His hand trembled. Then, at that moment—

"—!"

Holo lifted her head up.

Lawrence hastily withdrew his hand; Holo eyed him warily but soon turned her attention elsewhere. Lawrence wondered what was happening when he noticed that Norah had gotten to her feet, as had Enek, teeth bared.

Everywhere he looked it was the same—pitch-black forest.

"Mr. Lawrence, get back!" shouted Norah urgently, and mostly by reflex, the merchant tried to do as he was told, but he was caught on something and could not stand.

He turned only to find that it was Holo, holding fast to his clothes, keeping his hands behind him. He was about to protest when a warning glare from Holo over his shoulder pierced him. If he had to guess, the look meant something like "ignore the girl and get behind me."

Holo seemed to harbor an intense hostility toward Norah, and afraid to oppose her, when Holo stood, Lawrence stayed behind her.

Norah was absorbed in her own work, ringing the bell on her staff and directing Enek, rounding up the sleeping sheep and bringing them closer to the campfire, and then tapping the sleeping Liebert on the shoulder. Finally, she threw several more pieces of firewood onto the campfire.

Norah's movements were practiced and calm, and her awkward manner around other people reminded Lawrence of his own clumsiness when dealing with people outside of business.

Liebert finally awoke and, sensing the tense atmosphere, followed Norah's and Holo's gazes, searching for wolves.

He retreated, hand clutching his chest — no doubt feeling for the six hundred *lumione* note that was concealed there — as he got behind Enek, whose tail fur was standing on end as he bared his fangs.

The camp's defense arrangements settled, the only sounds that remained were the uneasy *baas* of the sheep, Enek's ragged breathing, and the crackling of the campfire.

There was no sound from the ebony woods. The moon was out, and there was no wind. Naturally being a mere merchant, Lawrence could hardly sense any presences in the forest.

But Norah, Enek, and Holo were utterly motionless as they looked into the woods.

For all he could tell, they might have been staring at catfish swimming in a black pond.

Strangely, he could not hear so much as a hint of a wolf's howl. Lawrence had been attacked by wolves many times in his travels, and such attacks always came with howls. And yet none were audible.

He wondered if there really were any.

Time crawled by with agonizing slowness.

There was no baying. The only reason Lawrence could keep his guard up was Holo — he trusted her implicitly, and she was still the very picture of seriousness.

Liebert, seeing Norah and Holo as mere girls, was another matter entirely.

The color returned to his previously frightened, pale face, and he began to cast his gaze here and there doubtfully.

There was movement the instant he opened his mouth.

Norah held her staff in the crook of her right arm and with her left hand took hold of the horn affixed to her side. Holo saw the gesture and was unamused — perhaps because wolves and hunting horns were ever in conflict.

Just as wolves howled and bears scratched themselves on trees, shepherds announced their presence with the blow of a horn. No animal could reproduce that long, drawn-out note, which unmistakably betrayed the presence of a shepherd.

The note rang out in the night and was swallowed by the forest. If there were indeed wolves nearby, they now knew that a skilled shepherd was among them.

But still, no howling rang out. The group's opponents maintained absolute silence.

"...Did we chase them off?" asked Liebert uncertainly.

"I'm not sure...At the very least, they seem to have backed away."

Liebert knitted his brow at Norah's vague answer, but seeing Enek stop baring his teeth and set about the work of rounding up the sheep, he accepted that the immediate danger had passed.

Perhaps he had decided that animals understood other animals.

"The wolves in this area are always like this. I hardly ever hear them howl, and they do not seem to attack — they just watch..."

The young employee of the Remelio Company paled at Norah's words, as though she had been talking about corpses returning to life and rising from their graves. Liebert was more timid than he looked.

"'Tis a bit strange they don't even howl," murmured Holo, still looking into the forest. Liebert gave her a skeptical look — this town girl who wasn't even a shepherd, what did she know of wolves?

It wasn't that Liebert had an especially bad disposition — many townspeople were like this, but their assumptions still grated on Holo's nerves.

"It could be aught besides wolves. For example, the spirit of a traveler who died here."

Liebert's face went sheet white. The wisewolf had exposed his cowardice.

"Still —"

Holo tugged at Lawrence's sleeve once she had finished teasing the poor lamb. Her voice was low, so Lawrence leaned down to put his ear level with her.

"I was half-serious. I have a bad feeling."

This journey was no ordinary one. They had to make it safely to and from Lamtra. If the group failed, whether they ran or met their fate, Lawrence's life as a merchant would be over.

He gave Holo a baleful look as if to say, "Don't try to frighten me with your foolish stories," but she just vaguely surveyed the forest.

Apparently she wasn't joking.

"Hmm, we seem to be out of firewood," said Norah brightly, perhaps to dispel the still-tense atmosphere. Lawrence agreed, and Holo finally averted her gaze from the forest and nodded. Liebert nodded as well, probably mostly out of a sense of obligation.

"I'll just go gather some more then, shall I?" said Norah, perhaps confident in her night vision.

Lawrence felt bad leaving it just to her. "I'll come as well."

Holo chimed in. "As shall I."

Not knowing the first thing about starting a campfire, Liebert had not raised a finger to tend it, but now he must have felt entirely ill at ease.

"I-I'll help, too!" he said, clearing his throat, afraid of being left all alone.

Holo smiled unpleasantly at him.

They walked into the forest to gather firewood, and Lawrence wondered if the bestial aura he felt was just his imagination.

Yet there were no further incidents, and the night passed quietly.

When Lamtra finally came into view, Lawrence breathed a sigh of genuine relief.

With the deep forest to their right and the rugged hills to the left, their passage had felt akin to going down an endless back alley.

But his sigh of relief did not come from reaching the end of that alley. He had experienced far worse trails many times in the past. No, the relief came from the fact that the strange gaze he had felt upon him the previous night was gone.

Lawrence knew it wasn't simply his imagination since Holo and Norah had been continuously on guard as well. There was definitely something within the forest that separated Ruvinheigen and Lamtra — something that even knight brigades feared.

Even so, they had made the trip out successfully, so the return trip should also be possible. Lawrence was still uneasy about it, but Norah was with them, and she had made the trek many times and never been attacked once. Relying on her shepherding skills — as well as Holo — would see them through somehow.

Then all they had to do was bring in the gold.

Lawrence was deep in thought as he watched Liebert head into town to make the purchase — there was no point in the lot of them filing into Lamtra.

"I hope everything goes well," said Norah, no doubt referring to Liebert's task.

So far, everything they did was perfectly legitimate, so there was little to worry about, but pointing that out seemed excessive.

"Indeed," replied Lawrence.

There was a reason he used his best merchant smile when he said this.

Norah was simply making small talk.

But in Lawrence's heart, misgiving mingled with regret.

He worried that Norah didn't truly understand the consequences that awaited them were they to fail. The shepherdess before him was the one who would be in the most danger when they moved the gold.

The gold would be hidden in the stomachs of her sheep when they passed the checkpoints. If one of the sheep should happen to cough up any of that gold, the shepherd responsible would face immediate punishment.

In contrast to that, if Liebert and Lawrence were to keep silent, they might be able make it through the checkpoint.

There was a huge difference in their risks. He wondered if Norah understood that.

Lawrence looked on as Norah tended to her flock as at any other time, petting Enek when he returned to her side after performing this or that task. The merchant felt he needed to ascertain Norah's awareness of her peril.

It simply did not seem as though she grasped the difference between what could happen to her compared to what the people around her might face.

If so, taking advantage of her ignorance was not far from fraud. Lawrence considered this and concluded that his conscience was most definitely somewhere near the pit of his stomach.

Were Norah to learn that she would be made to take the fall if caught, she might refuse to cooperate, turning a cold shoulder to them. That had to be avoided. Thus, Lawrence kept silent.

"Now that I think of it…," Norah piped up, jolting Lawrence out of his reverie.

However, when he lifted his head, he saw that she was not speaking to him.

Norah looked at Holo, who had plucked a single stalk of tall grass and was now wandering about aimlessly.

"Miss...Holo, I mean..." Norah hesitated after saying Holo's name, perhaps needing to muster up more courage to speak.

Lawrence had noticed Norah trying to engage her female companion several times, but Holo's curtness made her hesitate.

In his mind, he encouraged her, but he was genuinely surprised at the words that next came out of her mouth.

"Do...Do you know a lot about wolves?"

Lawrence was shocked for a moment, but Holo — ever the canny Wisewolf — did not alter her expression a bit. She finally tilted her head curiously at Norah.

"Um, I mean...I just, last night you noticed the wolves so quickly, so I..."

She trailed off there, perhaps because she wondered if Holo also had experience as a shepherd. Were that the case, it would be like one white crow finding another — one rare shepherdess meeting another would make for lively conversation.

If so, Holo's unapproachable attitude left few opportunities to speak up.

"What? I simply noticed them, that's all."

"Oh, I see..."

"I mean, the men are generally useless, after all," said Holo with a mischievous smile, glancing at Lawrence, who gave a small shrug in reply. "Don't you think?" she finished.

"Um, I, I don't..."

"Hmph. So you think you can count on that?" prodded Holo, pointing sharply. Norah followed where Holo indicated—

—only to meet Lawrence's eyes.

In that moment, Norah looked genuinely awkward as she

averted her eyes. Holo asked her again, and Norah glanced apol-
ogetically at Lawrence as she whispered something to Holo, who
had drawn near the shepherdess.

Given the cheeky wolf's smile, it had to be that kind of
answer.

Lawrence watched and realized the conversation was about to
turn farcical.

He waved his hand back and forth as if to admit defeat, while
Holo and Nora laughed.

"In the first place, 'tis not strange to ask if someone like me,
traveling alone with a man, knows a lot about wolves!"

Going by looks alone, Norah appeared to be the older of the
two girls, but as soon as Holo spoke, she took the upper hand.
She put one hand on her hip and held up the index finger of the other
looking for all the world like a theologian giving a lecture.

"You see, the answer is completely self-evident! Because —"

Because? Norah leaned forward as if to say.

"Because! Come nighttime, a wolf will always appear — tempted
by this helpless, adorable rabbit. Surely you'll agree that a rabbit
who is devoured by a wolf every night could not fail to know
something about wolves!"

Norah looked blank for a moment but soon understood what
Holo meant. Her face turned beet red as she searched back and
forth between Holo and Lawrence; then, embarrassed, she looked
at her feet.

Holo giggled. "Ah, 'twas a lovely reaction. But no — my first
answer is the one to remember," she said delightedly, at which
Norah blushed to her ears and averted her gaze as she seemed to
remember something.

It then sounded like she raised her voice in a quiet "Oh."

"In truth, it's my companion that's more like a rabbit. If I left
him on his own, he'd likely die of loneliness."

Holo whispered into Norah's ear, but her voice was loud enough to reach Lawrence quite distinctly. He gave Holo a bitter smile, but it was Norah's credulous nodding that hurt the most.

As if he really seemed that way.

"But, in any case, I just happened to notice the wolves last night."

In truth, it was not an obvious conclusion, but Norah had been sufficiently confused by Holo at this point that she seemed to accept it. She put her hands to her cheeks (the blush was now subsiding) and nodded.

Then taking a deep breath, she spoke, her nervousness evidently dispelled.

"Actually, I thought perhaps you were a shepherd, Miss Holo."

"Oh, because I was quick to notice the wolves?"

"Well, there is that, too," admitted Norah, pausing to look at her black-furred companion, who was content to pause in his work while his mistress had her chat. "Actually, it was because Enek seems to be very aware of you."

"Mm, is that so?" Holo — whose nerve was such that she had no trouble exposing her tail when she knew she would not be caught — smiled, totally unperturbed as she folded her arms and regarded Enek. "It's hard to say in front of a pet dog, but I daresay he's smitten with me."

As if he had heard her, Enek looked back to Holo and then struck out once again to tend to the flock of sheep.

His mistress, on the other hand, was struck dumb by Holo's words.

"Wha-what? Er, you mean, Enek is?"

"My, it's nothing to be sad about. Any male will get overconfident if spoiled. I'm sure he's quite important to you, but that only makes him feel secure that he's gained your affection. There's no mistake; he'll go looking for others to frolic with. No matter how delicious the bread, sometimes you want soup."

Perhaps feeling some sympathy with Holo's intricate argument, Norah nodded, apparently impressed.

"Put another way, sometimes you have to be cold. It's a good leash."

Norah nodded firmly, as if she had been told some deep truth, but then called Enek's name and crouched down to greet him.

She caught him head-on as he streaked over to her, then looked up to Holo, and smiled.

"If he ever has an affair, I'll keep that in mind."

"Good."

The wrongly accused Enek barked once, but Norah put her arms around him, and he was soon calm.

"I think I'd like to indulge him as long as I can, though," said Norah, lightly kissing Enek behind his dangling ears.

Holo looked on, a slight smile playing about her lips.

It was a somewhat bemused smile, inappropriate to the occasion, Lawrence realized, when Holo looked at him.

"Because...whether this job goes well or fails, I'll be giving up my work as a shepherd," said Norah quietly as she held Enek in her arms. It was clear that she had a firmly rational grasp of the situation and was prepared to act according to that understanding.

She understood both the position she had been placed in and the likely outcomes.

Lawrence's concern was unnecessary.

Though Norah might have looked frail, she had survived being cast out of an almshouse and lived through any number of difficulties. She was no pampered noble's daughter.

At the same time, Lawrence had renewed respect for Holo.

She had discerned Lawrence's misgivings and, after seizing the conversational initiative from Norah, casually drawn out evidence of how prepared the girl actually was.

That explained Holo's bemused smile earlier.

The merchant wondered if Holo's pronouncement that men were generally useless was not necessarily off the mark.

Lawrence covered his eyes in defeat and then sprawled out on the ground to rest.

The autumn landscape was cold with the approaching winter, but the scattered clouds in the sky looked warm.

The smuggling would succeed.

Lawrence muttered encouragement to himself as a sheep meandered over and peered down at him.

After some time, Liebert returned, riding his horse back at a leisurely pace.

When one carries a large amount of money, he will see everyone around him as a thief, but true to his position as a trusted employee of a trading company in a big city, Liebert appeared unperturbed.

He produced a bag of gold grains just large enough to be held in one hand, and after all present had confirmed the bag's contents, Liebert tucked it into the inside of his jacket, patting it lightly.

"Now all we have to do is make it safely back with this and feed it to the sheep at an opportune time," he said as if to emphasize that any real problems would be from here on out. "Then once we've gotten them through the gates, the sheep will be received as previously discussed. Are we agreed?"

"We are," said Norah with a nod.

Liebert faced straight ahead. "Then let us go. A golden tomorrow awaits us."

The small band headed back onto the narrow path between forest and hills.

The next morning, Lawrence opened his eyes as he felt something cold on his face.

Is a sheep licking me again? he wondered, but he saw only the lead-colored sky. Evidently there was going to be a rare autumn rain.

And it was *cold*. Lawrence lifted his head off the tree root he had been using as a pillow and saw that the fire had gone out. In order to have a small gap between the time Norah went to sleep and everyone awoke, one person had been tasked with having Norah awaken them early to tend the fire. That person was supposed to have been Liebert, but he lay there snoring away, firewood clasped in his arms.

It was so foolish that Lawrence could hardly be angry with him.

"...Mmph."

Lawrence sat up, apparently awakening Holo, with whom he had shared a blanket.

Without so much as a "good morning," she shot him a truly withering glare and yanked the blanket away.

"If you're awake, you don't need it" seemed to be her logic.

If he argued the point, she would likely become genuinely angry, so although it was a bit early for him, Lawrence forced himself up. He had to toss another log on the campfire. The sheep were all huddled together from the cold, and with no work to do, Enek slept stretched out by the cinders—nestled up to his beloved mistress, of course. Lawrence stood, joints creaking, and tossed a log onto the fire to get it started, glancing wearily at the comfortable-looking Enek.

As the dry wood began to crackle in the fire, Enek yawned contentedly. Lawrence smiled; it reminded him of Holo.

Still, it was cold. It was as if winter had suddenly arrived.

The cause was obvious to Lawrence, looking at the weather, but as they would be arriving in Ruvinheigen at midday the next day, he had wanted it to hold until then.

But the sky seemed unlikely to wait. Lawrence sniffed bitterly. Rain would likely fall by the afternoon, surely by evening.

The trees were thick enough in the forest that the group could probably take shelter under them, but with the sheep along, that was hardly an option. The forest was an ominous one, too. Lawrence was not terrified of it, but neither was he eager to spend the night there. Using the edge of the trees as a rain shelter would be quite close enough.

Lawrence thought it over as he gazed into the growing campfire, and then something suddenly loomed over his back.

He didn't have time to turn around before a familiar face appeared directly beside him.

It was Holo with the texture of the tree root she had slept on still imprinted on her face.

"'Tis warmer over here."

Lawrence was not so humble as to take those words purely at face value.

Holo wrapped the blanket around Lawrence's back and deliberately huddled under it with him again. Stealing the blanket away was all well and good, but perhaps she had decided that was excessive. Hunger and cold were every traveler's companions, after all.

But as Holo had said nothing to apologize, Lawrence said nothing by way of forgiveness.

He stirred up the embers with a stick, then tossed it into the fire.

"Oh, that's right," he said casually. "Didn't you say you could predict the weather?"

"Surely. It will rain just past midday today," she replied sleepily.

"Anyone could tell that, looking at this sky," teased Lawrence.

Instead of scowling, Holo bumped her head against his shoulder lightly.

"Wish we could take fast horses and make it to town before the rain. Anyway, what say you to some potato soup? It's been warming by the fire."

"I've no complaints. Also — "

"Your tail grooming, right?" said Lawrence, lowering his voice still further.

Holo sighed and nodded. "I want to return to the inn as soon as we can. Though…"

Her face was melancholy as she looked up at the sky.

A chill wind blew through her bangs, and she narrowed her eyes as though it had touched her long eyelashes.

"A rain is coming, though I haven't wished it so."

It was then that Lawrence remembered. When he had met Holo, she'd been the harvest god of a bountiful area. Farmers hated a chilly rain during the harvest months of autumn, so though she was far from the wheat fields now, such weather was not something she could welcome.

Though Holo herself hardly had good memories of the wheat fields, owing to the many things that had happened there, she had still been the god of the harvest.

It didn't take a harvest god to find the cold rain distasteful. In the worse case, the rain might turn to sleet.

Lawrence got cold just thinking about it, and he briskly tossed another log onto the fire.

There was a bit more time before everybody woke up.

Yet he still hadn't realized something.

Holo never said anything meaningless.

CHAPTER SIX

White breath trailed behind them as they walked. The exhalations warmed their cheeks momentarily, but with every breath, they soon turned to a painful chill.

The darkening sky had finally lost its patience, and just after midday, a thin drizzle began to fall as if shaved from some giant block of ice. Thus, Lawrence's face was so cold he wondered if it had actually frozen, but whenever a bit of air found its way into his clothes, it was just pleasantly cool.

They ran — the people, the horses, the sheep, and the dog.

There were eyes on them, many of them. There were presences, too.

But no matter how watchful the group was, not a single howl was heard nor a single clump of fur seen, and eventually the weather and the hard effort robbed them of their ability to worry about wolves.

It was as if something had aimed for that gap.

By the time Holo noticed this, they were already surrounded by the wolves.

"Enek!"

Norah's voice echoed, and Enek sprinted to the rear of the

flock in a blur of black fur and white breath, driving on a lagging lamb.

The lamb sprinted desperately but was unable to distinguish between dog and wolf, and a wolf's howls echoed as if to mock it.

The situation was clear. The cry had come from a wolf atop the rocky hills to the right as it tried to collect the sheep. In contrast, little howling could be heard from the forest on the left side — what *could* be heard were footfalls and panting.

On the far side of the ferns and undergrowth beneath the trees, Lawrence and the others ran side by side. Lawrence and Holo sat astride their horse; likewise, Liebert rode his. Norah's bangs were plastered to her forehead from the sleet and sweat as she used both Enek and her staff to control the sheep.

When it came to the wolves — well, if they were surrounded, that would be the end. Wolves hunted very carefully, making sure none in their pack was injured in the process. There would be no plan to use a single wolf as bait, nor would a single member make a heroic attack on its own. Wolves were cautious to the end and always conducted themselves with cunning.

Thus, if the group could put themselves in a position to kill just one wolf as the pack tried to tighten the noose, they could free themselves from any further harassment.

Lawrence listened to Holo's hasty explanation and saw that Norah moved to do just that.

A single wolf was visible in brief flashes, trying to get ahead and cut off their route, but it would be instantly diverted by either Enek being sent out ahead or Lawrence himself plunging ahead.

When the wolves moved to slowly close the loop, the sheep would be made to dash in some wild direction, breaking the line. For a shepherd, sheep are not poor children to be protected, but a shield — a weapon to be wielded like any other.

It was not Lawrence's or Liebert's time to act. Liebert was fully engaged holding his reins in one hand and keeping the gold within his jacket secure with the other.

For his part, Lawrence could only ask Holo what he should do.

"What to do, eh?"

The road was terrible and much worse on the back of a trotting horse. Impacts were constant, and it felt like one's head was about to separate from one's body. Keeping Holo, who sat in front of him, from being thrown off was work enough.

"What to do, indeed."

Her enunciation was bad, and not necessarily just because the bumpy ride made it easy to bite one's tongue when talking.

"Listen —"

"What?"

"About my explanation before — I take it back."

"Explanation before?" Lawrence was about to ask when the grass diagonally behind them in the forest rustled, and immediately thereafter came the sound of claws digging into dirt.

Lawrence felt an intense chill run down his back, as if wings were about to sprout there. It was not a chill that could be described as merely hot or cold. It was a message of danger from the very grave.

"Enek!"

With nearly superhuman intuition, Norah sensed the attack as she ran well ahead with the sheep. She quickly raised her staff to summon her black-furred knight, but their last hope was the hill that lay ahead.

Naturally the wolves realized this as well.

A brown whirl came streaking at the legs of Lawrence's horse.

It was do or die. Lawrence was about to pull back on the reins with all he had, but Holo put her hand out and stopped him.

Then looking over her shoulder, she spoke.

"Fall back."

The reason Lawrence understood that she had spoken to none other than the wolves themselves was that the surging pack suddenly wheeled aside and stopped, as if struck by arrows.

Norah, Lawrence, and the others weren't the only ones surprised. The bemusement of the halted wolves themselves was obvious just by looking at them.

Yet Lawrence could neither praise the feat as amazing nor give his thanks to Holo for saving them.

Holo's normally red-brown eyes flashed ruby bright.

To look on her was to be afraid; Holo the Wisewolf was among them.

"The humans, as well."

Her cold voice reminded Lawrence of when he'd first seen her true form.

"Youngsters these days, I suppose I could say."

Lawrence wondered for a moment what she was talking about, when suddenly he realized what she meant.

Though the immediate danger had passed, Norah did not understand why; doubt tinged her face. But there was no time to think. Preparing to face whatever crisis came next, Enek steadily carried out the rapid-fire orders given to him by his mistress.

Liebert clung desperately to his horse, trying only to avoid dropping the gold.

If they kept going at this speed, they would be able to put the forest behind them by sundown.

And to put this danger behind them, they had no choice but to try.

Then *it* resounded.

At first it seemed like the **wind** — there was a *whoosh* as the icy drizzle was blown back **momentarily** into the sky.

But it was soon clear that this was a strange wind indeed.

A normal gale didn't chill one's core the way this one did.

The wind was immediately followed by the sound.

A tremendous, forest-splitting roar battered their eardrums from one side.

"...!"

The overwhelming blast was enough to freeze a person's breath.

The horses stopped. The sheep stopped. Even the gallant sheep-dog was frozen in his tracks.

The violent roar seemed to nail everyone to the ground.

They stood as statues, looking into the forest.

"Listen —," said Holo quietly to Lawrence. Everything was still; the only sound was the drizzle falling on the earth. "This is a trouble I must bear. When I send the girl and the kid on, you'll have to stay back for a time as well."

"Wha — why?"

There in the stillness, Norah and Liebert did not seem to take notice of Holo and Lawrence's exchange as they glared unblinkingly into the forest.

But it wasn't that they hadn't noticed.

It was the same as a hound that had cornered a bird — even as the hunter moved its hand to strike, the bird could not fly away.

They were unable to take their eyes off the forest.

"Because what's in that forest is no normal wolf. You understand, yes?"

Holo slowly looked away from the forest, turning to Lawrence.

His legs went weak at those eyes.

Her expression was well past displeasure; her eyes flashed with such anger that Lawrence wondered if she might rage at the very cobblestones in the road.

Her breath was slow, like the breathing of a demon-horse in hell.

"If I go along with them, the pack will chase the sheep no longer. Those sheep are not their aim."

She turned back to the forest.

"Such cheap bluster. Such rough pride. Both prized by the young, I suppose."

Holo was still mostly within Lawrence's arms, and she seemed almost to swell as she spoke.

It took Lawrence a moment to realize that it was from the swishing of her tail beneath her robe.

"Go! They won't move until you speak. You're my partner — and partners cooperate, do they not?"

Holo's expression was suddenly softer, and Lawrence found himself nodding.

He was a merchant and generally hopeless at anything save business.

For Holo's part, there was none who knew more of wolves than she did.

"We'll take it from here. The two of you take the gold and go on as planned!" Lawrence hadn't planned to shout, but Norah and Liebert snapped out of their reveries as though they had heard voices in the middle of the night.

There were no objections. In situations like this, to leave the seemingly weak ones behind as a sacrifice so that the strong can live on was a well-used tactic.

But they did look at him questioningly — "Is it really all right?" their eyes asked.

No matter how established the tactic, what was possible for a grizzled mercenary band was not so for a regular traveler.

"We shall meet at the walls of Ruvinheigen. And we'll all be rich." Of course, Holo had no intentions of becoming a sacrifice, but there was no way for the others to know that. At the same time, she could not very well explain herself, so she just smiled lightly as she spoke.

She was taking advantage of human nature. People wouldn't waste the sacrifice of someone facing near-certain death with a smile and a faint hope. A clever wolf knew how to use that fact.

Liebert was the first to nod his agreement, followed by Norah.

Norah waved her staff, and time seemed to start moving again.

"The fortunes of war be with you," said Liebert. Norah gave Holo a look more eloquent than words and then soon turned away. As he heard the sound of the sheep starting to run, Liebert followed after them.

Holo watched all this, then turned to Lawrence.

"You'll need to stay away. If you get close, it could go badly. You understand, I know."

Instead of answering, Lawrence took Holo's hand before she dismounted from the horse.

"I won't let you lose," he said.

Her hand was surprisingly hot, and she returned his squeeze.

"Were you a proper male, I'd at least get a kiss for my trouble here." Holo grinned for a moment before her expression tightened, and she hopped off the horse.

"Oh, that's right. Here, take this for me," she said, undoing the sash at her waist and taking her robe off quickly.

Her flowing chestnut hair, pointed wolf ears, and fluffy wolf tail were all exposed.

As was the slightly swaying wheat-filled leather pouch around her neck.

"It is my hope that this will all conclude peacefully, but I don't know how it will go. When we meet up again, it will be cold if I'm naked, and a bit of a problem for you, too, I should think," she said with a smile and then looked to the forest, unmoving.

Her tail bristled as though struck by lightning.

Lawrence hesitated over what to say.

What finally came out was short: "Let's meet again."

He didn't wait for a reply before spurring the horse on.

Saying he didn't want to remain there would have been a lie.

But what could he accomplish if he did? Lawrence knew Holo's true form. Even if she were cornered by mercenaries or bandits, she could get away.

Lawrence drove the horse on. The sleet got heavier.

His face was strained and not just because of the cold.

For the first time in his life, he cursed himself for not being born a knight.

It appeared that Norah and Liebert had traveled some distance ahead in a short time. Lawrence did as he was told and had the horse at a gallop in order to put distance between himself and Holo, but even running at a fair pace, he had yet to catch sight of Norah or Liebert.

He no longer felt those unpleasant gazes, so this was probably a good opportunity to make progress. That was certainly true from Norah and Liebert's perspective — they would not want to waste Lawrence and Holo's deaths.

Lawrence smiled grimly to himself at the thought, and the concern about losing his way flitted in and out of his mind.

However, it soon dispersed. He was not especially familiar with the territory, but once the sun went down, he would have to stop, and he couldn't lose his way while at a standstill.

As long as he kept the hills to his right and the forest to his left, he would not stray too far off course.

Additionally, farther down the way the grass was clipped short and called a road, and if he followed that, it would take him straight to Ruvinheigen. Even if he never caught up with Norah and Liebert, there was little to be worried about.

Lawrence was more worried that his horse would stumble over a stone and fall, so he pulled back on the reins to slow the animal and then looked back over his shoulder.

Holo had long since disappeared behind him, but if the wolves changed their minds and came after him, they would cover the distance quickly.

He fought back the temptation to stay there and turned forward again, spurring the horse on to a walk.

He had Holo's robe; it was still warm. It seemed like a bad omen to leave clothing behind as a token. Lawrence felt himself grip the robe tightly.

But if Holo found it necessary to take wolf form, she would be in trouble if she had no clothes to change into.

She was even more rational than Lawrence the merchant.

Lawrence sighed deeply, shaking out the robe, which had a good deal of shed fur on it, probably from Holo's tail. He folded the garment up and stuffed it inside his own coat, which was already fairly wet, but that was better than holding it under his arm. Holo had taken the most dangerous role of all, so the least he could do was make sure her clothes weren't soaking wet when she returned.

The drizzle was getting heavier; it would be real rain by nightfall.

Lawrence continued on horseback for a bit, then stopped in the middle of the path, deciding that he had come far enough. Even if he had not put a lot of distance between them, it would require some effort for Holo to catch up with him — assuming she was in human form.

However, standing there in the middle of the road was tantamount to suicide. The cold had already numbed Lawrence's hands as they gripped the reins. It would be better to take shelter in the forest and keep an eye out for Holo coming down the road. He was worried about freezing to death before she ever found him.

Lawrence dismounted under the trees at the edge of the forest, looking back up the road. The space between the forest and the hills was mostly open. Norah and Liebert had probably already cleared the edge of the forest and were making their way straight to Ruvinheigen.

They were moving faster than normal, so it was entirely possible.

If so, then truly the only thing that remained to be done was feeding the gold to the sheep and entering the city.

As long as that went well, the gold smuggling would have wiped out his debt and turned a large profit for him to boot.

Lawrence's promised share would clear his debt and leave him with 150 *lumione*. That was a staggering amount of money, but still small in comparison to the total profit the smuggling would yield. They had bought up roughly six hundred *lumione* worth of gold, and avoiding the taxes on it meant that it would be multiplied tenfold. If he had been greedier, he probably could have gotten a larger share. After all, he was an accomplice to smuggling, a fact the rest could hardly ignore.

He stopped himself. Being greedy invited misfortune. It was the way of the world.

Lawrence tried to keep his mind off the cold as he gathered up what dry wood he could find, taking some tinder from a carefully waterproofed bag on the horse and starting a fire.

There was nothing around him. It was quiet without so much as a hint of an animal in the area.

As he dried his clothes, Lawrence wondered if Holo was all right, thinking of the robe she had taken off.

Such thoughts did him no good, he realized, but he couldn't help himself. His was the sin of helplessness, he felt.

He kept watch over the plains as the drizzle continued to fall.

How long had he stared at the unmoving scenery? His clothes were mostly dry. The first log he had set fire to was now ash.

Perhaps he would go check on her.

The seductive thought began to fill his mind.

There was a change in his field of vision. He rubbed his eyes. There was no mistaking it. It was a person.

"Holo!" he shouted, standing in spite of himself and grabbing Holo's now-dry clothes as he began to run. He would not possibly encounter anybody else in a place like this.

But as he ran out in the rain, he soon realized that it was not Holo.

There were three human forms, and they were on horseback.

"Mr. Lawrence, is that you?"

Apparently they had heard Lawrence's voice as he called out.

And, when they called his name, Lawrence realized they were from the Remelio Company.

But what where they doing here?

"Mr. Lawrence, are you all right?"

He had no recollection of any of their faces. One had a bow at his back, a sword hung from the belt of another, and the third carried a long spear. Their faces and postures showed that they were more used to travel than a town merchant like Liebert, and they wore rain gear as though they were used to it and were ready to fight at a moment's notice.

"We heard from Mr. Liebert—we couldn't just stay at the company—so we came out and waited at the edge of the forest. Thank goodness you're—"

The words cut off there.

The men, perhaps slightly older than Lawrence, had caught sight of the robe that he held.

It was Holo's and thus on the smallish side and obviously for a woman.

The obvious conclusion was not a good one.

They must be thinking he held on to the robe as a last memento, that she had met with tragedy. They had surely heard him call out Holo's name before.

As Lawrence expected, they looked at him sympathetically.

He tried to think of how he might clear up the misunderstanding when he noticed something strange.

The three men had simultaneously taken a deep breath, and Lawrence caught a glimpse of something like relief on their faces.

No doubt not a one of them thought this showed, but his merchant's eye caught it. They were probably glad that Lawrence had not succumbed to despair and become impossible to manage.

"And your things?"

If they felt pity for this poor man whose beloved companion had been killed by wolves, the point for broaching the subject had passed. If they dwelt on the topic too long, there was no telling when his emotions would explode. It was often the strangely composed ones who were dangerous.

Knowing it would be foolish to try and explain the misunderstanding, Lawrence merely gestured behind him.

"Over there. The horse, as well."

"I see. Let's take some shelter for a bit."

The tone was casual, but the three men's expressions were tight as they dismounted.

They were probably wondering if they were going to find the girl's wolf-mauled body.

Lawrence turned on his heel to lead them to his horse.

Some moments later, his mind went blank from shock.

"I won't ask you not to think badly of us," came a calm voice.

Lawrence's left arm was twisted from behind, and a spear pointed at his flank. There was a sword at his throat.

The droplets that ran down his face were not only rain.

"…So the Remelio Company is betraying me?" Lawrence

somehow managed to ask, stifling the cry as he felt his shoulder twisted.

It was luck that kept him from dropping Holo's clothes.

"It's insurance."

The sword at his throat was pulled away so that he could be tied up.

The men confiscated Holo's robe and bound Lawrence up like a piece of luggage.

"It weighed heavy on us to hear there would be a girl with you, so that's lucky, anyway."

The expressions of relief earlier were because Holo had not been there.

The men had known that if someone tried to be a hero, they would not pass the day without seeing blood.

"I know it will sound like an excuse, but we're on the brink here. We have to eliminate any danger we can."

The Remelio Company clearly assumed that Lawrence planned to blackmail them. Even if they did manage to come back from the edge of bankruptcy by smuggling gold, anyone who knew that fact had as good as a knife to the company's throat.

I would never do something so stupid, Lawrence thought to himself, but then he realized he had been thinking of it just a moment ago.

A large enough amount of money could cloud anyone's eyes.

Those who chose the path of the merchant knew this.

"You can keep the robe."

Holo's clothing was tossed at Lawrence's bound hands.

Lawrence grabbed at the robe with all his strength, somehow sealing away his anger at this betrayal.

The fact that they had tied him up meant that he was not going to find himself impaled on a blade immediately. He could not get himself killed for pointless resistance. However, it was plain to see that the men had no intention of letting him live, either.

They were probably wondering whether to simply leave him in the cold or in the forest, where the wolves might come. It was a reasonable question, as far as it went.

But there was something important the men had overlooked. They thought Holo was dead.

If Lawrence could rejoin her, all kinds of revenge became possible.

He could not die here. He had to repay this betrayal.

The anger was a cold stone in his gut as Lawrence feigned meek resignation.

"Don't think it doesn't wound me that I can't say we'll meet again."

Lawrence's forehead burned at the man's casual speech, but he bore it silently, not looking over his shoulder.

"It's depressing to think about what happens next."

"Hey," interrupted another of the Remelio Company men, as if to warn off unnecessary chatter.

What could possibly be depressing now at this last stage?

It was something that Lawrence mustn't hear apparently, even though he was about to die.

"C'mon, let us talk. I can't just keep quiet. You're the same, right?"

The one being addressed was at a loss for words for a moment. Lawrence ignored his own rage in order to listen.

What were they talking about?

"But that's the girl this guy had with him. Who cares if he hears —"

It can't be, his heart cried out within him.

"See, look —"

The man in front of Lawrence delivered a vicious kick to him at the same time that another punched his face.

Lawrence's head swam from the brutal shock, and when he came to, he was lying prostrate on the ground.

He couldn't tell whether the blockage in his nose was mud or blood. All he felt was a terrible fury that raced through him.

His vision sparkled from the shock, and he wasn't even sure what had happened to his body.

But he heard every word that was said.

"What if we just tie her up like this poor bastard? The wolves will just finish them off for us."

"Don't be stupid. Who knows what kind of pagan magic she used to get the sheep through that forest unharmed. We could blindfold her, tie both hands, and leave her here, and they'd still survive. And then *we'd* be the ones in trouble. But…it's depressing, I'll say that. Won't be able to eat for a while if we lay a hand on the girl, that's for sure."

They were clearly talking about Norah.

They were talking about killing her.

If the Remelio Company's solution to the risk of blackmail was murder, they could not very well let Norah live, either.

They would probably pass the checkpoint on the way to Ruvinheigen and then kill her after handing off the sheep to another shepherd. Norah was the only shepherd whose presence in this area wasn't suspicious, so they could not kill her until after the checkpoint.

"Shouldn't we finish this guy off?"

"What, you wanna do it?"

"Hey, the less killing the better, as far as I'm concerned."

"I'm with you."

"We've got the horse, so let's go. If we don't hurry, we'll catch it from Mr. Liebert."

Their footsteps receded only to be followed by the sound of horses' hooves.

After that, all Lawrence could hear was the sound of the drizzle. Pathetically, he began to cry.

The sin of helplessness.

Lawrence squeezed his eyes shut.

If only he were as strong as Holo, he would not have had to leave her to face danger alone, and he would not have to be resigned to this betrayal, to say nothing of having to listen while his enemies plotted the murder of the girl he himself had hired.

Norah was not like Holo. She didn't have pagan magic or any special powers. If sliced with a sword, her skin would split and her blood would flow.

Enek might be of some help, but it was a faint hope. No matter how gallant a dog, he would be helpless in the face of a surprise attack.

Lawrence wanted to at least spare Norah this.

He thought of her when they had spoken on the hill overlooking Lamtra.

She was smarter and tougher than she looked, and she knew her shepherding days were over. She had pinned her hopes on this unusual job.

She wanted to become a dressmaker after the severe life of the shepherd. It must have seemed a nearly impossible dream.

How much the possibility that it might come to pass must have thrilled her heart!

It was, of course, a fool's errand letting one's heart go aflutter at a mere hope, but for one's demise to be brought through treachery — that was another matter.

Norah would do the job given her. She had to receive her compensation.

This was true of Lawrence himself as well, of course, and once he reunited with Holo, he had the hope of exacting as much retribution as he wanted.

However, Norah's journey would end at the tip of a sword.

Using his maddening frustration as fuel, Lawrence forced his prostrate body to move. His hands were still bound behind his back, but by putting his face against the ground, he brought his knees under him to his chest, and in one movement, he raised his head and righted himself.

Apparently one nostril was blocked with mud and the other with blood. He snorted violently to clear his nose and then inhaled the cold air to cool his head — not that his head became any cooler.

He stood and began to walk unsteadily. He did not notice that his bound hands still held Holo's clothing until he came to the spot where his horse had been taken from him.

The fire had been kicked apart and scattered, but there were still some red glowing embers.

Lawrence left Holo's clothing where it wouldn't get wet and took a deep breath.

Then, he sat down very carefully next to the largest ember, checking his orientation to it several times.

He paused to ready himself.

Throwing himself down, Lawrence pressed his bound wrists against the hot coal.

The rope crackled as it burned, and a terrible heat assaulted his wrists. He squeezed his eyes shut and clenched his jaw to withstand the pain.

The next moment, his hands were suddenly free.

He had loosened his bonds.

Lawrence stood immediately and looked at his wrists. There were a few burns but nothing serious.

He was not so stupid as to grab the nearest handy stick and go chasing after his betrayers.

He knew that waiting for Holo was his best and only option. A simple traveling merchant was powerless alone.

A merchant did not have pride the way a knight or a townsperson did. He was prepared to lick anybody's boots if it meant turning a profit.

So whence came this feeling of humiliation?

Lawrence stood rooted to the spot and looked up at the sky.

The leaves on the trees shielded him from the rain and made him think of whatever cosmic force it was that allowed him only to crawl in the dirt; he couldn't bear it and looked down.

His eyes landed upon the robe Holo had worn.

Once again, he shed tears at his own helplessness.

"A tearful reunion, eh?"

Eventually unable to contain himself, Lawrence had run through the rain and encountered Holo just as he was running out of breath.

Holo was in her human form, uninjured and looking much the same as when they had parted ways. The knees of her trousers were dirty; perhaps she had tripped somewhere along the way.

"You look terrible," she said with an amused smile.

"We are betrayed."

"I'm not so naive as to think you saw that and *fell*," said Holo with a sigh. "I cannot say it didn't occur to me. They were from the company, yes?"

Her lack of surprise or shock suggested that she had vaguely anticipated betrayal, but since the entire plan was founded on mutual trust, she could not easily suggest the possibility. For Lawrence's part, even if he had been told in advance, he would not necessarily have known what to do. It was an unmistakable reality that nothing could happen without the Remelio Company's cooperation.

Holo smiled briefly and drew close to Lawrence, sniffing as she took his hands. She seemed to notice the burns. "Honestly, I would've found you soon enough. You didn't have to do this."

She twitched her nose again, then stuck her hand into Lawrence's coat, pulling her robe out.

Holo seemed surprised and wiped her face against the cloth. Her drizzle-soaked face was much improved.

She giggled. "You are a strange one, protecting my clothes with your life."

Holo's tail bristled in contrast to her delighted expression upon seeing the folded robe.

When she looked back at Lawrence, she still smiled, and he could have melted into her burning red eyes.

"There is something I need to say. I must be completely frank," she said, her fangs showing when she flashed a grin. "I may have to kill someone," she said, then continued before Lawrence could interrupt.

"I thought that if this plan didn't go well, I'd no longer be able to travel with you. The thought made me dreadfully lonely. Thus, I bore it. I let things go peaceably, I came along with you quickly, and I put up with things because I thought we'd soon be sipping hot potato soup in front of the fireplace. I am the Wisewolf of Yoitsu, Holo. I can forget the pride of a youngster if need be…"

Lawrence looked down at the mud on Holo's knees.

It had been no normal wolf in the forest, and it had not been after the sheep. There were few possibilities.

A territorial dispute.

Given that, the actions Holo took to "let things go peaceably" became clearer and clearer.

A wisewolf would never stumble clumsily over a stone, dirtying her knees.

"No, listen. That was all well and good. I am Holo the Wisewolf.

If I am made to act like a mere dog, I — I shall still not be angry. But what is this? This soaked mouse standing in front of me, face swollen, covered in mud? Has my companion been so foolish as to trip and fall? And with burns on his wrists! Oh, indeed. Before me is a fine fool, who doesn't give a second thought to his own appearance but protects my robe against the rain with his life. A dunce indeed! I've no idea what to do with such unbelievable softheartedness."

Holo gave her whole speech in one long breath, then inhaled deeply as she rubbed her eyes. "Well, then. I take it we're off to Ruvinheigen?" she said, suddenly back to her normal self.

Her arms and legs were covered with scratches and trembled. Lawrence didn't think it was because of the cold. This was Holo when she was truly angry.

"If we go now, we can enter the city under cover of darkness. The master always takes responsibility for betrayal. This is the truth of the world."

Holo thrust her robe back at Lawrence, then untied the opening of the leather pouch around her neck, and popped a few grains of wheat into her mouth. There was no hesitation.

"Wait, there's Liebert and Norah," interjected Lawrence, now that he finally had an opportunity to speak.

Holo's eyebrows shot up. "Think it through. Betrayal demands revenge. Sin must have punishment. But plunging in without thinking will give us no satisfaction. We can't be satisfied until we've taken everything from them. Do you not agree? Consider. If we attack the lot that came for you, dealing with the gold afterward becomes difficult. But we'll go first to the master's house and make him good and sorry, then strike at the ones who so happily betrayed you. Then, we have but to butcher the sheep, take the gold, and go wherever we may please. I daresay this is the best plan."

Despite her anger, Holo's mind was as clear and agile as ever. Her plan almost entirely eclipsed Lawrence's.

However, there was a reason he had to abandon this excellent plan.

"I feel the same way, but we must first get to Liebert — and quickly."

"You have a better plan?" asked Holo after gulping down the grains of wheat.

Her expression was unreadable, and Lawrence got the feeling that if he misspoke here, he would feel the full force of whatever swirled behind that mask.

Nonetheless, he could not abandon Norah.

"The Remelio Company plans to murder Norah."

Holo smiled thinly. "Yes, and those fools planned to kill you as well, yet you lived. She, too, may survive, don't you think?"

"If you go to save her, she will definitely be safe."

"Is that so?"

Lawrence found himself faintly irritated at Holo's mischievous look.

Why was she acting like this?

Time was short. If Norah and Liebert ran through the night, they might make it through the checkpoint to Ruvinheigen before dawn. And if it came to that, Norah would be killed shortly thereafter.

The probability was high.

"You could defeat a hundred armed men in a flash, could you not?" asked Lawrence impatiently, but Holo only shook her head slowly.

"That is not the problem."

Then what is *the problem,* Lawrence wanted to say.

"I am a wolf. The girl is a shepherd. We are eternal antagonists."

For just a moment, Lawrence wondered why Holo was dragging that out again now, but then he realized something important.

If Holo attacked Liebert and the others in her wolf form, it was quite possible that Norah would try to protect them.

In that case, there was a risk that Liebert would kill Norah, so could Holo explain that she was only there for the Remelio men? Would Norah even accept that?

If she didn't, Holo would wind up playing the villain.

Even in the best of times, Holo hated shepherds. It was obvious that she did not want to go to such lengths just to save Norah, and Lawrence couldn't force her to.

"I know there's nothing in it for you — far from it, in fact. But can I not ask this of you? An innocent person is about to die, and I can't just turn the other way."

Holo looked askance irritably as Lawrence tried to convince her. She was the only one who could save Norah.

"I'll owe you some thanks, of course."

Holo twitched one ear and looked at him.

"...What sort of thanks?"

"As long as you don't say anything like 'In exchange for her life,' I'll give you whatever I can," said Lawrence, trying to strike out the possibility of Holo making such a demand.

Upon hearing his words, her face turned severe; she had probably been planning to do just that.

"Please. You're the only one."

Holo's face stayed as irritated as ever as she lazily waved her sodden tail with discontent. She held her leather wheat pouch in her hand and folded her arms, exhaling whitely in the cold air.

"Holo..."

Lawrence knew there was a limit to what he could do. Moreover, Holo had endured humiliation in order that his gold smuggling could proceed. She had dirtied her knees and been made, she said, to act like a dog — he could imagine any number of awful appearances that might have been forced on her.

Then having endured that humiliation, she finds that her partner has been betrayed and made to look like a fool.

He couldn't criticize her and was already thankful that she was willing to assume her wolf form and strike at the Remelio Company. Asking for any more was the height of selfishness.

Holo exhaled a puff of air.

She smiled, looking almost resigned.

"Come now, don't use that voice with me," she said, heaving a sigh. "Here, take this. Also, I suppose I'd best take off my clothes. It would be troublesome to arrange for new ones."

"You'll do it?"

"There is a condition," said Holo as she undid the sash that held her trousers up. Her expression was unreadable.

Lawrence gulped and waited.

"You'll understand if I don't guarantee the lives of those who bother me."

If Norah took Holo for an enemy and protected Liebert and company, she would be spared no mercy, in other words.

He couldn't tell if she was joking or not.

No — she was surely serious.

Holo had spoken without particularly looking at Lawrence. Her breathing was neither fast nor slow.

Lawrence mustered all of his business cunning in response. "Very well. I trust you."

Puffs of white vapor appeared as Holo laughed as if giving in. "You've gotten quite clever. Exactly what sort of troublesome fellow am I traveling with?"

She shook her head lightly and quickly took off her blouse and trousers. She then kicked off her shoes roughly and, after collecting them, tossed them at Lawrence.

"What, no words of admiration yet?" she said, putting a hand to her hip, turning around, and looking over her shoulder.

It was a small price to pay.

"It's a magnificent tail," Lawrence said.

"Mm, that was a bit monotone, but I suppose it will do."

Holo turned to face him. "Now, then, be so kind as to close your eyes."

She had no problems being nude, but evidently she did not want him to witness her transformation.

Lawrence had no desire to oppose Holo on this. His feelings on the matter were complicated as he well knew from the Pazzio incident.

He closed his eyes and waited.

Soon there was a murmuring sort of rumble, like a great throng of mice running, and it was followed by the sound of something growing larger. Then he heard the shifting of something huge waving to and fro in the air and finally the heavy footfalls of a large animal.

Lawrence felt hot breath on his face.

When he opened his eyes, there was a gigantic mouth directly in front of him.

"If you'd flinched, I was thinking of eating your head first."

"Well, it is fairly frightening," answered Lawrence honestly as Holo's red-tinged irises seemed to stare right through him.

He trusted her, after all.

Perhaps she smiled a bit with her well-fanged mouth. There was a slight snarl.

"Shall I carry you in my mouth or on my back, then?"

"Spare me your mouth, please."

"You might find it surprisingly comfortable."

"I might be tempted by the warmth and find myself in your stomach."

"Hee-hee-hee. Come, on my back now. Grab on to my fur; it won't hurt. Hold on as tightly as you need."

Holo's body had a mysterious heat to it, like standing by a campfire.

Lawrence faltered a bit at her intimidating aura, which seemed to make even the rain move aside, but once he had roughly wrapped up her clothes and slung them under his arm, he did as he was told and, grabbing her fur, climbed atop the great wolf.

She had an animalistic scent to her, unlike a human, but it was distinctly Holo nonetheless.

"If you fall, I'll snatch you up in my jaws."

"I'll make sure not to."

He could tell that she smiled.

"You know — "

"What?"

"I truly hate shepherds."

For a moment, Lawrence didn't know why she bothered repeating this, but when he realized it was simply her true feelings, he pointed one thing out.

"Norah knows that whether this job succeeds or fails, she'll have to give up shepherding."

Lawrence felt a low rumbling; Holo was growling.

"By way of thanks, you'd best buy me more honeyed peach preserves than I can possibly eat."

Then Lawrence was assaulted by a terrible sensation that he was about to slip off as, beneath him, Holo's huge body began to run.

He held on to her fur for dear life, pressing himself down, desperate not to fall off the wisewolf, who accelerated with shocking force. The wind in his ears sounded like a rushing, flooding river.

But he also felt something else from the huge body that had left him so terrified when he had first seen it — it filled him with an indistinct warmth.

Holo's endurance was infinite, and she could run faster than any horse, but even so, they were unable to put the forest behind them until the sun was beginning to set.

Her feet bit into the earth and the landscape grew dimmer, as though candles were being put out one by one. The rain was relentless, and Holo's breath trailed behind them like a cloud.

Soon they found the road to Ruvinheigen. Holo turned right with no hesitation and gathered still more speed.

Occasionally, while on her back, Lawrence could hear a sound distinct from her breathing; perhaps it was her growling.

She had said she might kill someone.

At the time, Lawrence had thought she planned to stop just short of killing anyone.

If not, there was no "might" about it. There was not a human alive who could survive Holo's claws and fangs.

"*Hey,*" came Holo's sudden voice. There was too much tension in her voice for it to be idle chatter. "*We'll be upon them soon. I don't mind a bit if you stay on my back, but you might not like it. I'm going to jump clear over them. I'll crouch down right afterward, so you jump off then.*"

"Understood."

"*If you dillydally, I'll shake you right off.*"

Lawrence couldn't respond, and Holo plunged ahead, accelerating with terrifying speed.

He wondered if this was what it would be like to ride an arrow shot from a bow when he heard Holo take a deep breath.

Then it echoed, a thunderous howl.

Suddenly the steady pounding of Holo's stride ceased.

They were flying.

The only way to come close to the sensation would be to jump a horse off a cliff — but terrifyingly, the feeling lasted. Lawrence clung to Holo's body as they fell for an agonizingly long time. *Now? Now? Now?* Lawrence's mind cried out, wondering when the landing would come.

When he finally felt the impact of Holo's feet striking the ground, Lawrence wasn't sure if he was still alive.

He was afraid he would be flung off from the sudden deceleration when Holo suddenly wheeled around and crouched low.

"Off you go," she said quietly.

Lawrence remembered what he had been told before. The terror of the leap had not faded, but he managed to climb off Holo's back and make it to the ground without falling. There was a tiny moment of relief, then Holo got to her feet.

"Leave the rest to me," she said and dashed off, Lawrence scrambling to follow her.

Holo leapt into her hunting grounds in a twinkling, and despite the gathering gloom, Lawrence could clearly see the confusion caused by the giant wolf appearing in her prey's midst.

There were close to twenty people. The Remelio Company men raised a cry, and Lawrence somehow saw that Norah was among them. They had made it in time.

Holo stood in the middle of the maelstrom. Some of the men brandished long spears, but they might as well have been waving white flags. With the spear tips pointed high, they flourished the weapons uselessly back and forth; the extent of their disarray was obvious.

In the middle of all that, something that looked like a ball of mud would occasionally be sent flying. It was difficult to tell in the darkness, but they seemed to be people — Lawrence could see their hands flap wildly as they searched for the ground that had suddenly disappeared.

If Holo had been seriously striking people with her paws, they would surely be dead, so perhaps she was batting them aside on purpose.

One man was flung into the air — now two — and the long swords that were hurled at Holo in panic made high keening sounds as they were deflected away.

With the darkness beginning to take control, the swords were hit away from Holo so high and hard that Lawrence's eyes could not follow them. He got close enough to Holo to hear her breathing before the swords started to strike the earth near him.

Lawrence could tell they had been hurled quite high because the swords came down with such force that they buried themselves up to their hilts in the ground.

The Remelio Company had bet everything on this operation and had dispatched too many people to kill Lawrence and Norah.

However, the majority of them now lay unconscious, sprawled on the ground like stunned frogs, occasionally trampled on by the panicked sheep that ran around in circles.

"Protect the sheep and the shepherd!"

Lawrence drew a sharp breath at the voice.

It was Liebert.

He looked and saw that the young manager was one of the few taking rational action.

Keeping his panicking horse in check, Liebert waved a spear and shouted orders from a slight remove.

His timid nature while traveling with Lawrence and the rest had apparently been an act to get them to lower their guard.

If the man was cunning and careful enough to carry off this intricate betrayal, he was certainly capable of that much.

"Protect the shepherd! Run! Run!" Liebert called out again. Even if he planned to kill Norah eventually, she was still critical for getting the gold through the checkpoint.

Despite the resolute orders and the brave attempts of some Remelio men to carry them out, in the face of an attack by Holo obviously designed to smash their hopes, many of the men cried out and took flight. Holo ignored the stout few who still brandished their swords or spears and chased after the panicked.

It was a devilish tactic.

Once Holo pounced on one from behind, she would roll him over, then send the poor cowering fellow flying with a flick of her nose.

This all happened so quickly that it seemed it could not last much longer.

The number of men still standing had been steadily winnowed.

Now it was just Liebert on his horse, a petrified Norah, and Enek valiantly trying to protect her.

Holo shook her great head.

Something splattered — rain or sweat or blood.

"Sh-sh-shepherd! Protect me! Protect me!" Liebert cried out, clutching his chest, but it was unclear whether that was because his heart was on the verge of failure or to protect the gold in his coat.

Liebert screamed, looking not unlike the statues of sinners suffering in hell that decorated churches, but by some miracle, he controlled his horse and stayed behind Norah along with her sheep.

She may have been a shepherd, but Norah was a girl of delicate build.

The display made Lawrence nauseous — and Liebert had planned to kill both him and the girl.

Just as Norah was about to crumple from terror, the shepherdess seemed to remember her duty.

With an uncertain hand, she raised her staff aloft, ringing the bell at its end, and Enek crouched low, as though ready to receive directions.

Holo looked at Norah head-on, lowering her huge body like a loaded catapult.

Lawrence's breath caught. Holo was serious. At this rate, Norah could be killed.

Between the darkness and the sudden confusion caused by Holo's appearance, no one had noticed Lawrence some small distance away.

He thought if he identified himself, then at least Norah would recognize the giant wolf as Holo.

There was the risk of tipping Liebert off, but Lawrence was trying to think realistically.

There was no way that Holo would let him leave unharmed.

Lawrence had to make his presence known.

He was about to shout when —

"Shepherd! I'll give you three hundred *lumione* to protect me!"

In the midst of her fright, having raised her staff mostly by reflex, Norah's expression suddenly changed.

Three hundred *lumione* could do that to a person.

Norah silenced her bell. Her face began to fill with resolve.

Liebert, with his snakelike cunning, seemed to sense it.

He turned his horse's head around and began to gallop away at full speed.

Lawrence cried out in a strangled voice.

Norah, true to her profession, swung her staff.

It was too late.

The realization exploded in Lawrence's head as time seemed to slow down.

Enek and Holo, though their sizes were vastly different, assumed the same posture, like arrows in a bow the moment before taking flight.

Norah's staff was still, pointing straight at Holo.

Lawrence thought he heard a bell ring, quietly — *ting!*

" — !"

Lawrence shouted something, but whether it was Holo's name or Norah's, he didn't know — if it even was a name.

His strained eyes watched Enek and Holo for the barest hint of movement.

Thus, he saw the instant when the gallant sheepdog and the huge, godlike wolf pounced.

He was sure that in the next instant he would see Enek's body ripped through by Holo's massive claws before those same claws were turned on his mistress.

Then those paws would stretch farther out and render their judgment on another unworthy existence, turning it into a mass of gore not even fit to be butchered.

Regret.

Lawrence didn't even know what or how he regretted, only that regret now filled his soul.

And then—

"Enek, wait!"

Those words were like some magic signal, restoring time to its normal flow.

Holo's huge form leapt through the air like a stone hurled from a catapult, clearing both the dog and his mistress and landing among the sheep, which scattered chaotically.

Immediately upon landing, Holo sprung forward after the fleeing Liebert, whose desire for money had reduced him to a swine.

When the man turned back and saw the wolf pursuing him, Lawrence caught a glimpse of his pathetic face.

A short scream tore the air, but it was soon silenced.

Holo ran lightly for a few more paces, then stopped.

Norah still held Enek.

However, Lawrence could tell that it wasn't from fright that she clung to him.

Somehow, Norah knew. She either knew that the giant wolf was Holo or that it wasn't trying to attack them, but in either case, she knew not to let Enek give chase.

254

She had cast aside her staff — something no shepherd ever did — and desperately held on to Enek to stop him.

That wasn't fear.

"Norah!" Lawrence shouted and ran toward her, still worried that she was hurt.

Still restraining Enek, Norah looked up, shocked, and was doubly so upon seeing Lawrence. She then turned slowly to Holo, this time unsurprised.

Her aspect suggested that she both did and did not understand.

The emotion in Lawrence's chest practically exploded from his mouth. "I'm so glad you're all right!"

Norah could see that the giant wolf responsible for all of this was still unhurt, so she had no idea how to react to these words. She looked to Lawrence with a dazed expression on her face, overwhelmed.

"The wolf is Holo. My companion, I mean."

Norah smiled awkwardly; she probably thought it was some kind of joke.

She gave a little gasp as Holo came bounding up to them. A pair of legs protruded from Holo's mouth.

"You didn't kill him?"

Lawrence himself had felt a certain homicidal urge when he had seen Liebert use Norah as a shield. If it had been up to Lawrence, he would have killed the man.

Given the legs dangling from Holo's mouth, the matter would seem to be settled, but instead of replying, Holo shook her head slightly and let the man drop to the ground. Soaked with saliva, Liebert fell with an unpleasant *splat*.

"*I thought about swallowing him, I'll admit.*" Holo seemed to smile. "*But gold doesn't agree with my stomach.*"

She sniffed lightly and inclined her chin toward Liebert.

"Take the gold," she seemed to be saying.

"I think it was in his coat...Ugh, he's soaked," Lawrence complained, when a huge snout poked him. He begrudgingly peeled back Liebert's warm, wet clothes and easily found the bag of gold.

"There it is. The genuine article," he said upon opening the bag and seeing the gold grains inside.

"Norah," he said, tossing the bag to the shepherdess.

Holo gave Lawrence an aggravated look, which he ignored.

"The job's still not done. You're the one that has to get that gold into the city."

The massive wolf heaved a huge sigh. Surprised, Norah glanced at Holo but then turned back to Lawrence. "B-but...how are you still alive?"

Lawrence gave a pained grimace. After meeting up with his comrades, Liebert had sent men back to the forest to "save" Lawrence.

But those same men had returned without him, which meant that Lawrence and Holo had surely died.

Lawrence tried to think of where to begin his explanation of events when he felt the air stir and, looking over his shoulder, saw Holo raise her front leg and bring it down hard.

"— Urghyaaaaa!"

There was a loud crack, like a thick tree branch breaking, followed by an ear-splitting shriek that echoed in the darkness.

It seemed excessive to Lawrence, but also well deserved.

After his shriek died down, Liebert — whose left leg had just been broken by Holo's forepaw — flapped his mouth wordlessly, eyes open.

"Good evening, Mr. Liebert! And how fare you tonight?"

"Wh-wha...Uh? H-how are youuuugghghh!"

"Holo. Honeyed peach preserves."

As if by magic, those words dispelled Holo's reinvigorated anger, and she reluctantly took her paw off the man's broken leg.

"Mr. Liebert. Mr. Liebert! Would you be so kind as to explain to Norah how while you were getting dressed you, shall we say, got the buttons wrong, please?"

Liebert wiped the sweat from his forehead, and for a minute, his merchant sense showed past the terror and pain — it was the shrewd face of a merchant who understood the situation and was trying to discern how to save his own life.

"Mr. Liebert!"

"It — it wasn't me! It was Remelio's orders. I told him not to do it. I told him betrayal would call down God's wrath. I swear, I was against it — "

"As you can see, this is no ordinary wolf. Think of it as a representative of almighty God. In other words, lies will not avail you," said Lawrence.

Liebert's mouth snapped shut, and he looked up at Holo with despair in his eyes.

Slowly, very slowly, Holo's white breath emerged from between her teeth.

"I-I-I, I th-thought, I thought we were paying too much compensation. Remelio, too. At this rate we'd use all the p-profit paying our debts and have nothing to keep. Remelio told me to do something about it. I h-had to. I had no choice. Y-you understand, don't you? After all, we're both merch — "

He was cut off when Lawrence punched him in the nose.

"I'm nothing like you."

"*Ha-ha-ha-ha!*" Holo laughed heartily, taking her paw off the again unconscious Liebert.

"So that is how it is. The Remelio Company had planned to kill you, Norah. I swear this to you — they betrayed us."

Norah's expression was blank, but the situation seemed to be slowly seeping into her head nonetheless.

She looked up slowly at Lawrence.

"B-but, what about the wolves in the forest...?"

"*That was something else,*" interjected Holo, causing Norah to give a small yelp of surprise. Holo's voice carried well, after all.

"*I am Holo, the Wisewolf of Yoitsu. What was in that forest was nothing more than a brat whose only redeeming feature was its sense of territory. I've prudence enough to avoid a pointless fight over something like that.*"

Norah listened to Holo with a half-credulous expression, then smiled helplessly as she slowly let go of Enek. "I don't know why, Miss Holo, but somehow when you say it, I kind of believe you."

"*Incidentally, your dog was never smitten with me. He simply realized my true form. I thought I should let you know.*"

"Wha — ?" said Norah, surprised, at which point Enek gave a single angry bark.

"Now then, Norah, back to the issue at hand," said Lawrence. He felt bad about changing the subject yet again, but the affair was not yet settled.

The gold was still in transit, and Lawrence's debt was yet unpaid. There was also the issue of what to do about the Remelio Company.

"We're in the middle of a kind of storm right now. However, by the grace of God, somehow we've recovered the gold. If Liebert is to be believed, it's worth six hundred *lumione*. However, if we can bring it into Ruvinheigen and sell it to a broker, we should get close to ten times that — six thousand *lumione*."

Norah seemed to quail at the huge figures, which were so big that even Lawrence had trouble wrapping his head around them.

"Six thousand is far more than we could possibly take receipt

258

of, and even without facing that danger, we have six hundred in hand right now. However…"

"How…ever?"

"However, while it is true that it's the Remelio Company's fault that this plan has been more eventful than anybody would've liked, it is also true that without their investment, we never would have been able to buy the gold. And if we take the gold and run, they will be left ruined, bankrupt immediately. Thus —"

Holo nudged the side of Lawrence's face with her nose and not in a playful fashion.

Lawrence understood what she was trying to do.

"Thus, I propose the following."

"*Now, hold —*," Holo began, her tone displeased, but Lawrence would not yield.

"Holo. We do not live in a fairy-tale world. We cannot simply take revenge on those who have betrayed us and say, 'The end.' We have to live on after this. And taking revenge for betrayal only invites more revenge."

"*Well, then —*"

"Are you going to tell me you'd kill the entire ruined company?"

"*Um —*"

"In the end, I don't want the bread I buy tomorrow to have been paid for in blood. There are many ways to end this, but if we want to have a life tomorrow, we have to choose to do so."

Holo's amber eyes closed.

She looked away.

"If it weren't for you, I'd be freezing to death by the forest right now. I'm well aware that if you hadn't been here, all would be lost, and I thank you for hearing my plea. But —"

"*Enough. Enough, I say. Ah, my travel companion is tiresome beyond words!*" said Holo, hitting Lawrence's head lightly with her chin. It hurt, but if this satisfied her selfishness, it was a small price to pay.

"Then here's what I'll have you do."

"You may as well! Let me just say this — I'll carry out whatever duties your undoubtedly tiresome plan asks of me, so you may as well ask away."

Lawrence smiled, thankful beyond words, and took a deep breath before turning back to Norah.

"Sorry to keep you waiting. Here's what I propose we do."

Having listened to the strange exchange between Holo and Lawrence, Norah straightened herself and looked up.

"I'd like you to decide whether or not to bring the gold into Ruvinheigen."

"Wha — ?"

It was an obvious question. Without any further risk, she had six hundred *lumione* on hand. Of course, six thousand was an unimaginable gain over that, but it would mean risking her life again.

"However, if you bring it into Ruvinheigen, the huge profit will save both us and the Remelio Company."

At this, Norah let slip a small "Oh."

"On the other hand, if you decide to take it, then all of these fallen men here, along with their families in Ruvinheigen and the other remnants of the company, will all glimpse hell. Some of them will not be spared its wrath. But in their hearts, they will bear a grudge against three demons — that is to say, me, Holo, and you, Norah."

Even for someone who lived by travel, being the object of such animosity from so many people could make life far more dangerous. Business consisted of exchanges between people. The location of Lawrence, Holo, and Norah would eventually be found and swords put to their throats.

There was another important point to make.

"Of course, if we flee to some foreign land with a foreign tongue, we can live as though nothing happened. But even living without the fear of revenge, suppose you came across a slave with a familiar face being whipped like a workhorse? Would you be able to sleep that night?"

Lawrence paused, allowing the words to sink in.

"However, I will have the Remelio Company make amends."

Holo grinned unpleasantly.

"We're headed there next. For your part, Norah, please make your decision by tomorrow morning. If you decide to bring the gold into Ruvinheigen, we'll meet at the same plaza where we first discussed this. I'll go into the city first, secure a trustworthy butcher, and wait by the eastern gate for one day. If you decide not to bring it in…Hm. Let us meet in Poroson."

This plan did, of course, leave room for another betrayal.

Norah could take all of the gold herself and set off for some other town.

For all of them to live on without regret, though, it would be best if she brought the gold into Ruvinheigen so the Remelio Company could be saved and the money divided equitably.

Lawrence had to consider what to do if Norah were caught at the checkpoint, though. Without exception, gold smugglers were executed in the plaza, so he would just have Holo rescue her if need be. Holo had promised to do as he asked, after all, no matter how tiresome the task.

Lawrence wasn't particularly trying to give Norah time to think, but in any case, while waiting for her reply, he went among the unconscious Remelio men and tied them up. He had no rope, so he used the sleeves of their coats. Even if the men cooperated to undo the knots, none of them seemed in any condition to do anything strenuous.

"Well then, Norah. We'll meet again," said Lawrence once he finished binding the men and had Holo knock out the few who were regaining consciousness.

He didn't say that to try and persuade her of anything in particular.

It was merely to ascertain her trust and bring about a favorable outcome for all.

The moon shone vaguely through the thick clouds.

"M-Mr. Lawrence!"

He stopped as she called his name.

"We-we'll meet again!"

He looked over his shoulder to see her holding her staff.

"We will," he said. "And we'll be rich."

Norah smiled and nodded.

Enek barked and began to round up the sheep.

"Well, now."

After they walked for a while, Lawrence starting thinking about riding on Holo's back, but she had apparently already anticipated that and spoke up just in time to cut him off.

"What?" he said, just slightly irritated. He was sure she had chosen that exact moment on purpose.

"Might I hear the truth now?"

Holo looked at him evenly with her large eyes. Lies would not avail him — he had told Liebert the same thing.

Lawrence was aware of the pained grimace that distorted his face.

"Let me keep up the pretense a bit longer."

"Heh-heh. No."

Looking at her happily wagging tail, Lawrence knew she would keep asking until he relented.

He quickly gave up the deception.

"That's not enough gold."

"*Oh ho.*"

"There is no way that's six hundred *lumione*. It's a hundred, at best."

"*Your share would be used up just paying your debt. If she doesn't smuggle it in, there'll be no profit at all.*"

The tip of her big tail brushed against the back of his neck. He slapped it away; she growled playfully.

"The Remelio Company must be up against the wall. They must have scraped together a hundred *lumione* hoping just to get by on that. Of course, they knew from the start they'd have to pay us enough to keep our mouths shut, but that's precisely why they got on board the plan with us in the first place."

And yet Lawrence's position was such that he had no choice but to trust and rely on that same company.

"*Hmph. Still, that was certainly a skillful excuse you gave her. You're like unto a saint.*"

"It was mostly sincere."

" . . . "

Holo chuckled through her nose, then stopped, and crouched down.

"*Get on.*"

"What, no more interrogation?"

"*I tire of your foolishness.*"

Narrowing her amber eyes, she nudged him with her muzzle.

It was but a light touch, yet Lawrence nearly stumbled and fell, though his fear at Holo's wolf form was by now entirely gone.

"Still, we're not just saving the Remelio Company out of charity."

"*Oh?*"

Lawrence grabbed on to Holo's fur and brought his legs up.

"No. We're doing it to make more money for ourselves."

He swung his legs quickly over her back.

"*More money, eh? I cannot say I follow you.*"

"Merchants can convert all sorts of things into money. I have to be of *some* occasional use."

At first, he thought she was teasing him, but Holo's laugh was genuine.

"*I look forward to observing your skill, sir!*"

Holo got to her feet and began to walk, soon breaking into a run.

The golden moon was occasionally visible in the dark sky.

Perhaps owing to the rain that had fallen since noon, the Ruvinheigen night was exceptionally quiet.

"…Th-there must be some kind of problem. Right? Like when you've forgotten to put salt in the soup."

Lawrence knew only too well that merchants were people who, no matter the circumstance, lived by telling lies.

However, trust was important, even among liars — merchants were strange creatures indeed.

Lawrence pondered this.

"I-I don't know what Liebert said. I'm sure it sounded like heaven's own truth, as if he were confessing before an altar. But it was a lie! He lies about everything! I've been thinking about firing him — I swear!"

The man's voice was hoarse and difficult to hear through the emotion, but this was no delicate business negotiation. As long as Lawrence could understand the gist, it was good enough.

"Mr. Remelio."

"Y-y-yaaagh!"

Remelio gave a short cry because his head was firmly clamped between Holo's jaws, and he felt her increase the pressure just a bit.

Lawrence and Holo were fortunate that he had been alone in the office, waiting for his employees to return.

Just a moment ago, Holo had jumped over the city walls with unbelievable ease. Lawrence had planned to reenter the city with Holo in human form and simply claim they had been waylaid by bandits, but Holo, who could sense any presence on the other side of the wall, said simply, "*It's safe,*" and cleared it with a single leap. It had been so easy that Lawrence wondered if they could have avoided all this trouble in the first place and smuggled the gold in themselves.

They entered the city unseen and, once Holo had temporarily returned to her human form, stole quietly to the Remelio Company.

Remelio had been expecting the return of his men, so when he saw Holo and Lawrence, he made quite a face.

He was now tied up and on the floor, head trapped between Holo's terrifying teeth, looking as though he might die from terror.

It seemed imprudent to let Remelio see Holo's wolf form, but he and Lawrence both shared the secret of the gold smuggling. If Remelio wanted to go to the Church with the revelation, let him — there was a mountain of circumstantial evidence.

No merchant would speak of his opponent's weakness when his opponent could easily do the same to him.

Also, letting Holo terrify Remelio would make her feel better, and the overwhelming terror would discourage the master from trying to exact revenge on them later.

Unsurprisingly, the results had been immense.

"The jaws that now hold your head between their teeth are the jaws of truth, my friend. If you lie, they will know. Also, this wolf is hungry from being made to run all night, I hear. If you lie, your head may just be devoured."

Holo's fangs squeezed just slightly harder against Remelio's temple.

He couldn't even scream anymore.

"All right, Mr. Remelio. Know that I have not returned to take revenge for your betrayal. I've come to talk business."

A bit of light returned to Remelio's eyes at the word *business,* perhaps realizing that business was about making deals, and if a deal could be made there was the possibility that he would not die here.

"Our negotiations begin now. Feel free to lie in your interest as much as you wish. However, the wolf here is far more discerning than I and can see the hidden meaning behind your every word. If you do anything clumsy, you may wind up a head shorter. Are we clear?"

With his head stuck in Holo's jaws, Remelio couldn't very well nod, but he tried to, and that was good enough.

"Then let's begin," said Lawrence frankly. "In the event that we succeed in the gold smuggling, might I ask you to purchase it from us at five hundred *lumione*?"

Remelio's eyes were literally dots.

"We are still accomplices to smuggling. Surely you didn't think we'd come back to take revenge on you after making off with the gold?"

The salt-and-pepper-haired Remelio nodded like a chastened child, at which Lawrence grinned bitterly. "Well, I won't say there's no chance of that, but no, I don't think so. But if we don't talk about what to do when we succeed — well, we might wind up disagreeing, mightn't we?"

Holo chuckled deep in her throat, causing Remelio's head to quiver along with her mouth; his face tensed in a nervous grin.

"So, I'll say it again. Might I ask you to purchase the gold from us at five hundred *lumione*?"

Remelio's face was distorted with despair — he knew how much the gold bought in Lamtra was really worth.

"I can't possibly do —"

"Of course, I don't expect it all in cash up front. Let's see. Perhaps you could write me an IOU?"

In that moment, the master of the Remelio Company showed the intelligence that had gotten him his position.

He made a pained expression when he understood what Lawrence was saying and begged for mercy. "F-five hundred, that's simply — "

"Too much? Well, hmm. In that case, I'll just take whatever you've hidden away here and sell the gold to someone else." Lawrence exchanged a look with Holo, then added, "Also, I'll let that demon there have your life."

Holo hated being called a god, but she apparently didn't mind being called a demon.

Her tail swished through the air, and she panted dramatically.

All expression drained rapidly from Remelio's face.

If Lawrence's guess was right, it meant Remelio would now do whatever they asked.

"You see, Mr. Remelio, I don't think it's fair to lose everything because of a single failure. We can't perfectly predict every price drop, can we? So I want to give you another chance. But I want you to be grateful for it, and I want that to take the form of five hundred *lumione*. You've built a wonderful company with a magnificent loading dock in a city like this. If you think in terms of decades, surely five hundred is a bargain."

Remelio's eyes opened wide, and after a moment, he began to cry.

If he could rebuild his business, paying five hundred *lumione* back over the course of ten years was far from an unreasonable proposition. A traveling merchant was no match for a trading company in that regard.

Perhaps those tears were from the prospect of managing a revived company.

267

"So you'll write the note, then? Holo —"

Upon hearing her name, Holo sighed and reluctantly released Remelio, nudging his head with the tip of her nose.

Lawrence untied the rope that bound Remelio and continued. "The terms will be yearly installments over ten years. The first will be ten *lumione*. The last will be one hundred. You understand, yes?"

It meant that the debt would increase every year. Added all up it came to 550 *lumione,* but that was still an excellent interest rate.

If Remelio could get his company running successfully again, it would not be a difficult amount to manage.

"You can write it out at that desk."

Remelio nodded and accepted Lawrence's hand to get to his feet. His feet were still tied, so he tottered over to the desk and sat.

"S-so, should this be payable to...," began Remelio, turning around.

Lawrence smiled and answered, "The Rowen Trade Guild."

Remelio grinned almost sadly, realizing he would never be able to run from this debt.

If Lawrence held the loan personally, then as the years passed and Remelio gained strength, he could get revenge or default on the repayment. Also, Lawrence dreaded the thought of having to return every year to the people who had wronged him in order to demand his money.

And more important still was the Remelio Company's current utter lack of assets. No matter how many IOUs he might hold, Lawrence would see none of this money for a year. Even if the debt he had originally owed the company was now gone, the profits from the gold smuggling might be used up compensating Norah and paying obligations for the Remelio Company's recovery. In the worst case, Norah might not even get her consideration.

But all those problems were solved by having the trade guild to which Lawrence was attached hold the loan. By selling the IOU to the Rowen Trade Guild relatively cheaply, he could cut his ties with the Remelio Company and convert ten years of repayment into immediate cash.

Also, defaulting on a loan held by a trade guild was like declaring war on another city. The Remelio Company would never dare to default.

"You're a formidable man."

"Not as formidable as the wolf," Lawrence answered smoothly. The wolf found the joke funnier than anyone.

"Now, all we need to do is pray the smuggling succeeds."

EPILOGUE

Afterward, things were busy.

First, Lawrence and Holo had to borrow changes of clothes from the Remelio Company while the dirt and blood were washed from their own clothes. While those clothes dried, Lawrence took the IOU to the Rowen Trade Guild, leaving Holo (who said she was hungry) at a late-night tavern. Apparently, it was Lawrence's job to take care of the details.

Lawrence was greeted heartily by the members of the trade guild, who had gathered there to drink after the end of the business day. He endured many vulgar questions about the wound on his face before finally reaching Jakob.

It wouldn't have been at all strange for people from the Remelio Company to come beating down the door demanding repayment, but neither they nor Lawrence had been seen. Jakob had probably been worried sick ever since Lawrence's debt had been incurred.

Unsurprisingly, Jakob's first reaction upon seeing Lawrence's face was to angrily give his skull a sound rapping.

But then his face split in a tearful smile, and he threw his arms wide, relieved that Lawrence was safe.

Lawrence turned the IOU over to Jakob, who could probably

guess, in a broad sense, at what had happened. He brought a purse full of seldom-seen gold *lumione* coins out from within the guild and bought the IOU on the spot.

Of course, now there was a merchant who had entered his term of service. It had been entirely possible that the gold smuggling would not succeed, in which case the Remelio Company's physical assets and accounts receivable would have been sold off to pay its debts. Normally, when a company failed, its assets were liquidated and divided proportionally among the creditors, so a five hundred *lumione* note from the Remelio Company would not be immediately worthless even if the gold smuggling had failed. In short, Jakob bought the IOU up at an amount that corresponded to the smuggling gamble.

Taking all those possibilities into account, Jakob had valued the IOU somewhat conservatively at thirty *lumione*.

If the smuggling succeeded, there was the promise of an additional hundred *lumione*. That was significantly less than the face value of the IOU, but there was a high probability that the recovered Remelio Company would still go bankrupt within ten years. It was a reasonable price.

Lawrence gave twenty *lumione* to Jakob as a way of compensating him for the damage caused to the Rowen Trade Guild's good name. He intended to use the rest that Jakob gave him as a bribe to keep the butchers quiet if they had to slaughter the sheep.

With the hundred additional *lumione* he might have from the success of the smuggling, Lawrence had to compensate Norah the twenty *lumione* she was due, and he planned to give more by way of apology to the various trading companies he had begged for loans. If that came to thirty *lumione*, that still left him with fifty for himself.

Somehow, he would be back to where he was when he had sold off his pepper in Poroson.

Given that at one point he had resigned himself to dying aboard a slave ship, this could only be called a miracle.

Next, Lawrence used his guild connections to get introduced to a butcher whose discretion could be trusted. He secured a promise from the butcher to receive the sheep from Norah and butcher them, no questions asked, for ten *lumione*. He was paying the butcher very well and had every expectation that things would proceed smoothly.

After making the various preparations, Lawrence returned to the Remelio Company to retrieve his clothes and then left Remelio to round up and rehire his former employees, who were probably all huddled together, shivering in the cold weather. Lawrence also ordered Remelio to return his cart horse, which he had forgotten about entirely. He was a bit sharp in saying so, as he expected his orders to be carried out quickly.

By the time Lawrence finished all his preparations, the night sky was beginning to pale with the dawn.

He walked along the street quietly in the early morning, a chill still in the air from the previous day's rain.

His destination was a tavern that was able to remain open all night, courtesy of bribes paid to the appropriate authorities.

The distinctive pale blue sky of dawn hung over the city. An out-of-place lamp, still burning, marked the tavern.

"Welcome."

The voice that greeted him was listless — not from illegality necessarily, but rather from the exhaustion of staying up all night.

The tavern was perhaps half-full, though surprisingly quiet; the patrons drank their wine quietly, perhaps mourning the inevitable daybreak.

"Ho there."

Lawrence turned to face the voice and found Holo, who had appeared at his side holding a small cask and some bread. If a priest had spotted Holo (who was dressed again as a town girl) in the all-night tavern, there might have been some real problems — but nobody seemed to mind her presence.

Holo caught the eye of the tavern master behind the counter, and he sleepily waved to her. Holo had probably charmed the goods she was carrying out of the master with some sweet talk.

"Come, let's go."

Lawrence had actually wanted to sit and rest for a moment, but Holo took his hand and would not be argued with.

"Come again," said the tavern master as they left.

The two had no particular destination and for the time being were content to walk.

It was cold outside. Thanks to the humidity, their breath hung in the air.

"Here. Bread," Holo said, and Lawrence's stomach groaned as he realized that he had not eaten since midday the day before. Lawrence took the bread—actually a bacon and vegetable sandwich—from the happily smiling Holo and bit into it without hesitation.

"Also, this." Holo held out the small cask.

Once he uncorked and put his lips to the cask, it proved to contain a warm mixture of mead and milk.

"'Tis good for what ails you."

The warm, sweet liquor was perfect.

"Now, then," said Holo. She probably hadn't meant the food and drink to loosen his tongue per se, but as he finished eating, she began to speak.

"I have two questions to put to you."

Lawrence braced himself for the worst.

Holo paused for a moment.

"How far do you trust that girl?" she asked, not looking at him.

It was a question he both had and had not expected. The fact that Holo had left the time, place, and circumstances unclear meant that there was probably some vague doubt in her own mind.

Lawrence took another drink from the cask. "I don't know how far I trust her," he said without glancing at Holo. "However, I do know that if Norah were to take the gold and disappear some-where, she would be easily followed. I don't trust her enough to think that would happen and still have handed her the gold."

Holo was silent.

"Unless she travels a significant distance, no one will buy it up at a reasonable price, and tales of a shepherdess just happening to sell off gold are rare enough to travel far and wide. She would be easy to follow."

It was certain that he did not trust Norah absolutely. As a merchant, Lawrence was always thinking of the contingencies.

"I see. I suppose that is the size of it, then."

"And the other question?" Lawrence asked.

Holo faced him with an inscrutable expression.

It wasn't anger. It was, perhaps, hesitation.

But hesitation about what? Lawrence wondered.

He found it hard to imagine that she was vascillating over whether or not to ask the question at all.

"Whatever it is, I'll answer it. I owe you a huge debt, after all."

He took a bite of the now-cold sandwich, washing it down with liquor.

The golden light of the dawn began to reflect on the cobble-stone streets.

"Are you not going to ask?" inquired Lawrence.

Holo took a deep breath. She grabbed his sleeve. Her hand trembled — either because of the cold or something else.

"Hm?"

"Do — do you remember…" Holo looked at him with uncer-tain eyes. "When I was facing the dog and the girl…, whose name did you call out?"

She did not appear to be joking.

Her eyes were seriousness itself.

"The blood was rushing in my head, and I couldn't hear. But it's been gnawing at me. I am quite sure you called someone's name. Do you remember?"

Lawrence hesitated as they walked slowly through the city streets, the sun now beginning to rise.

How should he answer? The truth was that he didn't remember.

But what if Holo actually *did* remember, and she was only trying to get him to confirm it?

If he had called Holo's name, that would be fine. The problem would come if he had called for Norah.

In that case, saying he didn't know would mean he'd blurted out Norah's name without really knowing or remembering what he was saying.

And in *that* case, Holo would certainly be angry. It would be better to honestly admit he had called Norah's name and come up with some vague reason as to why.

There was another possibility, of course — that Holo really hadn't heard at all.

In which case, it would be best to say he had called her name.

Having thought it through so thoroughly, Lawrence realized the extent of his own stupidity.

The girl next to him was the Wisewolf Holo. She would see right through any lies.

In which case, the correct answer was —

"I called your name."

After looking for a moment like the eyes of an abandoned puppy, Holo's eyes flashed with hatred.

"That is a lie."

She tightened her grip on his sleeve, and Lawrence answered immediately.

"It is. The truth is I don't remember. However — "

Holo's ears flicked underneath the kerchief on her head faster than her facial expression could change.

She should know that what he had just said wasn't a lie.

" — In those circumstances, I certainly think I would've called your name," he said, looking steadily back at her.

As quickly as her eyes had flashed with hatred, Holo now looked back at him with a hint of doubt in her gaze.

There was no way to tell whether or not that was the truth; she would have to decide.

For his part, Lawrence put forth the most persuasive argument he could think of.

"Time was of the essence. I'm sure I would've unconsciously chosen to call your name. After all — "

Holo's grip tightened.

"After all, it's one letter shorter."

He could almost feel the expression drop from her face.

"Also, if I'd shouted 'Norah' even hastily, you'd be able to tell. But Holo takes but a moment to say — it would be easy to miss with blood roaring through your head. What do you think? Quite a persuasive argument — "

He didn't finish his sentence because Holo struck him in the mouth.

"Shut up."

Even her small, soft hand hurt quite a bit since Lawrence's lip was split slightly where the Remelio Company mook had struck him.

"So you called my name because it was *shorter*? Dunce! Fool!" she said, yanking on his sleeve. "It's infuriating that you would even *think* that!" She looked flatly opposite him as if to turn him away.

Lawrence wondered if it would have been better to just tell an obvious lie, but he had the feeling Holo would've been angry either way.

As they walked, they approached the east gate; there were more people around now busily setting about their day.

Holo walked slightly in front of him, alone.

Just as he wondered what she was going to do, she stopped.

"Just —" she stood there —

"— call it out," said Holo, her back turned to Lawrence.

Past her, Lawrence saw a bell at the end of a long staff.

He heard the bleating of the sheep behind a figure.

What he saw beyond Holo was a shepherd girl leading a black sheepdog.

In that very instant, he knew the smuggling had succeeded. He couldn't help but be happy. He might easily have called out Norah's name.

Lawrence smiled at Holo's clever, bald-faced actions.

The moment he opened his mouth to call out *the* name, he sneezed.

"*Achoo!*"

Now the truth of which name he called out would remain forever a mystery.

Holo looked over her shoulder, chagrined. He had gotten the better of her.

Lawrence ignored her and waved broadly three times just as when he had first met Norah on the road.

Norah noticed and returned the wave.

Holo regarded Norah over her shoulder.

That was the moment Lawrence was waiting for.

"Holo."

Her wolf ears twitched.

"Holo really *is* easier to call."

A puff of vapor appeared at Holo's mouth as she exhaled, admitting defeat.

"You dunce."

Lawrence loved her ticklish smile even more than the warm late-autumn sunshine.

AFTERWORD

It has been a while! This is Isuna Hasekura. Well, here's volume 2. I know; I'm shocked, too.

But if you wish to know what is most shocking of all, it's that when I started to write this second volume, I utterly forgot the personalities of the two main characters.

I know it sounds unbelievable, but it's true, even though I myself can barely believe it. You always hear about birdbrained people who forget everything after taking three steps, and that definitely fits a chicken who reads a horror story on the Net and gets so freaked out he can't even go to the bathroom, right?

Now that I think about it, there's one more surprising thing. What is it, you ask? Well, I bought stock. Having won a prize for writing a novel with a merchant as the protagonist, I put half the prize money into a certain stock. I wrote about it in the afterword for volume 1, too, and I get this evil grin on my face when I think about multiplying my money in the stock market. This time my delusions have just gotten wilder, but perhaps as a consequence of some shadowy group's trap, the stock dropped steadily for two weeks. It even fell on a day when 90 percent of the stocks on the market rose. Right behind the window I'm writing this afterword in, there's a stock tool that tells me every minute change in the price, and today it seems to be trading in a very narrow range. Although it *is* dropping. It seems that it's not going well, just like the novel. How odd...

I'm a sad piece of work, but I hope you've enjoyed this book.

Once again Jyuu Ayakura provided wonderful illustrations; they fit the images in my head perfectly. Thank you so much. Also, to my editor — I am so sorry for all the mistakes in my Japanese. Next time — next time, I promise! — I'll try to write the novel so we can finish in a single meeting.

And of course, to all those who hold this book in your hands, my heartfelt thanks.

I hope to see you all again in volume 3.

— Isuna Hasekura

Isuna Hasekura

Born December 27, 1982, Isuna Hasekura is a physics student and spends his days lamenting the cruel nature of the world ever since studying spherical surface harmonics failed to give him the correct result on his income tax return. However, due to mitigating circumstances, he is unable to provide a satisfactory explanation of spherical surface harmonics.

Illustrations: Jyuu Ayakura

Born 1981. Birthplace: Kyoto. Blood Type: AB. Currently living a free, spartan life in Tokyo, he has been thus far unsuccessful in putting his temple-hiking plans into action.

THE JOURNEY CONTINUES IN THE MANGA
ADAPTATION OF THE HIT NOVEL SERIES

OUT NOW!
SPICE
&
WOLF